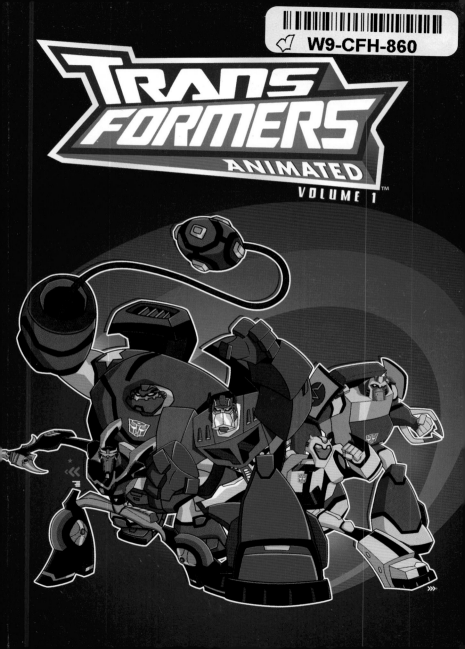

TRANSFORMERS
ANIMATED
VOLUME 1™

BASED ON THE SCREENPLAY BY:
MARTY ISENBERG

ADAPTATION BY:
ZACHARY RAU

LETTERS BY:
ROBBIE ROBBINS

EDITS BY:
JUSTIN EISINGER

Licensed by:

Special thanks to Hasbro's Aaron
Archer, Elizabeth Griffin, Sheri Lucci,
Richard Zambarano, Jared Jones,
Michael Provost, Michael Richie,
and Michael Verrecchia for their
invaluable assistance.

IDW Publishing is:
Ted Adams, President
Robbie Robbins, EVP/Sr. Graphic Artist
Chris Ryall, Publisher/Editor-in-Chief
Clifford Meth, EVP of Strategies/Editorial
Alan Payne, VP of Sales
Neil Uyetake, Art Director
Justin Eisinger, Editor
Tom Waltz, Editor
Andrew Steven Harris, Editor
Chris Mowry, Graphic Artist
Amauri Osorio, Graphic Artist
Matthew Ruzicka, CPA, Controller
Alonzo Simon, Shipping Manager
Kris Oprisko, Editor/Foreign Lic. Rep.

To discuss this issue of *Transformers*, or join
the IDW Insiders, or to check out exclusive Web
offers, check out our site:

www.IDWPUBLISHING.com

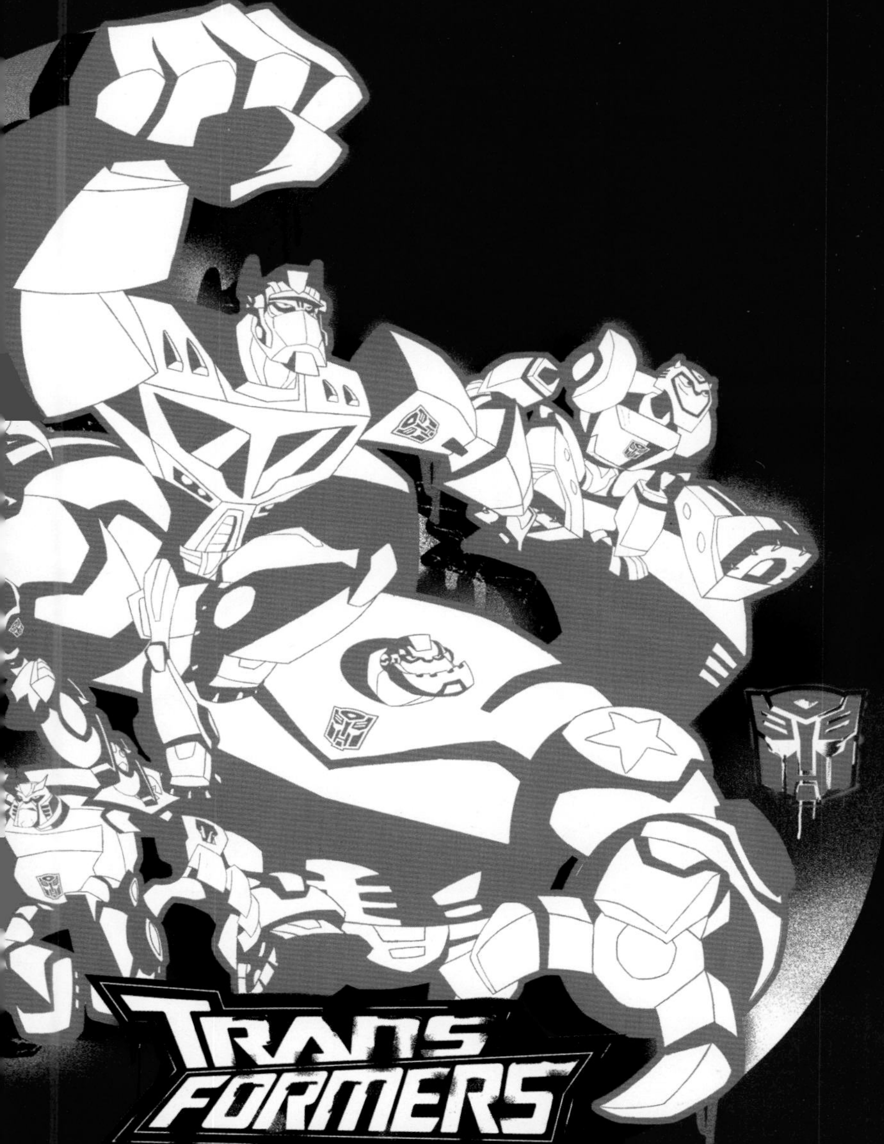

TRANSFORMERS ANIMATED™

VOLUME 1

Roll Call

Optimus Prime

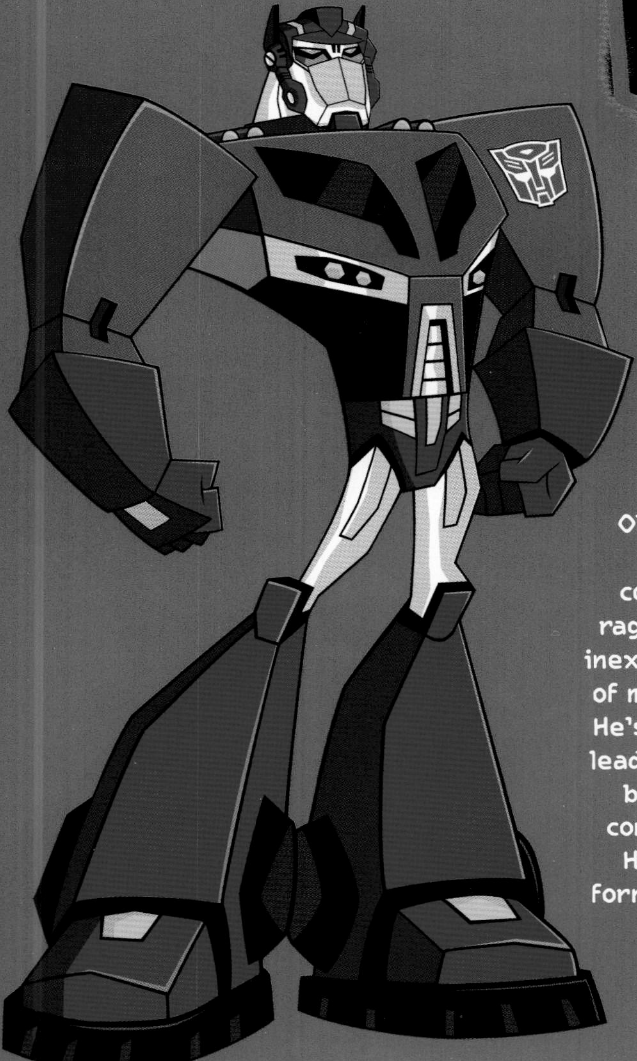

OPTIMUS PRIME is the young commander of a ragtag and largely inexperienced group of misfit AUTOBOTS. He's not the kind of leader who needs to bark orders to command respect. His mechanized form is a fire truck.

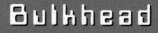

Bulkhead

Every team needs its "muscle" and BULKHEAD is it. Designed primarily for demolition, BULKHEAD is a bull in a china shop. He is tough as nails in both his robot and S.W.A.T. assault cruiser forms.

Ratchet

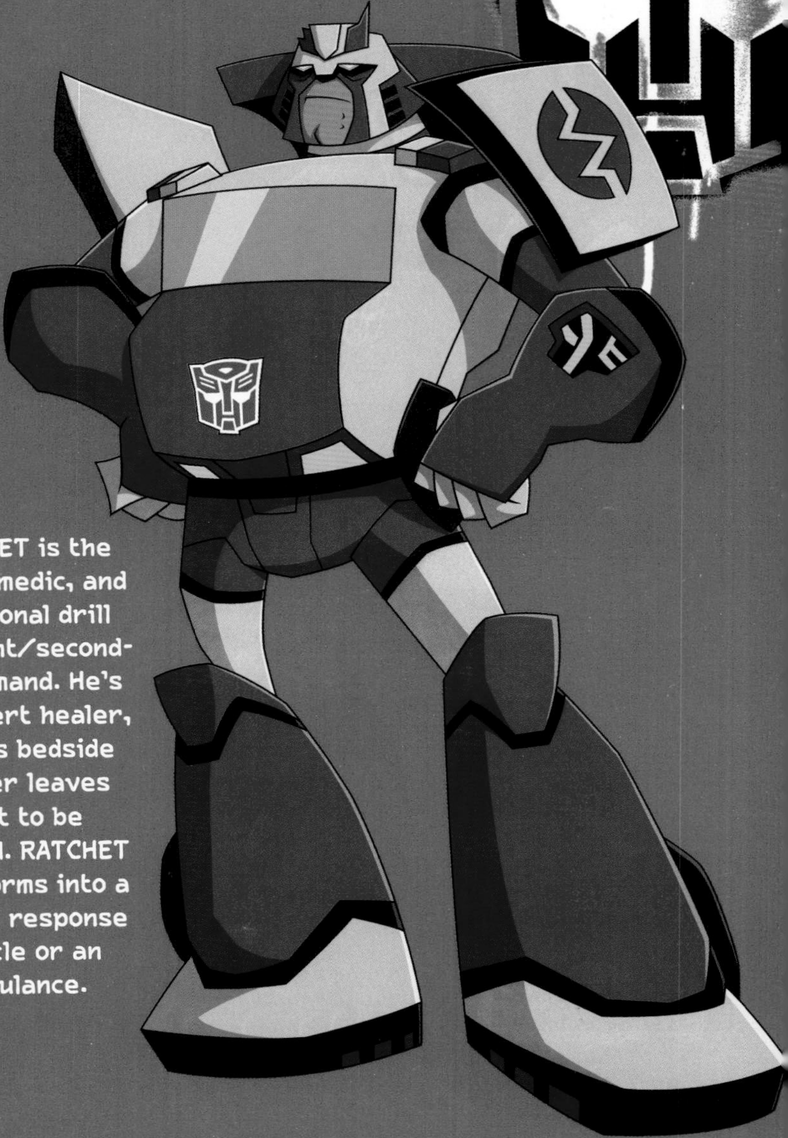

RATCHET is the team's medic, and occasional drill sergeant/second-in-command. He's an expert healer, but his bedside manner leaves a lot to be desired. RATCHET transforms into a medical response vehicle or an ambulance.

Bumblebee

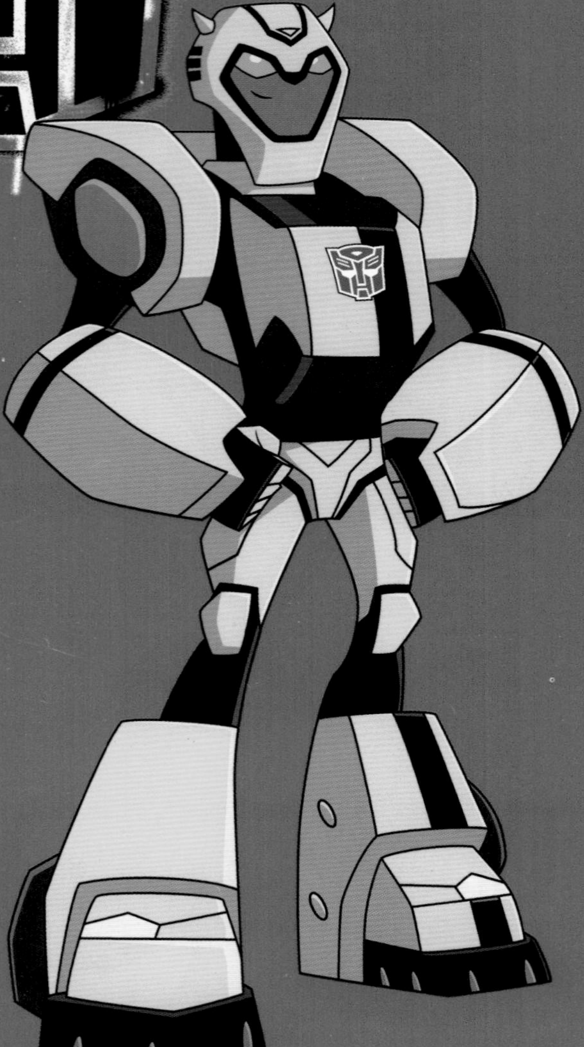

BUMBLEBEE is the "kid" of the team, easily the youngest and least mature of the AUTOBOTS. He's a bit of a showoff, always acting on impulse and rarely considering the consequences. But he looks awesome in his undercover police cruiser form.

Prowl

PROWL is the silent ninja of the group. He speaks only when he has to, and even then as briefly as possible. Of all the AUTOBOTS, he's the most skilled in direct combat. He is also the only member of the team with a motorcycle as his mechanized form.

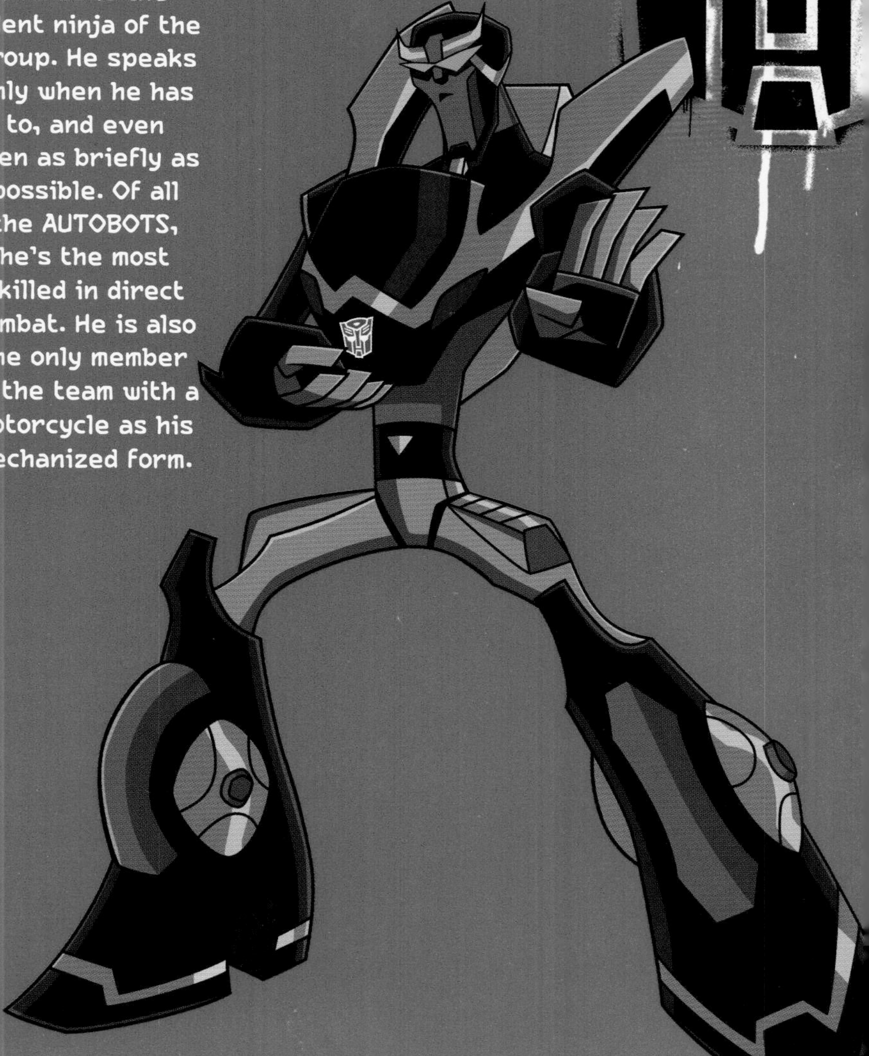

Megatron

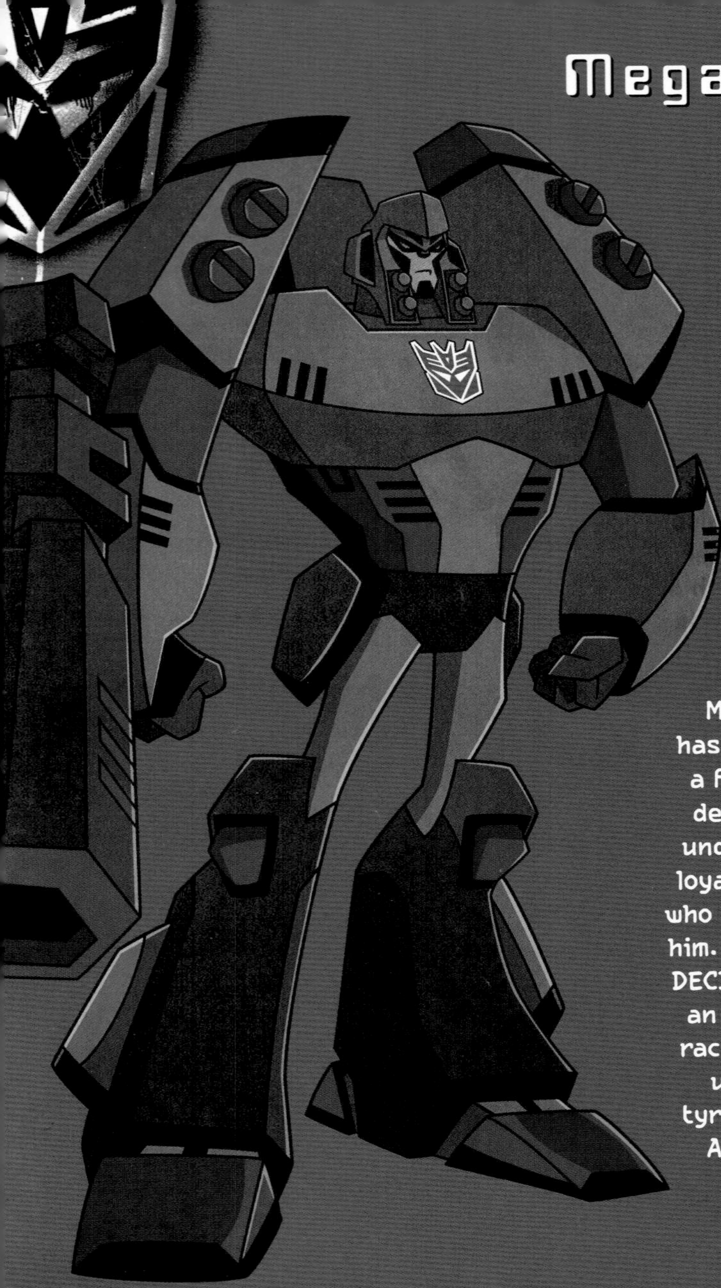

MEGATRON has the zeal of a fanatic and demands the unquestioning loyalty of those who serve under him. He sees the **DECIPTICONS** as an oppressed race suffering under the tyranny of the **AUTOBOTS.**

Starscream

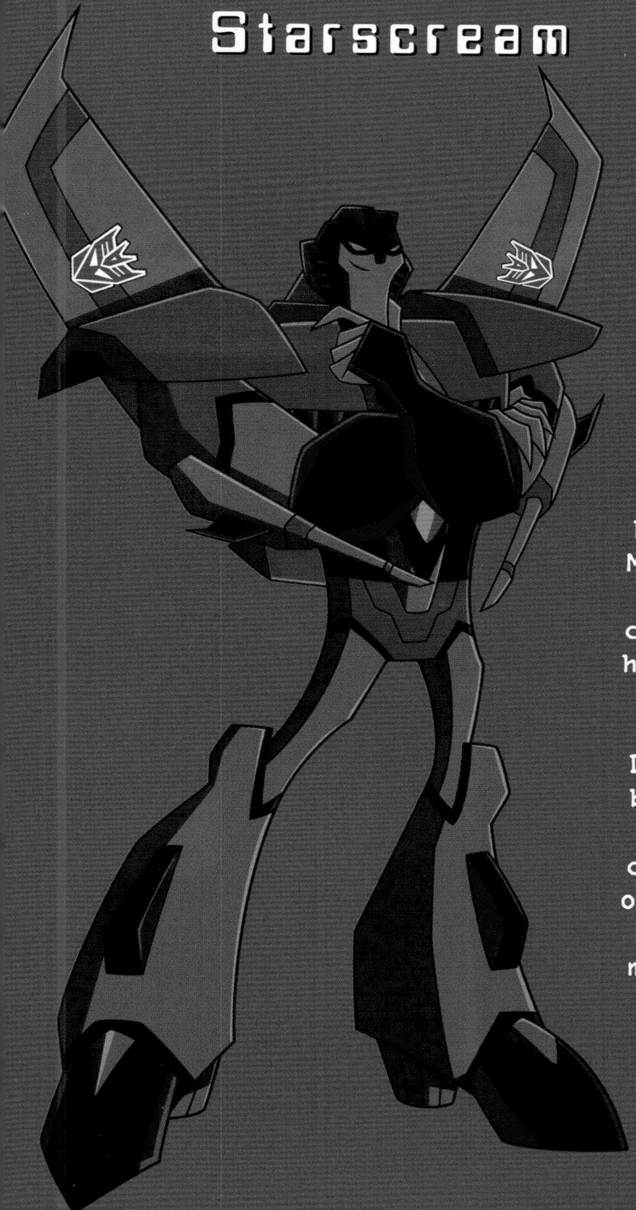

STARSCREAM has always lived in MEGATRON'S shadow and it burns him constantly. He feels he has done as much as MEGATRON in the name of the DECEPTICON cause, but he simply lacks MEGATRON'S charisma to inspire others to follow him. He is deadly in his mechanized fighter jet form.

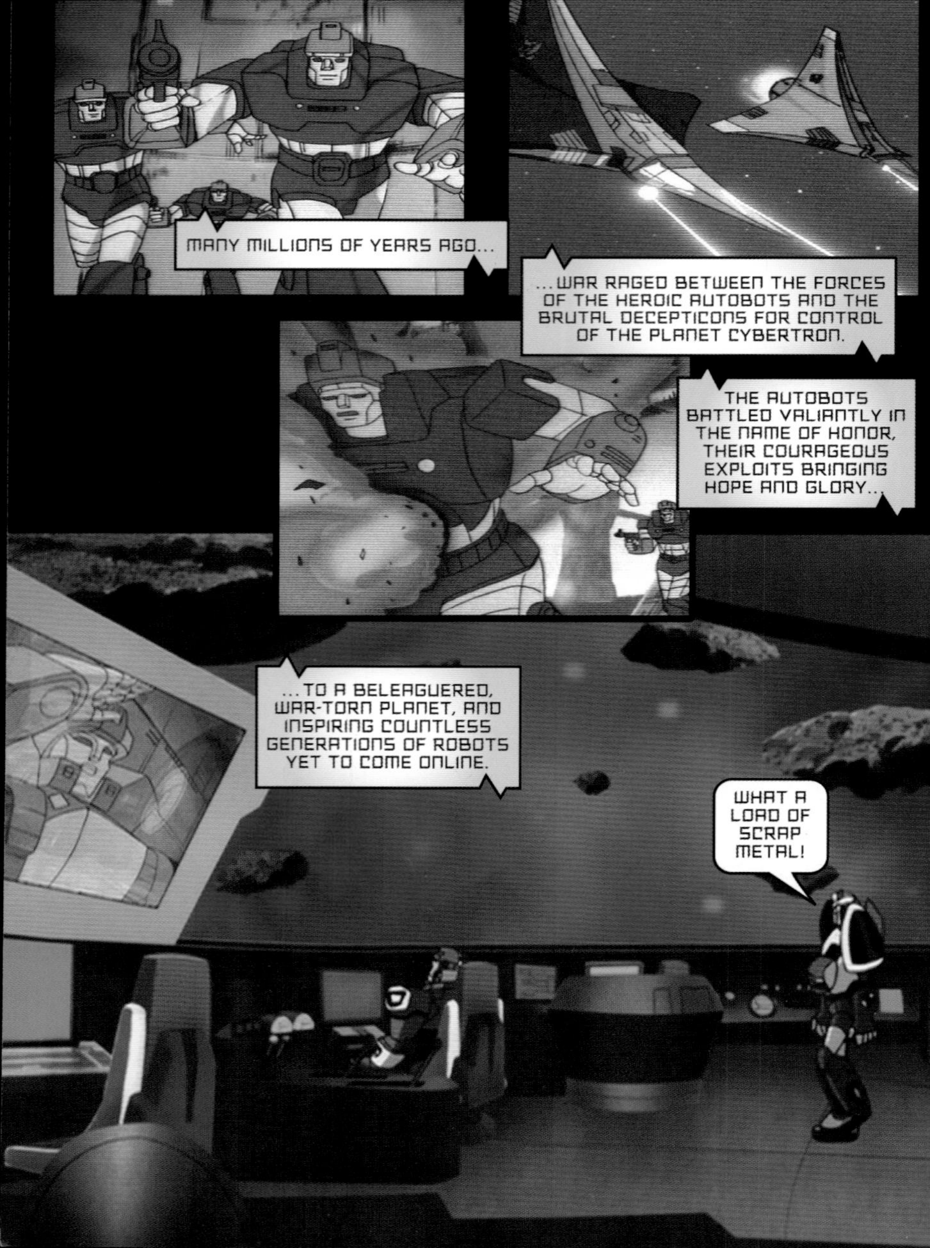
MANY MILLIONS OF YEARS AGO...
...WAR RAGED BETWEEN THE FORCES OF THE HEROIC AUTOBOTS AND THE BRUTAL DECEPTICONS FOR CONTROL OF THE PLANET CYBERTRON.
THE AUTOBOTS BATTLED VALIANTLY IN THE NAME OF HONOR, THEIR COURAGEOUS EXPLOITS BRINGING HOPE AND GLORY...
...TO A BELEAGUERED, WAR-TORN PLANET, AND INSPIRING COUNTLESS GENERATIONS OF ROBOTS YET TO COME ONLINE.
WHAT A LOAD OF SCRAP METAL!

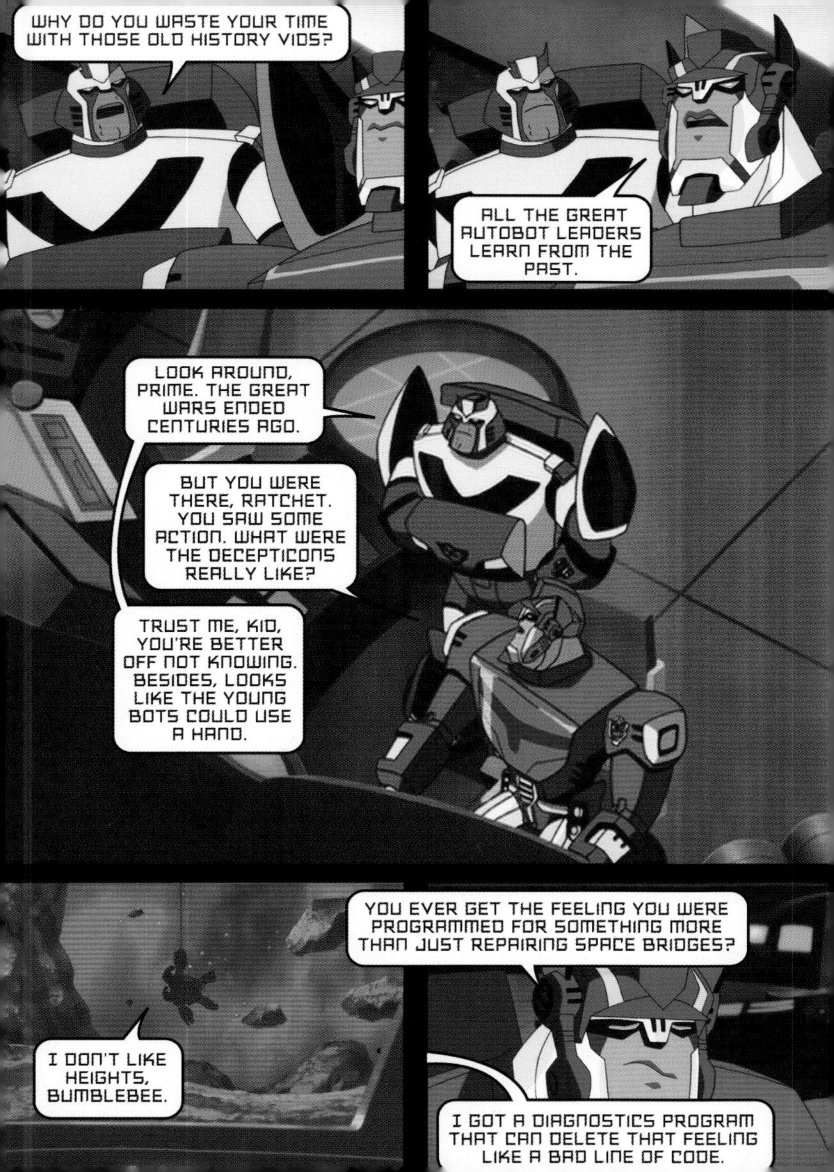

WHY DO YOU WASTE YOUR TIME WITH THOSE OLD HISTORY VIDS?
ALL THE GREAT AUTOBOT LEADERS LEARN FROM THE PAST.
LOOK AROUND, PRIME. THE GREAT WARS ENDED CENTURIES AGO.
BUT YOU WERE THERE, RATCHET. YOU SAW SOME ACTION. WHAT WERE THE DECEPTICONS REALLY LIKE?
TRUST ME, KID, YOU'RE BETTER OFF NOT KNOWING. BESIDES, LOOKS LIKE THE YOUNG BOTS COULD USE A HAND.
I DON'T LIKE HEIGHTS, BUMBLEBEE.
YOU EVER GET THE FEELING YOU WERE PROGRAMMED FOR SOMETHING MORE THAN JUST REPAIRING SPACE BRIDGES?
I GOT A DIAGNOSTICS PROGRAM THAT CAN DELETE THAT FEELING LIKE A BAD LINE OF CODE.

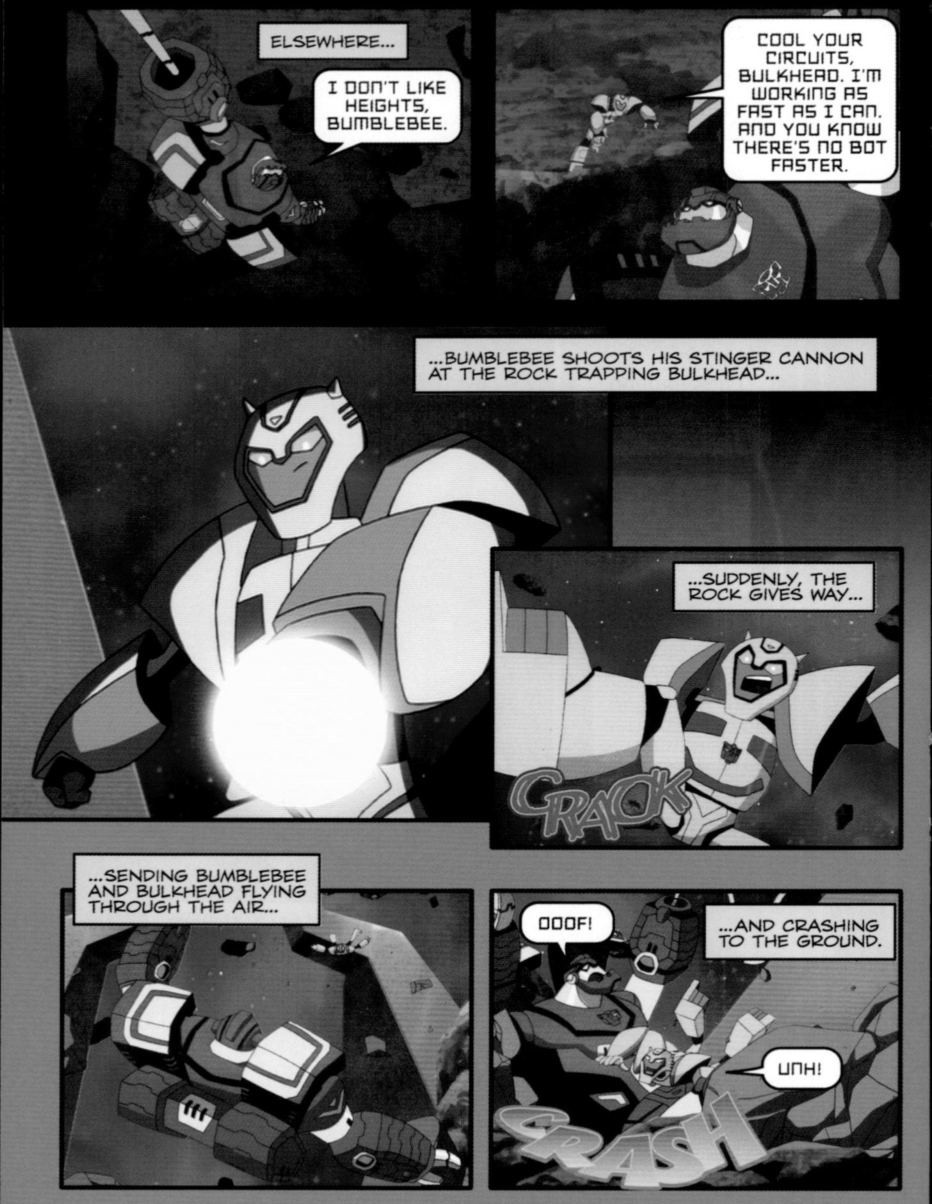
ELSEWHERE...
I DON'T LIKE HEIGHTS, BUMBLEBEE.
COOL YOUR CIRCUITS, BULKHEAD. I'M WORKING AS FAST AS I CAN. AND YOU KNOW THERE'S NO BOT FASTER.
...BUMBLEBEE SHOOTS HIS STINGER CANNON AT THE ROCK TRAPPING BULKHEAD...
...SUDDENLY, THE ROCK GIVES WAY...
CRACK
...SENDING BUMBLEBEE AND BULKHEAD FLYING THROUGH THE AIR...
OOOF!
...AND CRASHING TO THE GROUND.
UNH!
CRASH

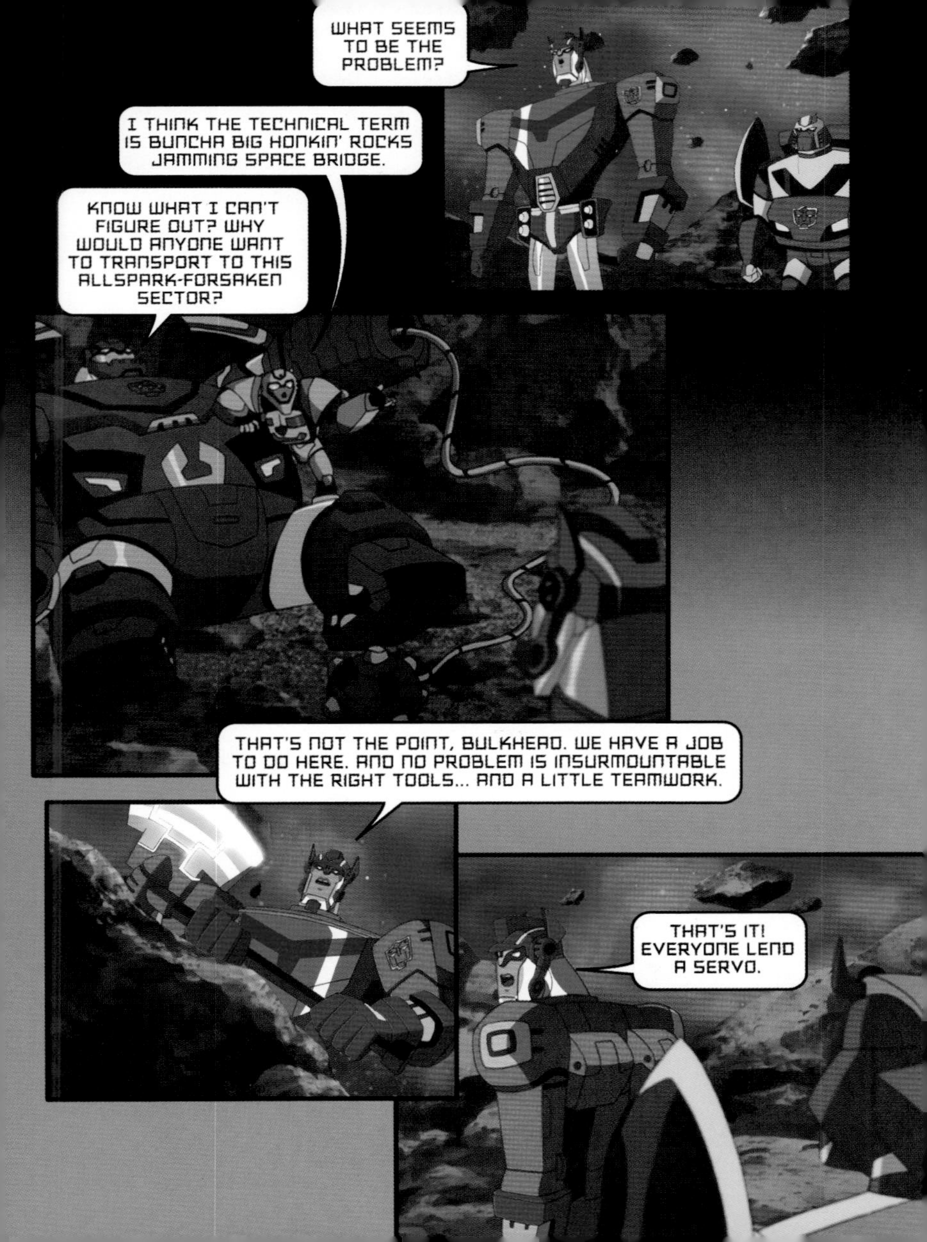
WHAT SEEMS TO BE THE PROBLEM?
I THINK THE TECHNICAL TERM IS BUNCHA BIG HONKIN' ROCKS JAMMING SPACE BRIDGE.
KNOW WHAT I CAN'T FIGURE OUT? WHY WOULD ANYONE WANT TO TRANSPORT TO THIS ALLSPARK-FORSAKEN SECTOR?
THAT'S NOT THE POINT, BULKHEAD. WE HAVE A JOB TO DO HERE. AND NO PROBLEM IS INSURMOUNTABLE WITH THE RIGHT TOOLS... AND A LITTLE TEAMWORK.
THAT'S IT! EVERYONE LEND A SERVO.

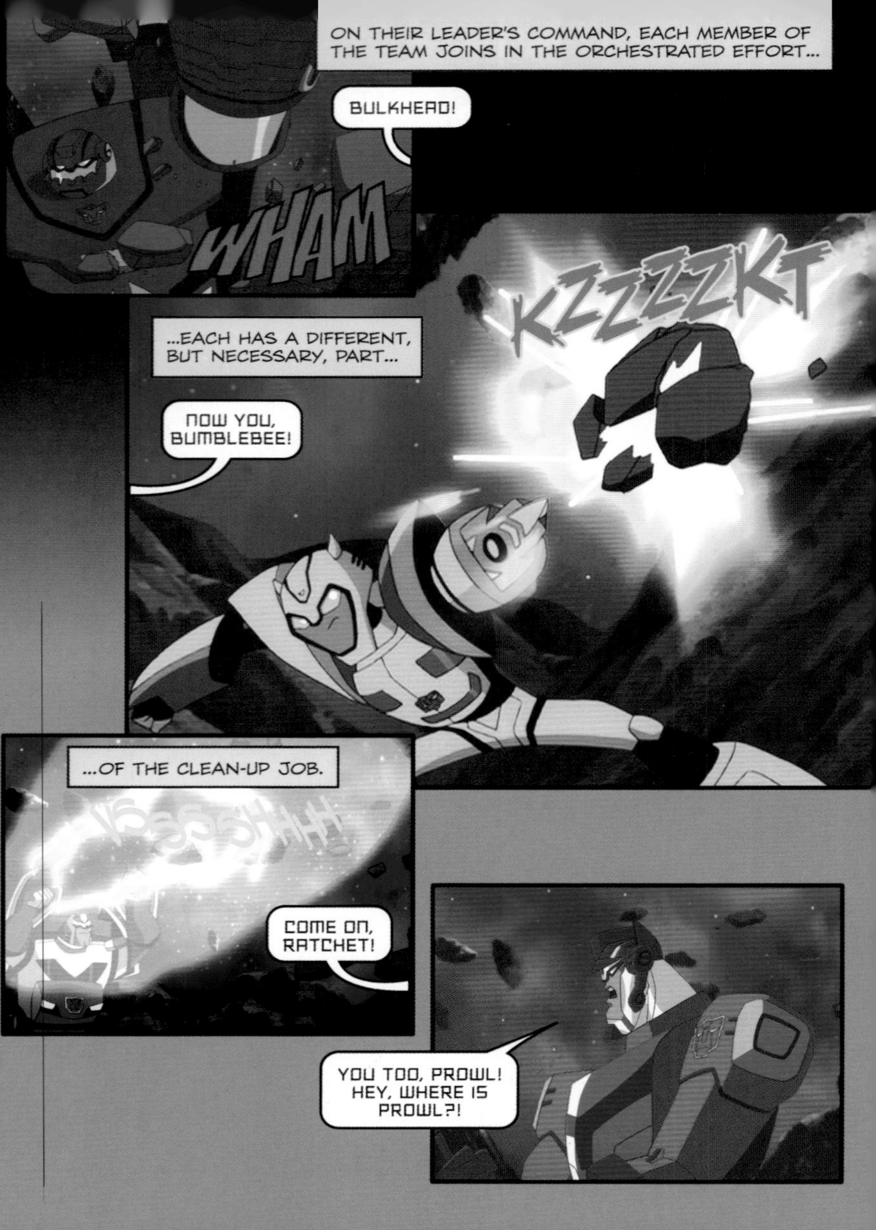
ON THEIR LEADER'S COMMAND, EACH MEMBER OF THE TEAM JOINS IN THE ORCHESTRATED EFFORT...
BULKHEAD!
WHAM
KZZZZKT
...EACH HAS A DIFFERENT, BUT NECESSARY, PART...
NOW YOU, BUMBLEBEE!
...OF THE CLEAN-UP JOB.
COME ON, RATCHET!
YOU TOO, PROWL! HEY, WHERE IS PROWL?!

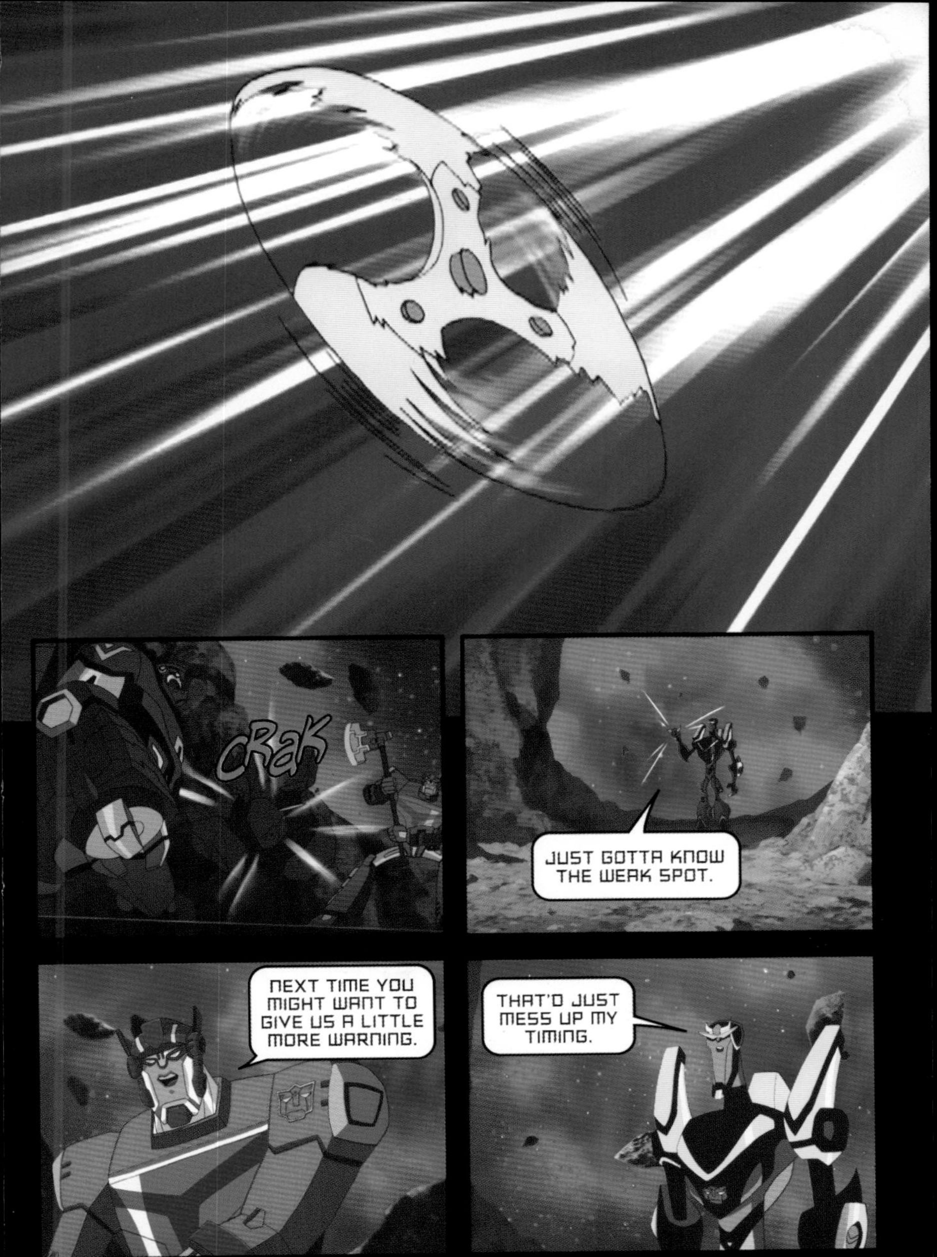
CRAK
JUST GOTTA KNOW THE WEAK SPOT.
NEXT TIME YOU MIGHT WANT TO GIVE US A LITTLE MORE WARNING.
THAT'D JUST MESS UP MY TIMING.

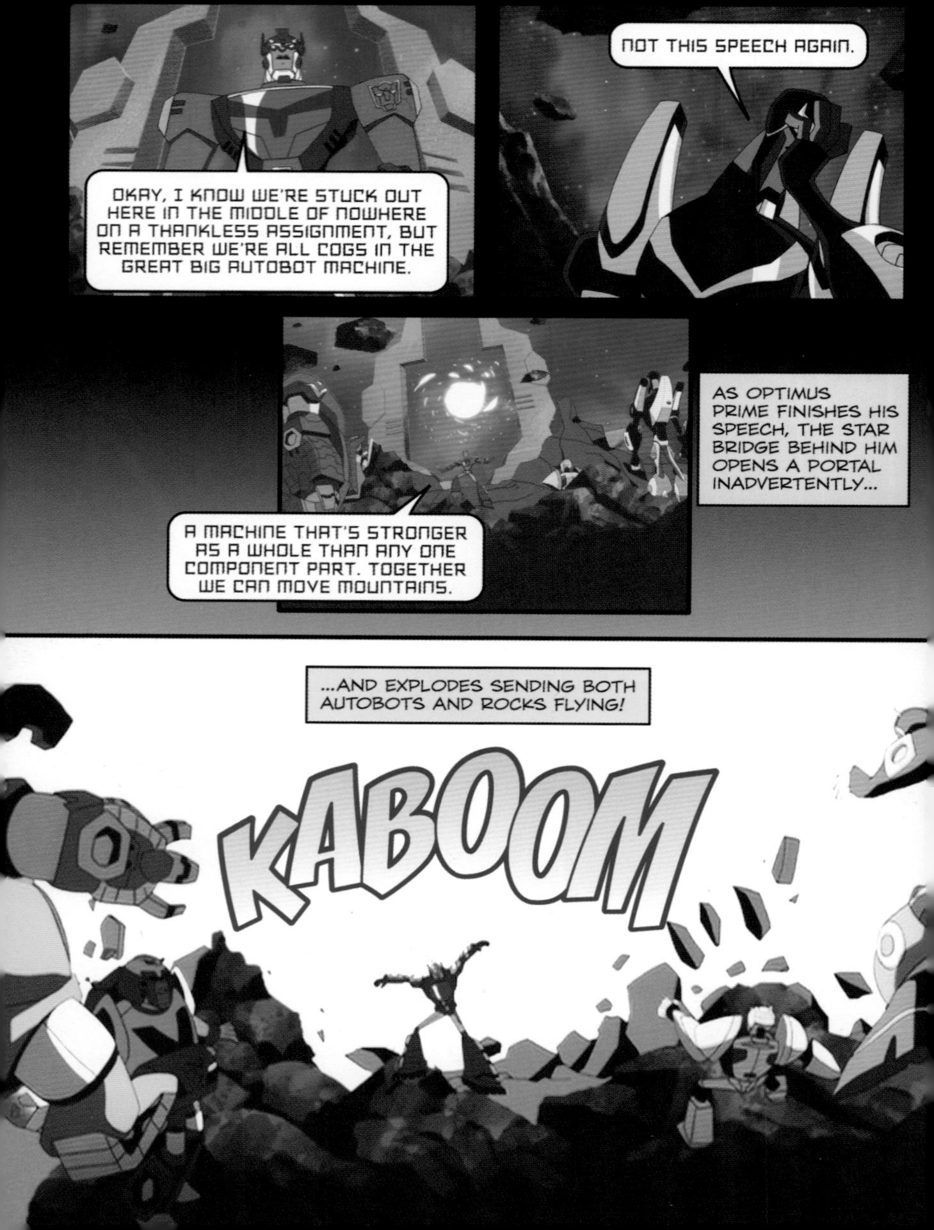
OKAY, I KNOW WE'RE STUCK OUT HERE IN THE MIDDLE OF NOWHERE ON A THANKLESS ASSIGNMENT, BUT REMEMBER WE'RE ALL COGS IN THE GREAT BIG AUTOBOT MACHINE.
NOT THIS SPEECH AGAIN.
A MACHINE THAT'S STRONGER AS A WHOLE THAN ANY ONE COMPONENT PART. TOGETHER WE CAN MOVE MOUNTAINS.
AS OPTIMUS PRIME FINISHES HIS SPEECH, THE STAR BRIDGE BEHIND HIM OPENS A PORTAL INADVERTENTLY...
...AND EXPLODES SENDING BOTH AUTOBOTS AND ROCKS FLYING!
KABOOM

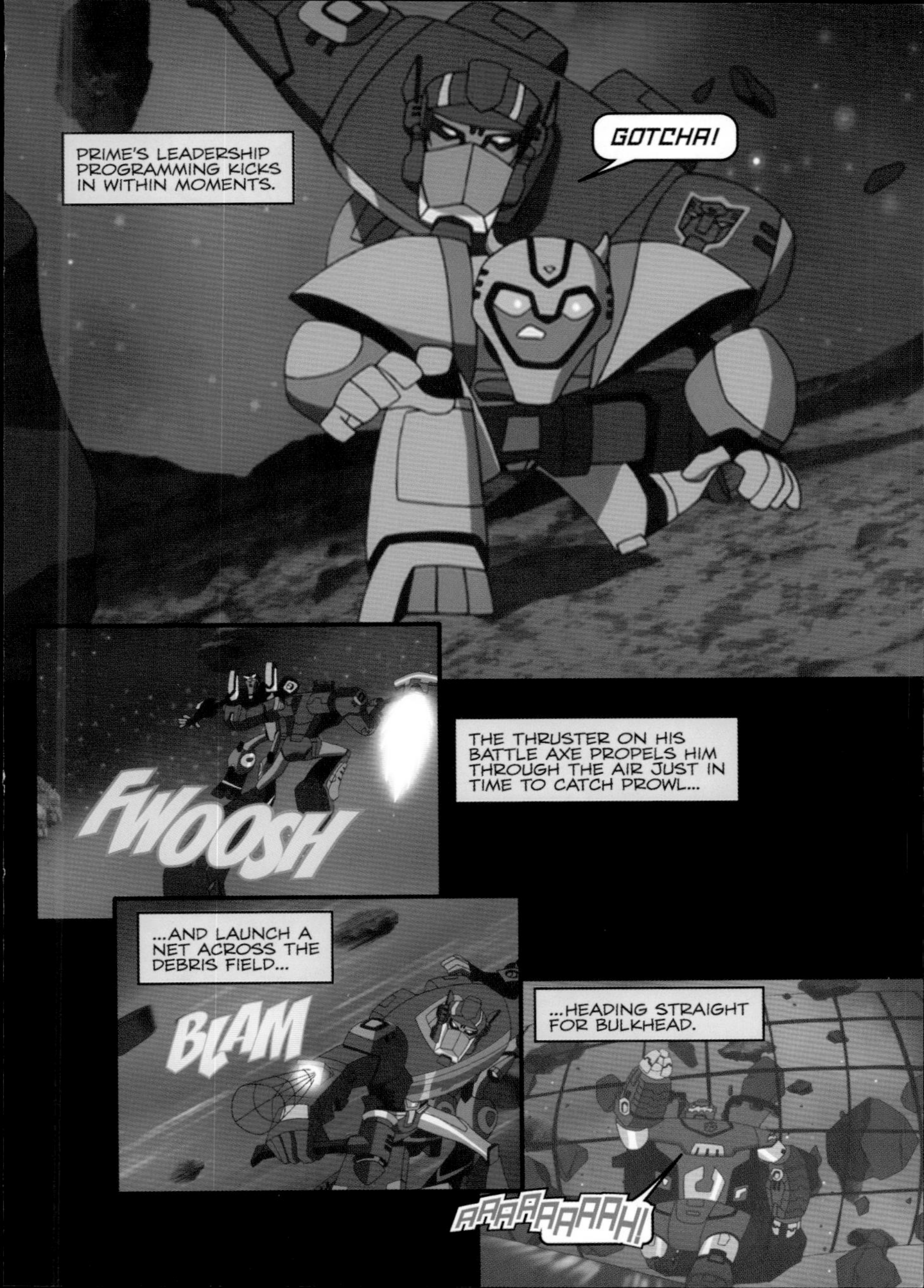

PRIME'S LEADERSHIP PROGRAMMING KICKS IN WITHIN MOMENTS.
GOTCHA!
FWOOSH
THE THRUSTER ON HIS BATTLE AXE PROPELS HIM THROUGH THE AIR JUST IN TIME TO CATCH PROWL...
...AND LAUNCH A NET ACROSS THE DEBRIS FIELD...
BLAM
...HEADING STRAIGHT FOR BULKHEAD.
AAAAAAAAAH!

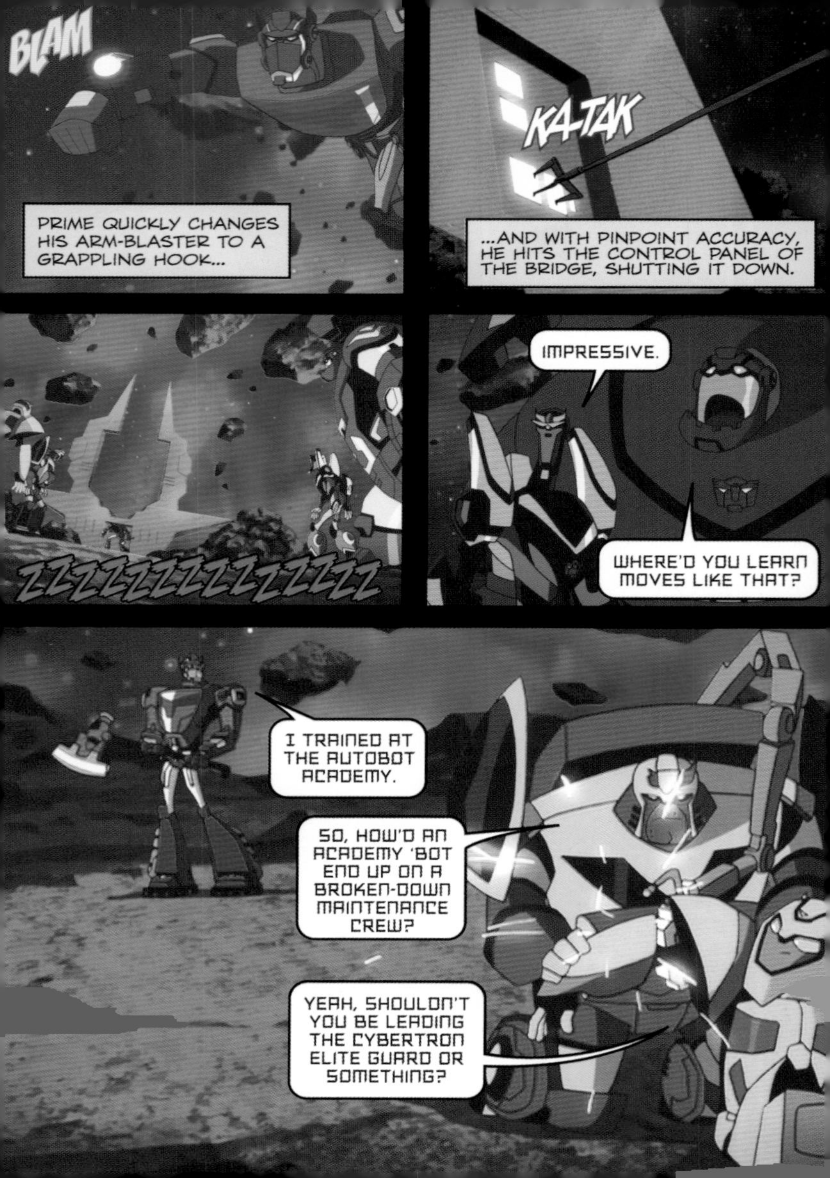
BLAM
PRIME QUICKLY CHANGES HIS ARM-BLASTER TO A GRAPPLING HOOK...
KA-TAK
...AND WITH PINPOINT ACCURACY, HE HITS THE CONTROL PANEL OF THE BRIDGE, SHUTTING IT DOWN.
ZZZZZZZZZZZZZZZZZZ
IMPRESSIVE.
WHERE'D YOU LEARN MOVES LIKE THAT?
I TRAINED AT THE AUTOBOT ACADEMY.
SO, HOW'D AN ACADEMY 'BOT END UP ON A BROKEN-DOWN MAINTENANCE CREW?
YEAH, SHOULDN'T YOU BE LEADING THE CYBERTRON ELITE GUARD OR SOMETHING?

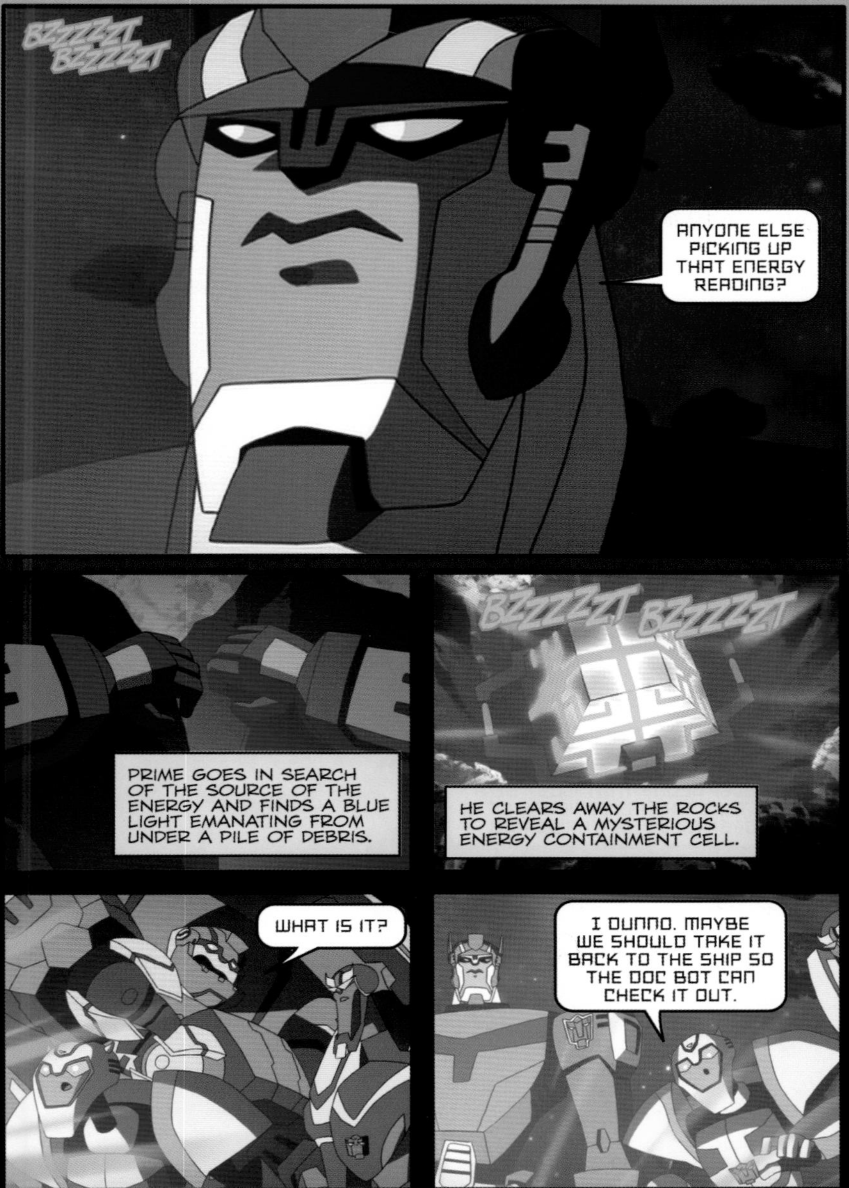
BZZZZZT BZZZZZT
ANYONE ELSE PICKING UP THAT ENERGY READING?
PRIME GOES IN SEARCH OF THE SOURCE OF THE ENERGY AND FINDS A BLUE LIGHT EMANATING FROM UNDER A PILE OF DEBRIS.
BZZZZZT BZZZZZT
HE CLEARS AWAY THE ROCKS TO REVEAL A MYSTERIOUS ENERGY CONTAINMENT CELL.
WHAT IS IT?
I DUNNO. MAYBE WE SHOULD TAKE IT BACK TO THE SHIP SO THE DOC BOT CAN CHECK IT OUT.

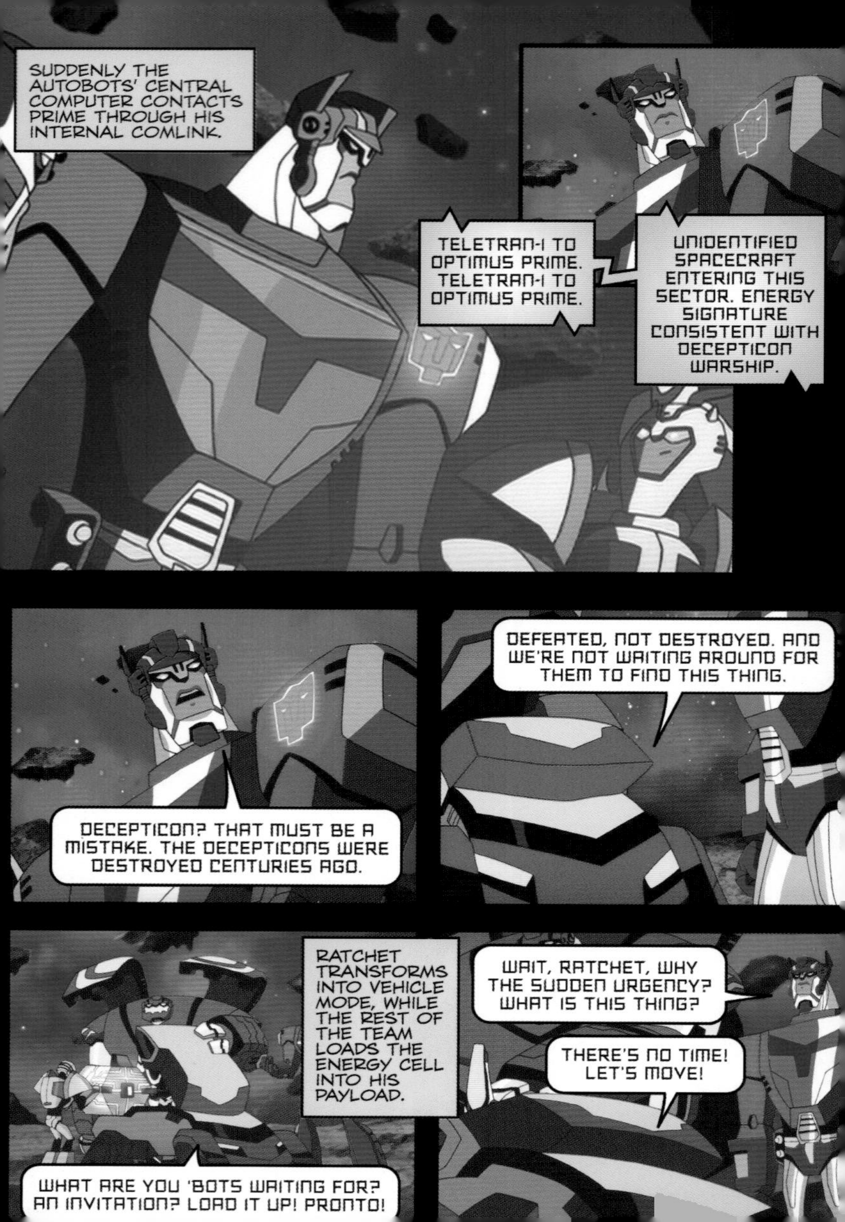
SUDDENLY THE AUTOBOTS' CENTRAL COMPUTER CONTACTS PRIME THROUGH HIS INTERNAL COMLINK.
TELETRAN-1 TO OPTIMUS PRIME. TELETRAN-1 TO OPTIMUS PRIME.
UNIDENTIFIED SPACECRAFT ENTERING THIS SECTOR. ENERGY SIGNATURE CONSISTENT WITH DECEPTICON WARSHIP.
DECEPTICON? THAT MUST BE A MISTAKE. THE DECEPTICONS WERE DESTROYED CENTURIES AGO.
DEFEATED, NOT DESTROYED. AND WE'RE NOT WAITING AROUND FOR THEM TO FIND THIS THING.
RATCHET TRANSFORMS INTO VEHICLE MODE, WHILE THE REST OF THE TEAM LOADS THE ENERGY CELL INTO HIS PAYLOAD.
WHAT ARE YOU 'BOTS WAITING FOR? AN INVITATION? LOAD IT UP! PRONTO!
WAIT, RATCHET, WHY THE SUDDEN URGENCY? WHAT IS THIS THING?
THERE'S NO TIME! LET'S MOVE!

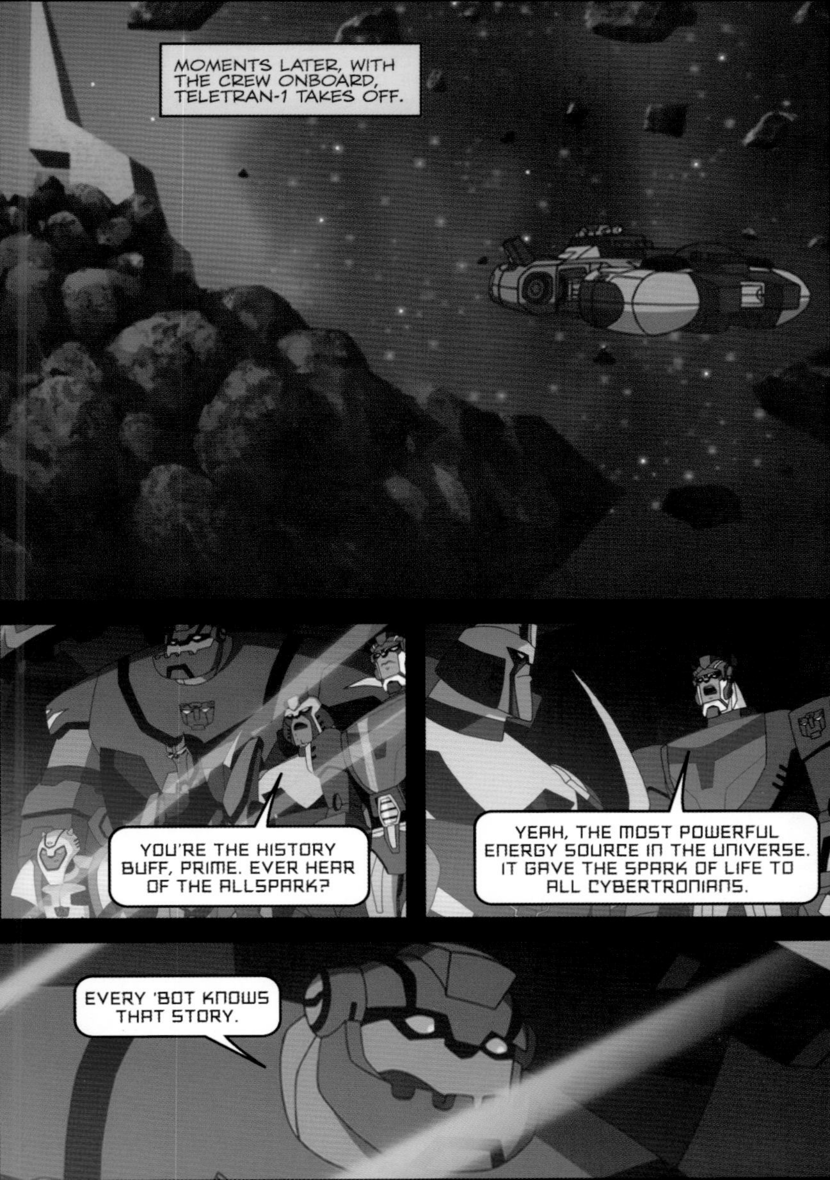
MOMENTS LATER, WITH THE CREW ONBOARD, TELETRAN-1 TAKES OFF.
YOU'RE THE HISTORY BUFF, PRIME. EVER HEAR OF THE ALLSPARK?
YEAH, THE MOST POWERFUL ENERGY SOURCE IN THE UNIVERSE. IT GAVE THE SPARK OF LIFE TO ALL CYBERTRONIANS.
EVERY 'BOT KNOWS THAT STORY.

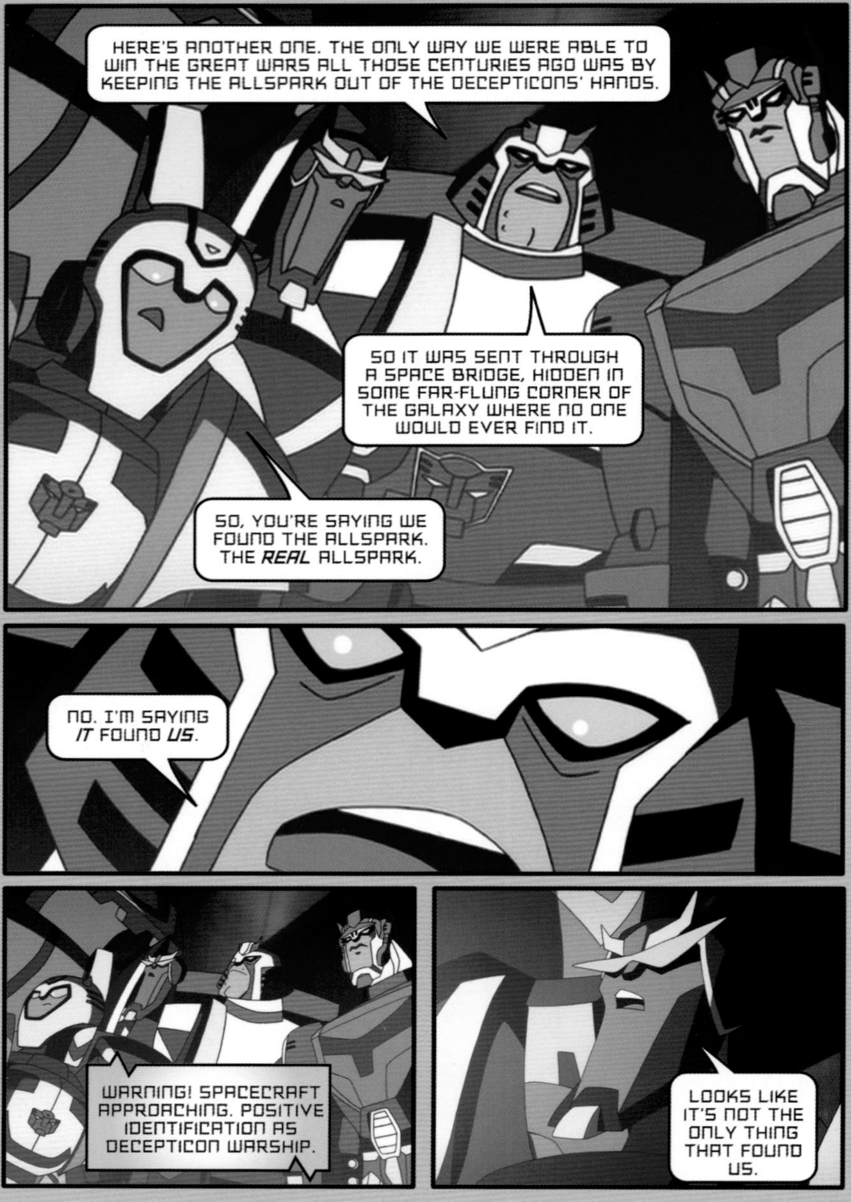
HERE'S ANOTHER ONE. THE ONLY WAY WE WERE ABLE TO WIN THE GREAT WARS ALL THOSE CENTURIES AGO WAS BY KEEPING THE ALLSPARK OUT OF THE DECEPTICONS' HANDS.
SO IT WAS SENT THROUGH A SPACE BRIDGE, HIDDEN IN SOME FAR-FLUNG CORNER OF THE GALAXY WHERE NO ONE WOULD EVER FIND IT.
SO, YOU'RE SAYING WE FOUND THE ALLSPARK. THE *REAL* ALLSPARK.
NO. I'M SAYING *IT* FOUND *US*.
WARNING! SPACECRAFT APPROACHING. POSITIVE IDENTIFICATION AS DECEPTICON WARSHIP.
LOOKS LIKE IT'S NOT THE ONLY THING THAT FOUND US.

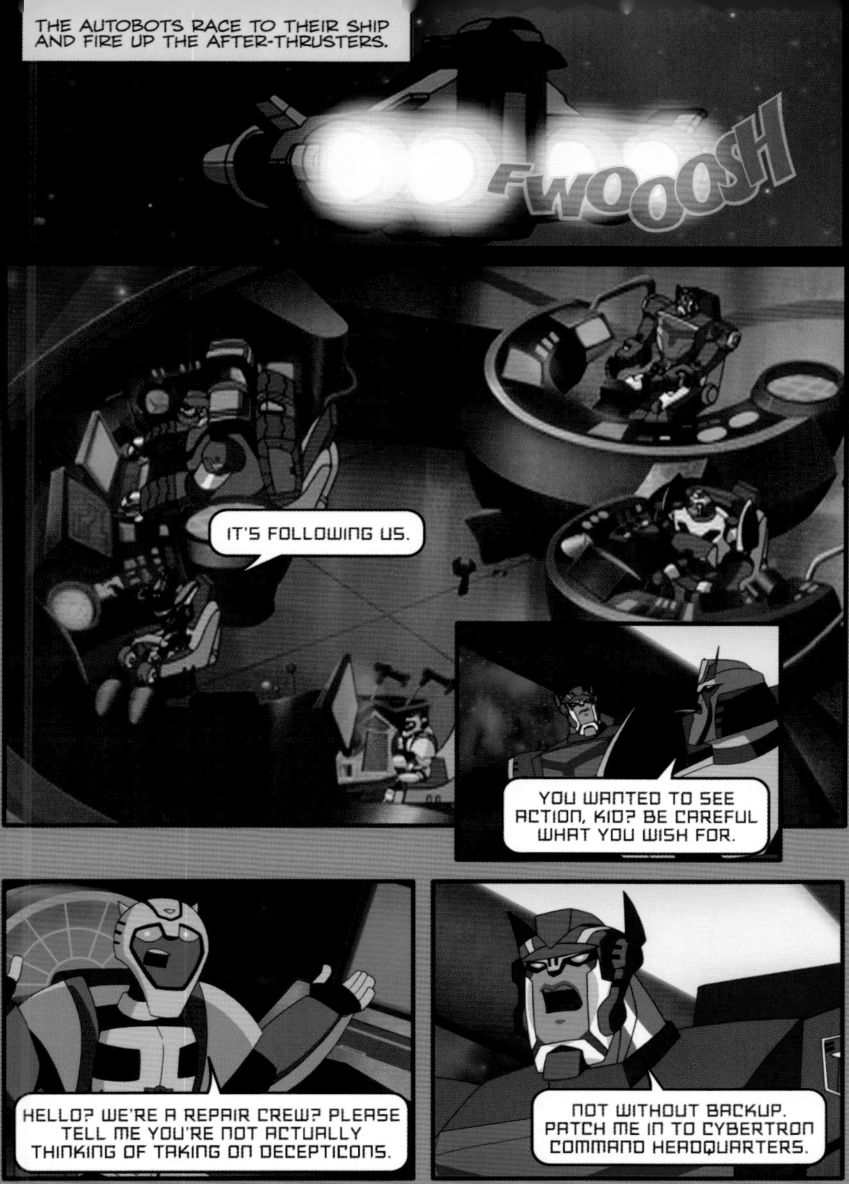
THE AUTOBOTS RACE TO THEIR SHIP AND FIRE UP THE AFTER-THRUSTERS.
FWOOOOSH
IT'S FOLLOWING US.
YOU WANTED TO SEE ACTION, KID? BE CAREFUL WHAT YOU WISH FOR.
HELLO? WE'RE A REPAIR CREW? PLEASE TELL ME YOU'RE NOT ACTUALLY THINKING OF TAKING ON DECEPTICONS.
NOT WITHOUT BACKUP. PATCH ME IN TO CYBERTRON COMMAND HEADQUARTERS.

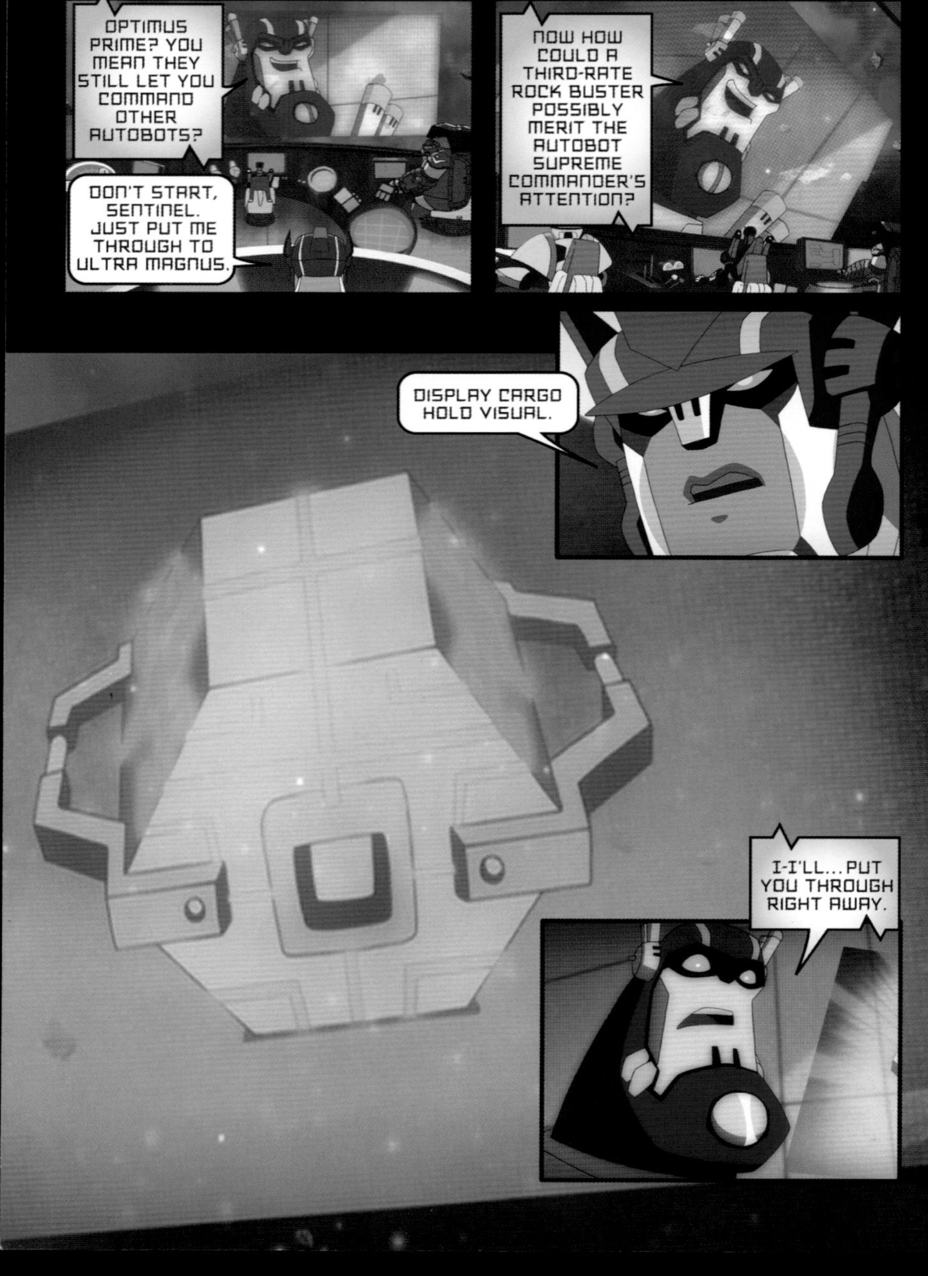
OPTIMUS PRIME? YOU MEAN THEY STILL LET YOU COMMAND OTHER AUTOBOTS?
DON'T START, SENTINEL. JUST PUT ME THROUGH TO ULTRA MAGNUS.
NOW HOW COULD A THIRD-RATE ROCK BUSTER POSSIBLY MERIT THE AUTOBOT SUPREME COMMANDER'S ATTENTION?
DISPLAY CARGO HOLD VISUAL.
I-I'LL...PUT YOU THROUGH RIGHT AWAY.

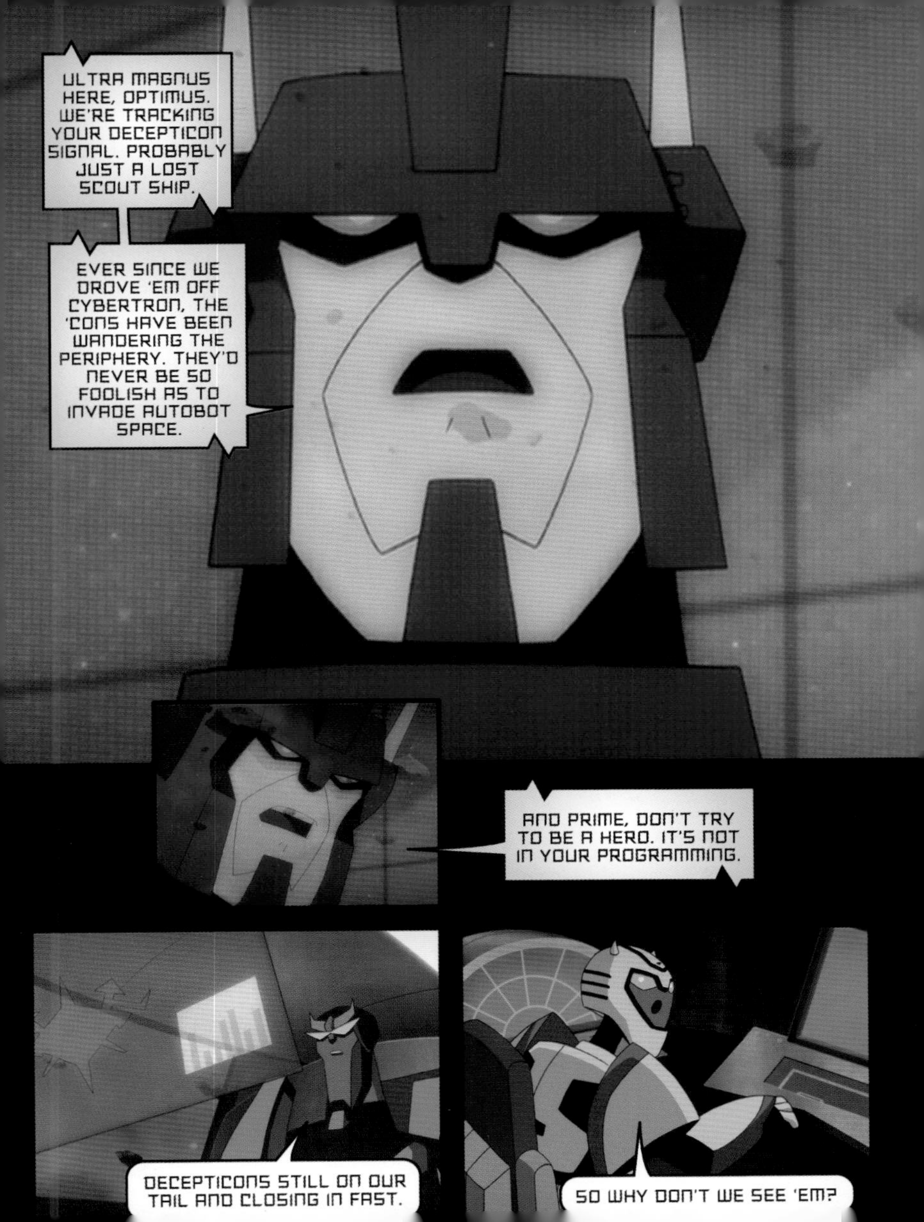
ULTRA MAGNUS HERE, OPTIMUS. WE'RE TRACKING YOUR DECEPTICON SIGNAL. PROBABLY JUST A LOST SCOUT SHIP.
EVER SINCE WE DROVE 'EM OFF CYBERTRON, THE 'CONS HAVE BEEN WANDERING THE PERIPHERY. THEY'D NEVER BE SO FOOLISH AS TO INVADE AUTOBOT SPACE.
AND PRIME, DON'T TRY TO BE A HERO. IT'S NOT IN YOUR PROGRAMMING.
DECEPTICONS STILL ON OUR TAIL AND CLOSING IN FAST.
SO WHY DON'T WE SEE 'EM?

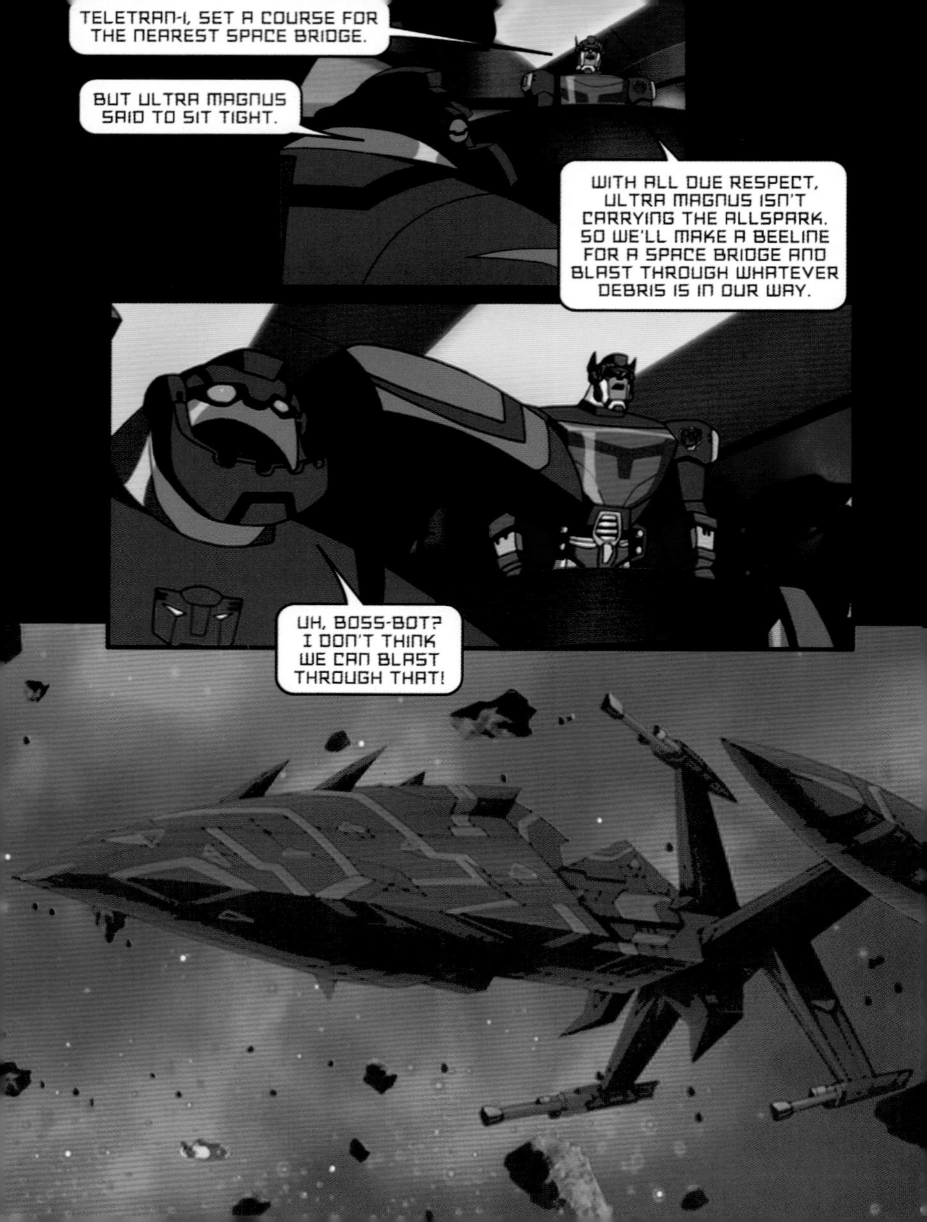
TELETRAN-1, SET A COURSE FOR THE NEAREST SPACE BRIDGE.
BUT ULTRA MAGNUS SAID TO SIT TIGHT.
WITH ALL DUE RESPECT, ULTRA MAGNUS ISN'T CARRYING THE ALLSPARK. SO WE'LL MAKE A BEELINE FOR A SPACE BRIDGE AND BLAST THROUGH WHATEVER DEBRIS IS IN OUR WAY.
UH, BOSS-BOT? I DON'T THINK WE CAN BLAST THROUGH THAT!

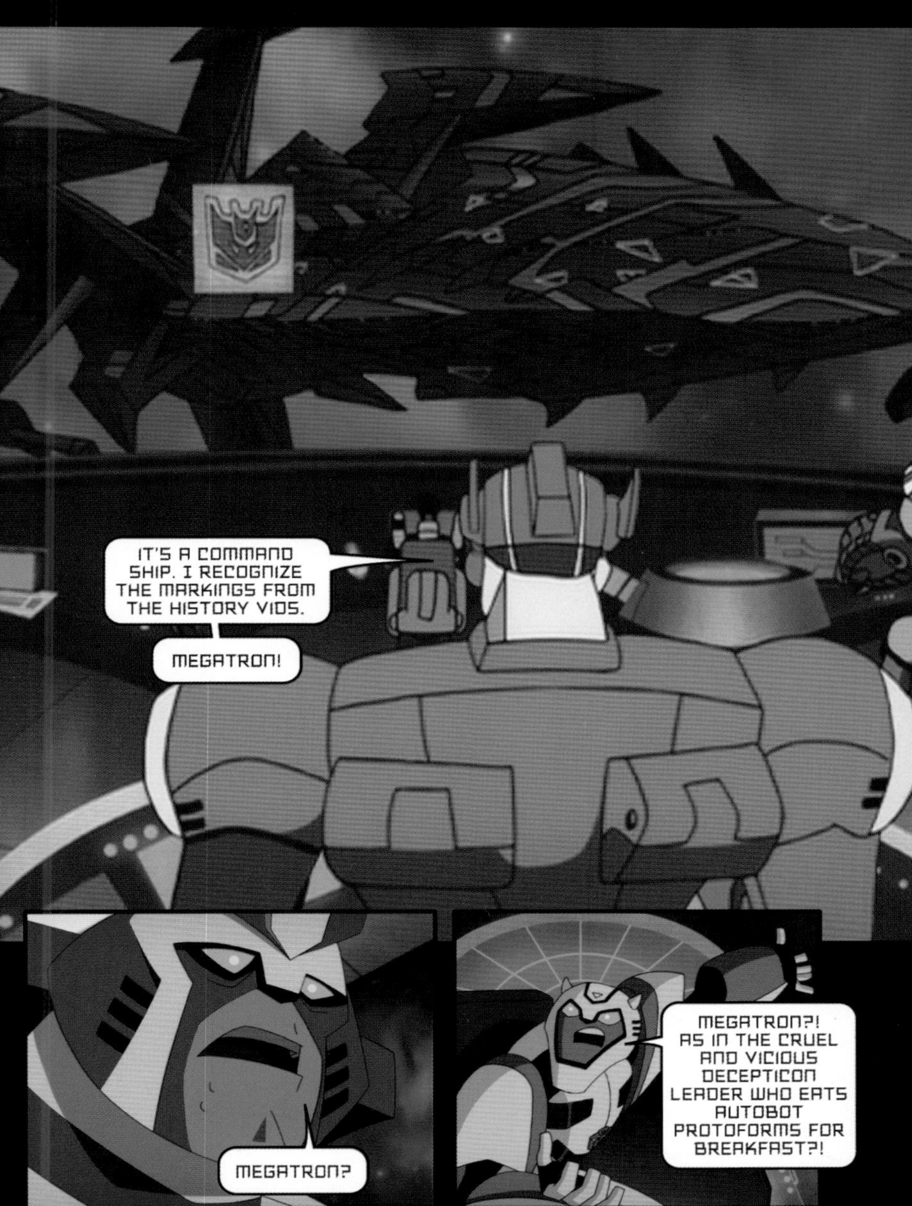
IT'S A COMMAND SHIP. I RECOGNIZE THE MARKINGS FROM THE HISTORY VIDS.
MEGATRON!
MEGATRON?
MEGATRON?! AS IN THE CRUEL AND VICIOUS DECEPTICON LEADER WHO EATS AUTOBOT PROTOFORMS FOR BREAKFAST?!

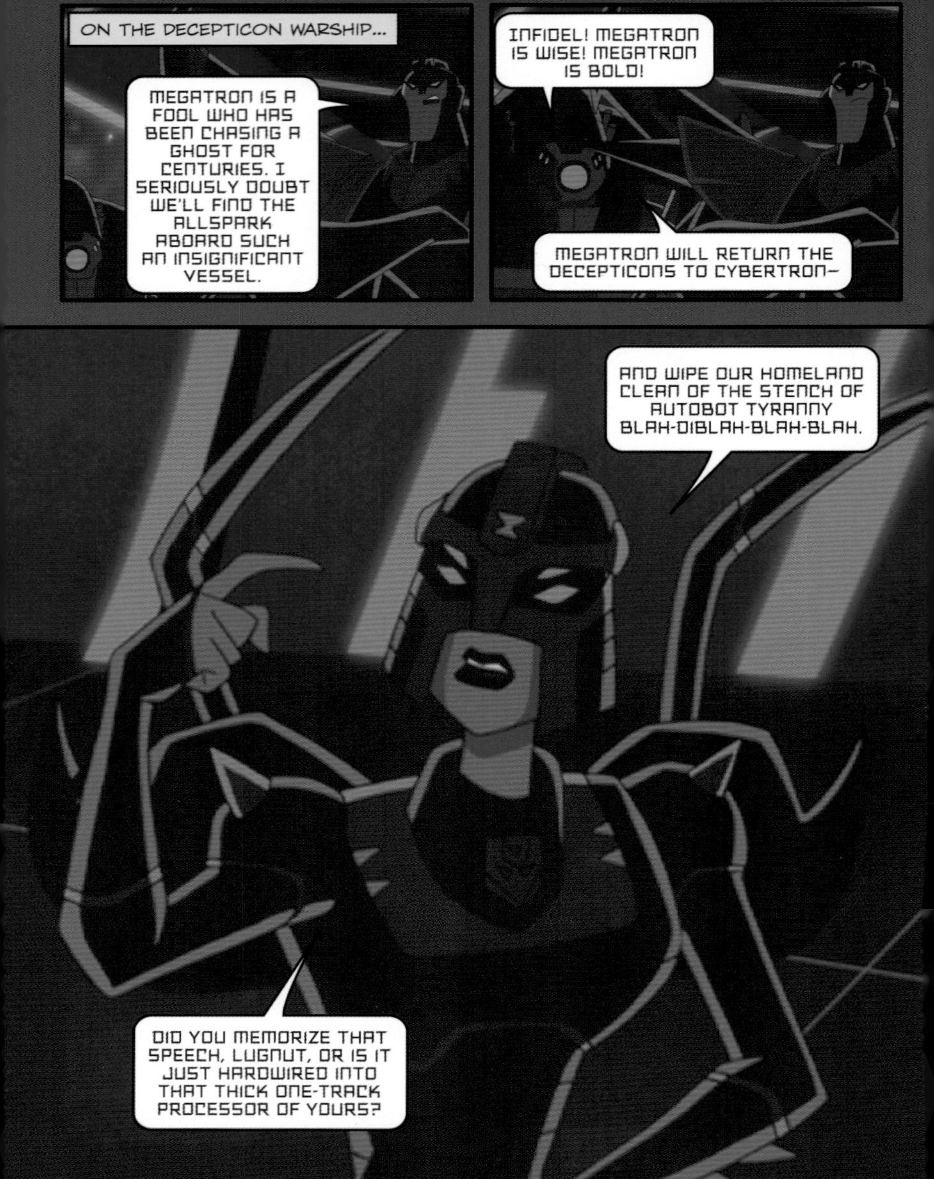
ON THE DECEPTICON WARSHIP...
MEGATRON IS A FOOL WHO HAS BEEN CHASING A GHOST FOR CENTURIES. I SERIOUSLY DOUBT WE'LL FIND THE ALLSPARK ABOARD SUCH AN INSIGNIFICANT VESSEL.
INFIDEL! MEGATRON IS WISE! MEGATRON IS BOLD!
MEGATRON WILL RETURN THE DECEPTICONS TO CYBERTRON—
AND WIPE OUR HOMELAND CLEAN OF THE STENCH OF AUTOBOT TYRANNY BLAH-DIBLAH-BLAH-BLAH.
DID YOU MEMORIZE THAT SPEECH, LUGNUT, OR IS IT JUST HARDWIRED INTO THAT THICK ONE-TRACK PROCESSOR OF YOURS?

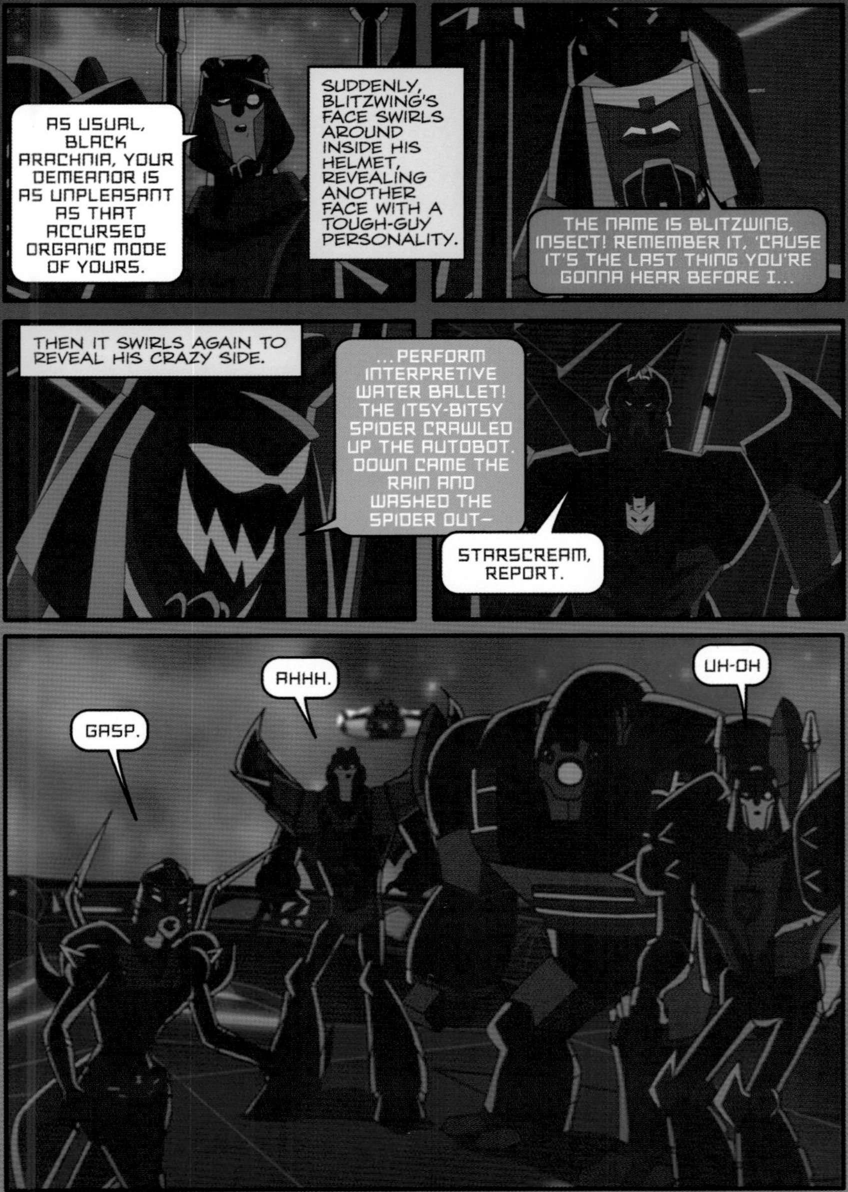

AS USUAL, BLACK ARACHNIA, YOUR DEMEANOR IS AS UNPLEASANT AS THAT ACCURSED ORGANIC MODE OF YOURS.
SUDDENLY, BLITZWING'S FACE SWIRLS AROUND INSIDE HIS HELMET, REVEALING ANOTHER FACE WITH A TOUGH-GUY PERSONALITY.
THE NAME IS BLITZWING, INSECT! REMEMBER IT, 'CAUSE IT'S THE LAST THING YOU'RE GONNA HEAR BEFORE I...
THEN IT SWIRLS AGAIN TO REVEAL HIS CRAZY SIDE.
...PERFORM INTERPRETIVE WATER BALLET! THE ITSY-BITSY SPIDER CRAWLED UP THE AUTOBOT. DOWN CAME THE RAIN AND WASHED THE SPIDER OUT—
STARSCREAM, REPORT.
GASP.
AHHH.
UH-OH

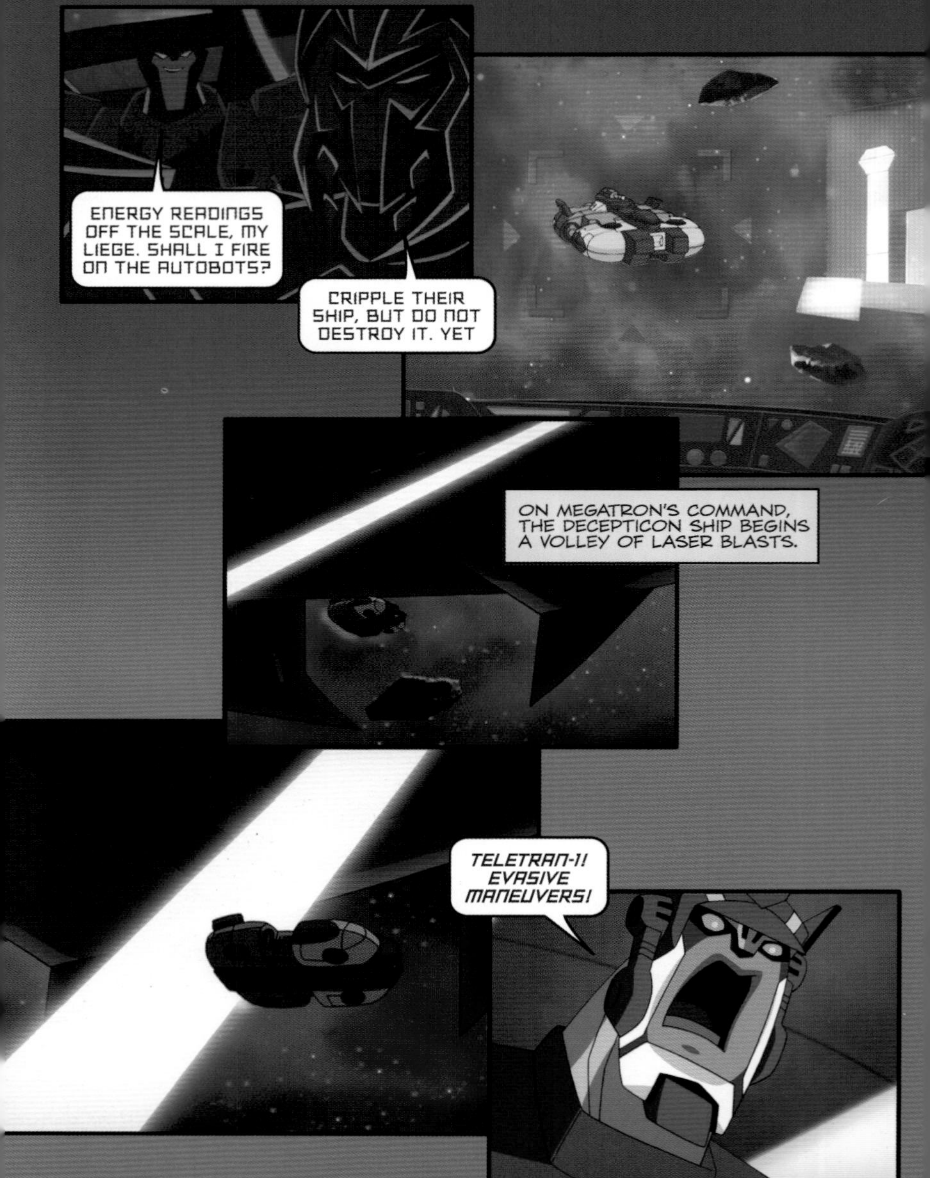
ENERGY READINGS OFF THE SCALE, MY LIEGE. SHALL I FIRE ON THE AUTOBOTS?
CRIPPLE THEIR SHIP, BUT DO NOT DESTROY IT. YET
ON MEGATRON'S COMMAND, THE DECEPTICON SHIP BEGINS A VOLLEY OF LASER BLASTS.
TELETRAN-1! EVASIVE MANEUVERS!

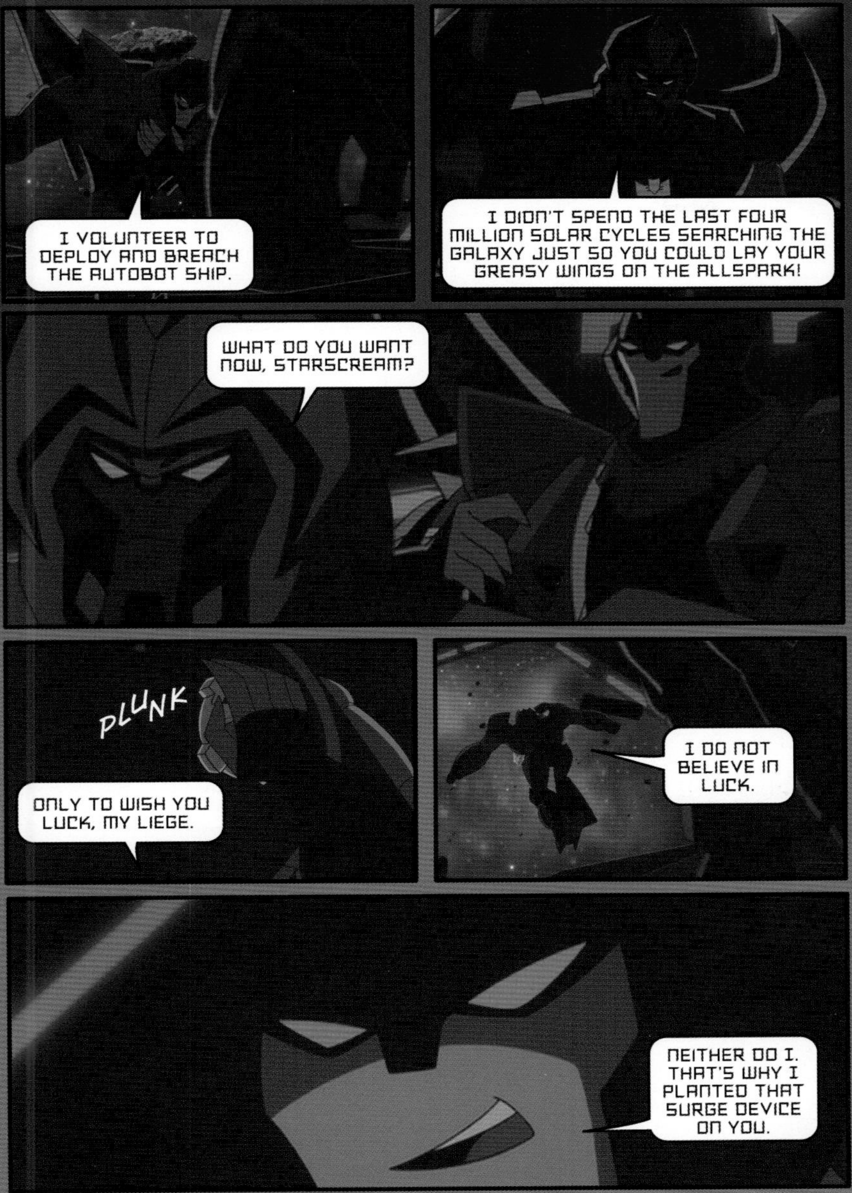
I VOLUNTEER TO DEPLOY AND BREACH THE AUTOBOT SHIP.
I DIDN'T SPEND THE LAST FOUR MILLION SOLAR CYCLES SEARCHING THE GALAXY JUST SO YOU COULD LAY YOUR GREASY WINGS ON THE ALLSPARK!
WHAT DO YOU WANT NOW, STARSCREAM?
PLUNK
ONLY TO WISH YOU LUCK, MY LIEGE.
I DO NOT BELIEVE IN LUCK.
NEITHER DO I. THAT'S WHY I PLANTED THAT SURGE DEVICE ON YOU.

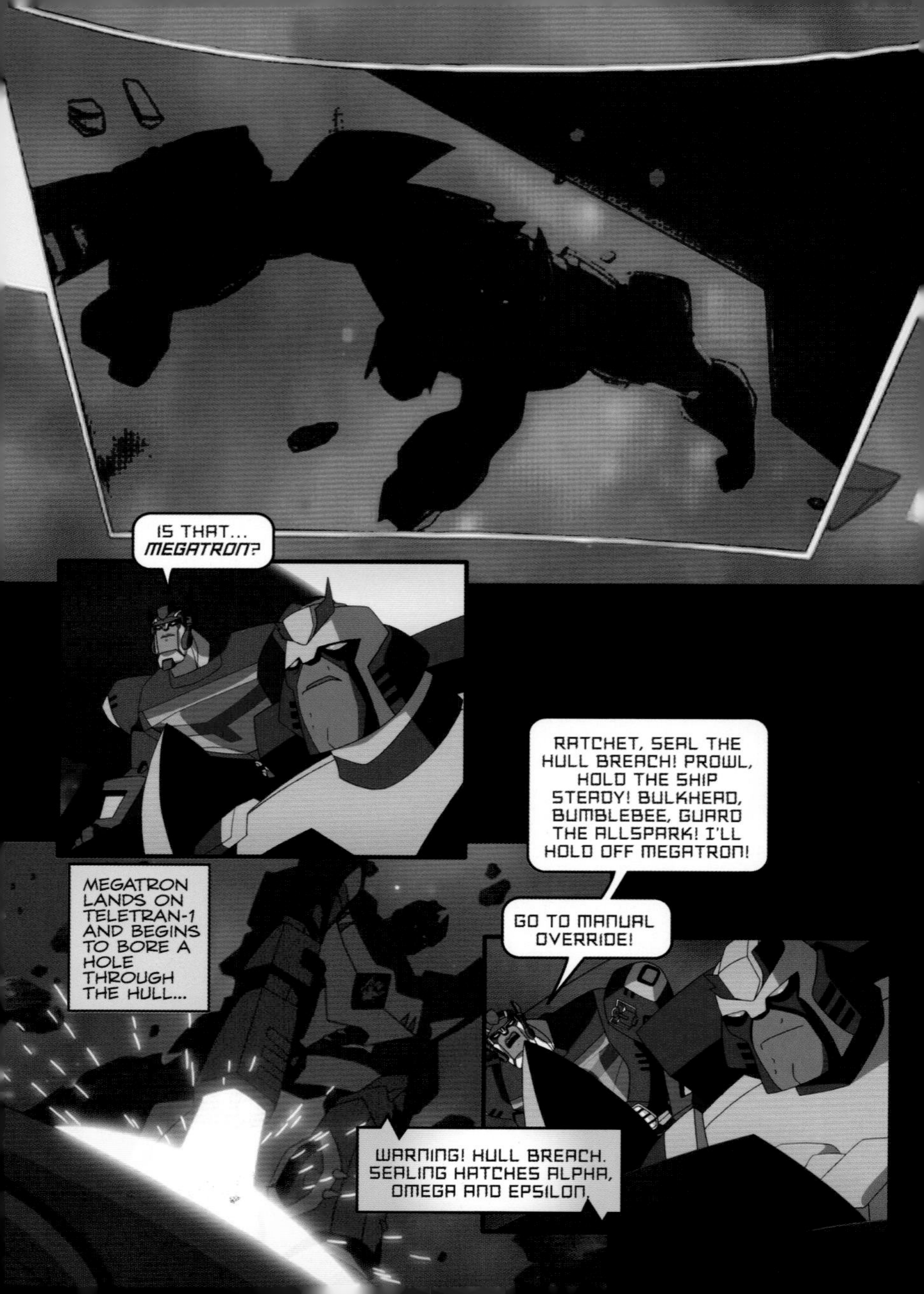
IS THAT... MEGATRON?
RATCHET, SEAL THE HULL BREACH! PROWL, HOLD THE SHIP STEADY! BULKHEAD, BUMBLEBEE, GUARD THE ALLSPARK! I'LL HOLD OFF MEGATRON!
MEGATRON LANDS ON TELETRAN-1 AND BEGINS TO BORE A HOLE THROUGH THE HULL...
GO TO MANUAL OVERRIDE!
WARNING! HULL BREACH. SEALING HATCHES ALPHA, OMEGA AND EPSILON.

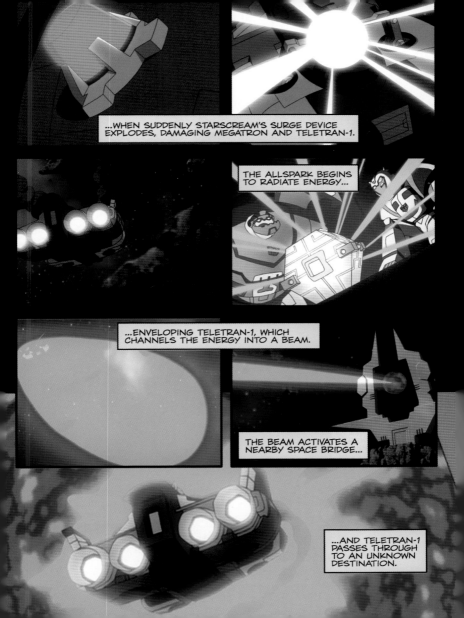

...WHEN SUDDENLY STARSCREAM'S SURGE DEVICE EXPLODES, DAMAGING MEGATRON AND TELETRAN-1.

THE ALLSPARK BEGINS TO RADIATE ENERGY...

...ENVELOPING TELETRAN-1, WHICH CHANNELS THE ENERGY INTO A BEAM.

THE BEAM ACTIVATES A NEARBY SPACE BRIDGE...

...AND TELETRAN-1 PASSES THROUGH TO AN UNKNOWN DESTINATION.

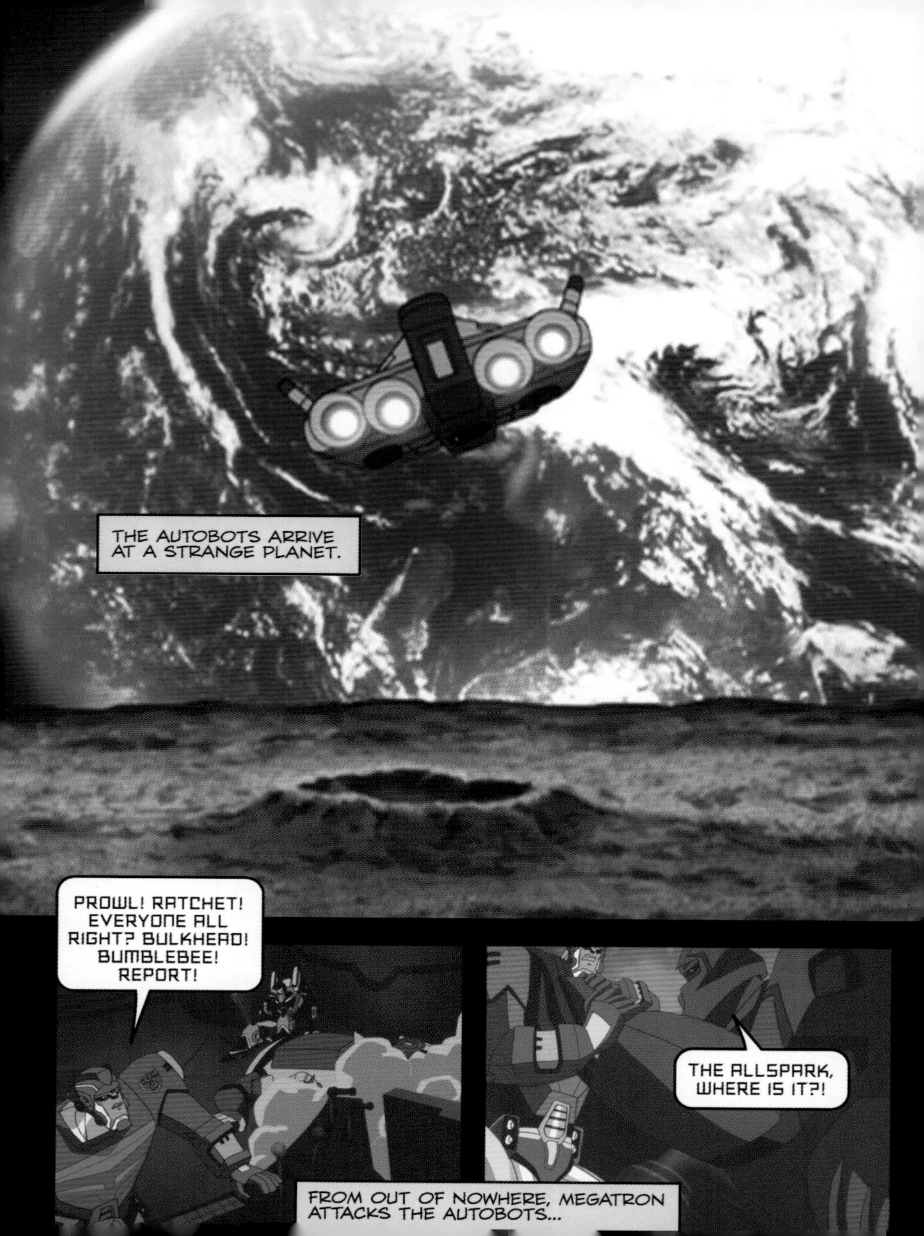
THE AUTOBOTS ARRIVE AT A STRANGE PLANET.
PROWL! RATCHET! EVERYONE ALL RIGHT? BULKHEAD! BUMBLEBEE! REPORT!
THE ALLSPARK, WHERE IS IT?!
FROM OUT OF NOWHERE, MEGATRON ATTACKS THE AUTOBOTS...

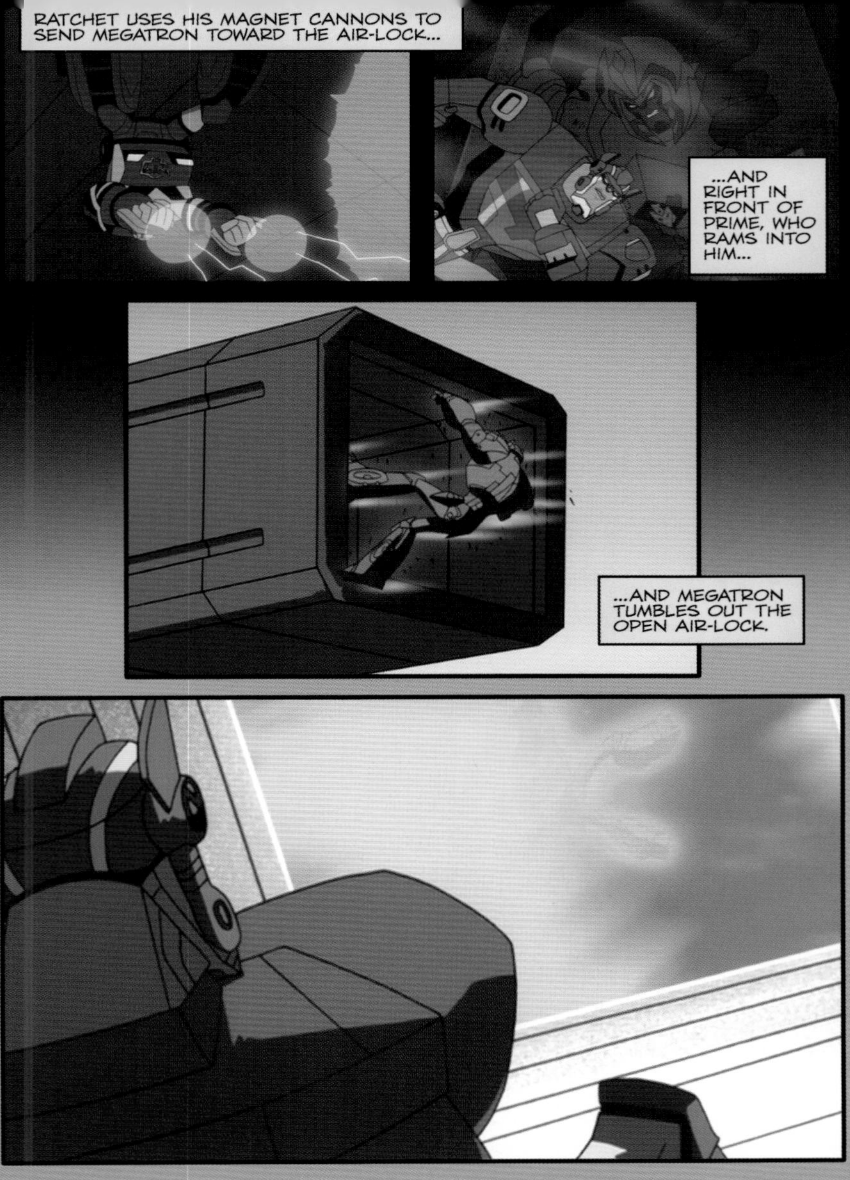
RATCHET USES HIS MAGNET CANNONS TO SEND MEGATRON TOWARD THE AIR-LOCK...
...AND RIGHT IN FRONT OF PRIME, WHO RAMS INTO HIM...
...AND MEGATRON TUMBLES OUT THE OPEN AIR-LOCK.

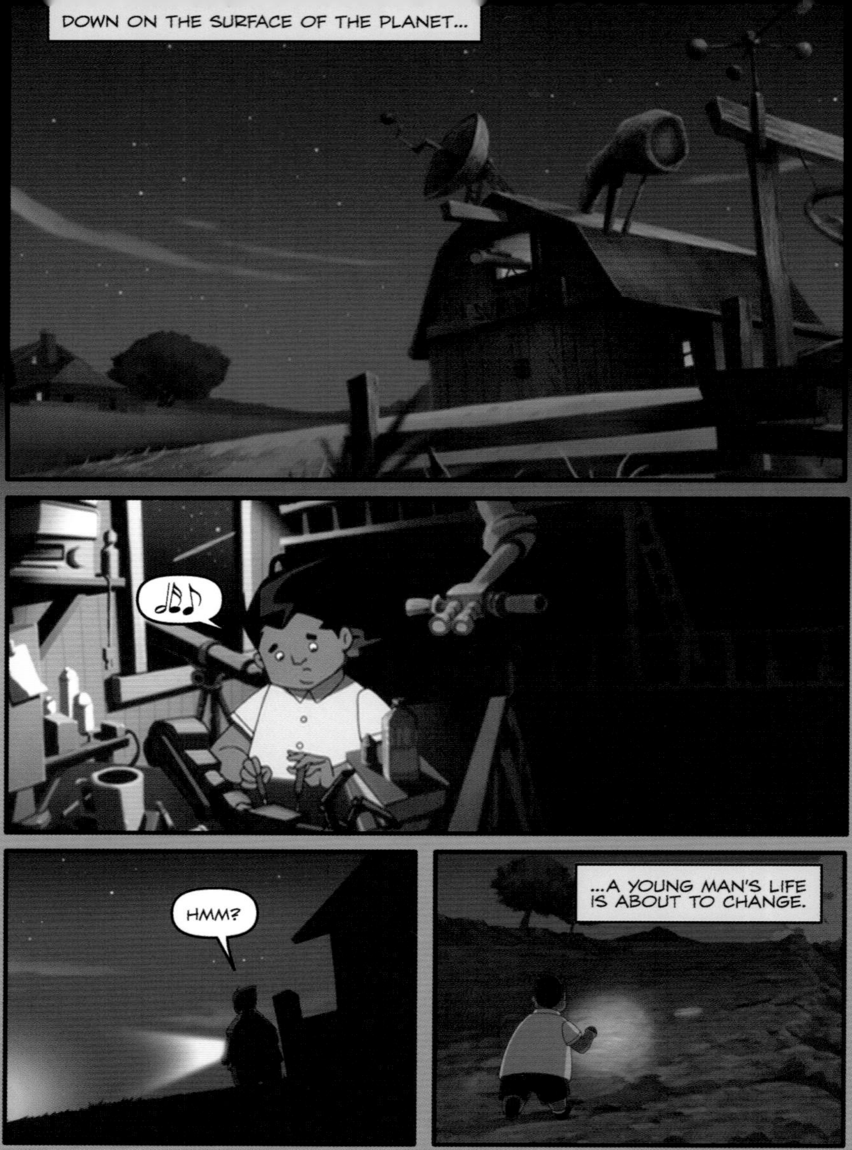
DOWN ON THE SURFACE OF THE PLANET...
HMM?
...A YOUNG MAN'S LIFE IS ABOUT TO CHANGE.

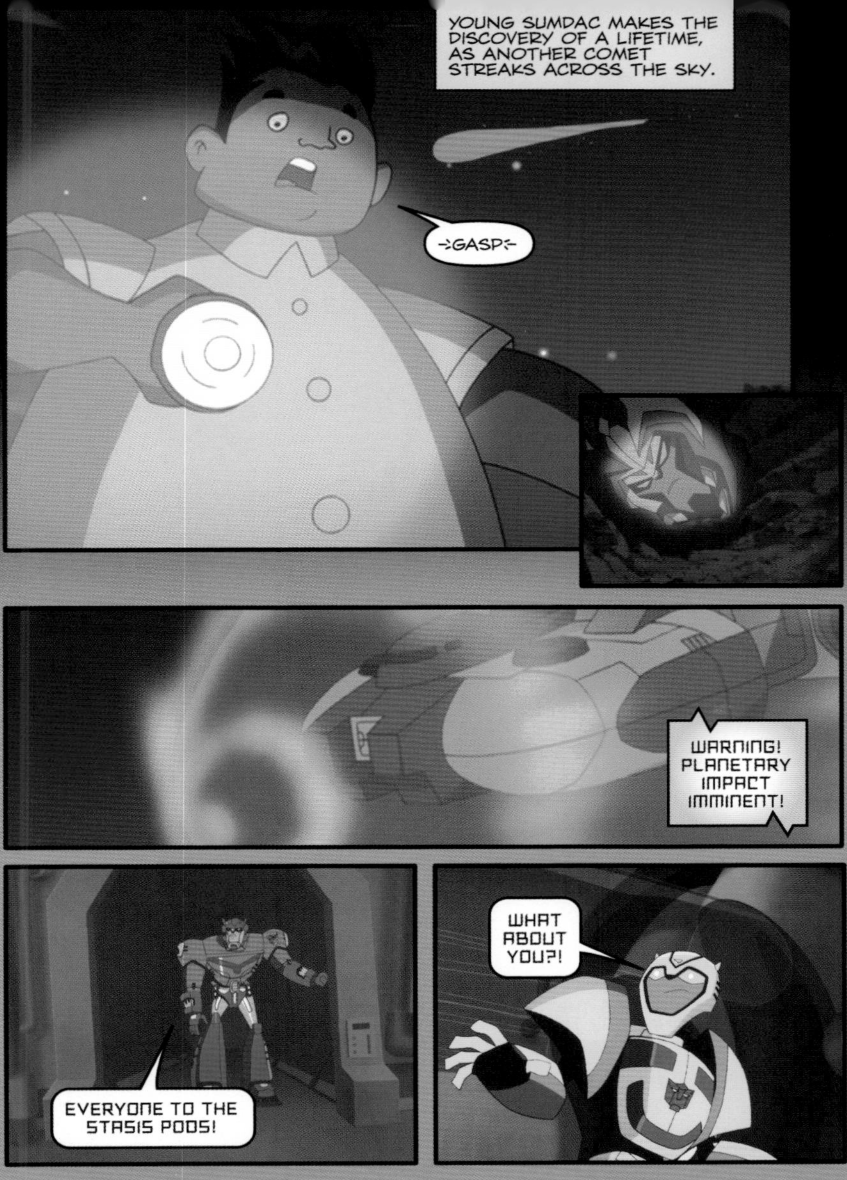
YOUNG SUMDAC MAKES THE DISCOVERY OF A LIFETIME, AS ANOTHER COMET STREAKS ACROSS THE SKY.
-GASP-
WARNING! PLANETARY IMPACT IMMINENT!
EVERYONE TO THE STASIS PODS!
WHAT ABOUT YOU?!

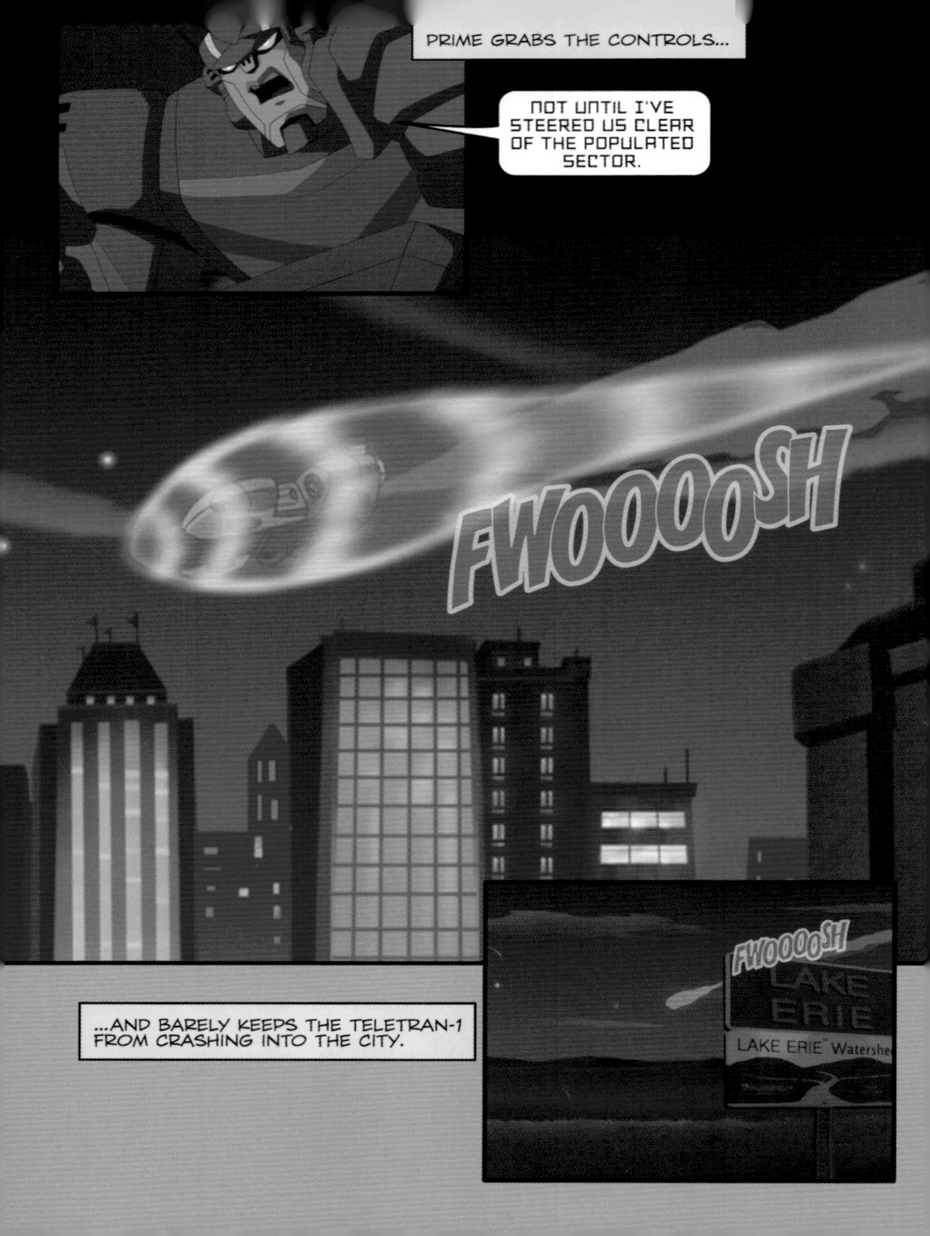
PRIME GRABS THE CONTROLS...
NOT UNTIL I'VE STEERED US CLEAR OF THE POPULATED SECTOR.
FWOOOOSH
...AND BARELY KEEPS THE TELETRAN-1 FROM CRASHING INTO THE CITY.
FWOOOOSH
LAKE ERIE
LAKE ERIE™ Watershe

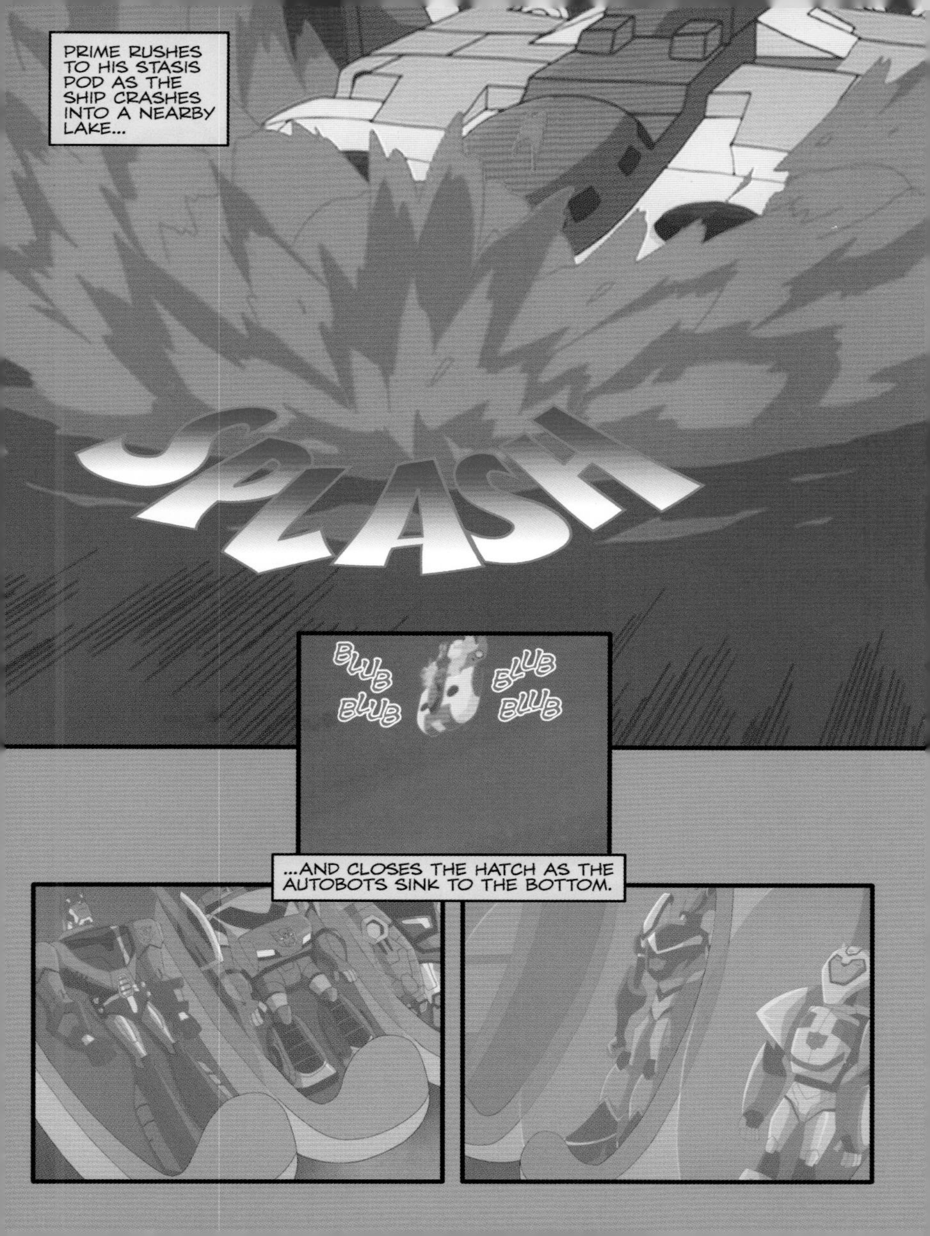
PRIME RUSHES TO HIS STASIS POD AS THE SHIP CRASHES INTO A NEARBY LAKE...
SPLASH
BLUB BLUB
BLUB BLUB
...AND CLOSES THE HATCH AS THE AUTOBOTS SINK TO THE BOTTOM.

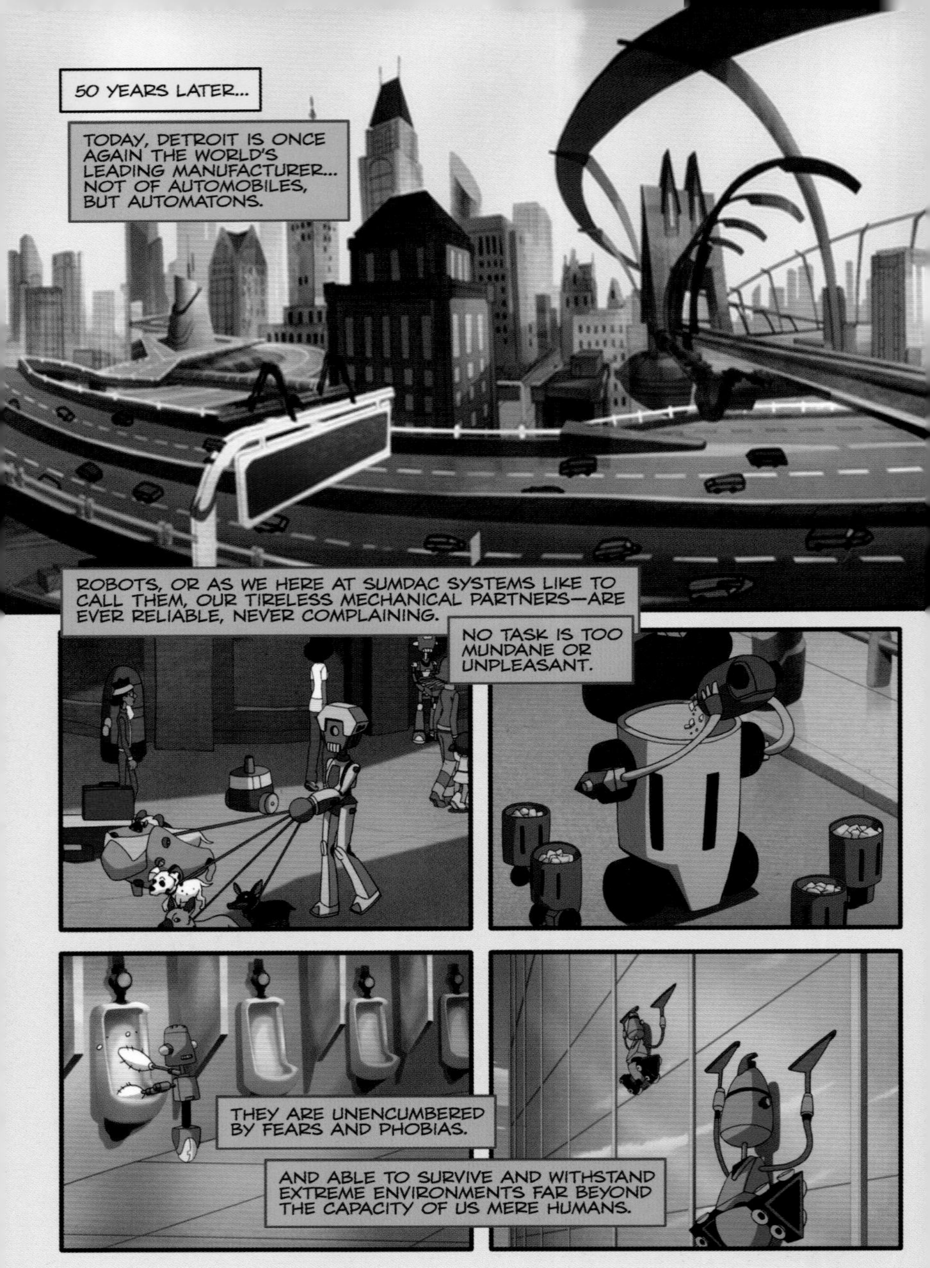
50 YEARS LATER...
TODAY, DETROIT IS ONCE AGAIN THE WORLD'S LEADING MANUFACTURER... NOT OF AUTOMOBILES, BUT AUTOMATONS.
ROBOTS, OR AS WE HERE AT SUMDAC SYSTEMS LIKE TO CALL THEM, OUR TIRELESS MECHANICAL PARTNERS—ARE EVER RELIABLE, NEVER COMPLAINING.
NO TASK IS TOO MUNDANE OR UNPLEASANT.
THEY ARE UNENCUMBERED BY FEARS AND PHOBIAS.
AND ABLE TO SURVIVE AND WITHSTAND EXTREME ENVIRONMENTS FAR BEYOND THE CAPACITY OF US MERE HUMANS.

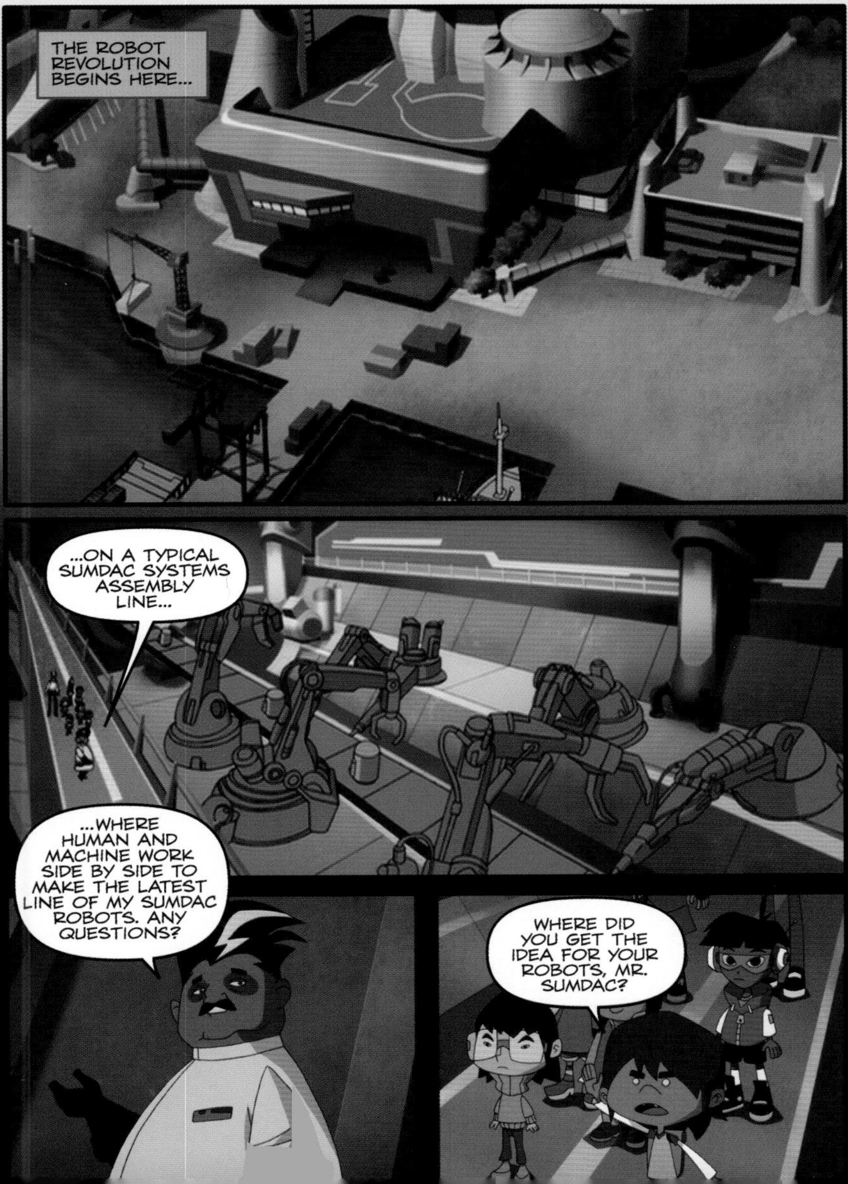
THE ROBOT REVOLUTION BEGINS HERE...
...ON A TYPICAL SUMDAC SYSTEMS ASSEMBLY LINE...
...WHERE HUMAN AND MACHINE WORK SIDE BY SIDE TO MAKE THE LATEST LINE OF MY SUMDAC ROBOTS. ANY QUESTIONS?
WHERE DID YOU GET THE IDEA FOR YOUR ROBOTS, MR. SUMDAC?

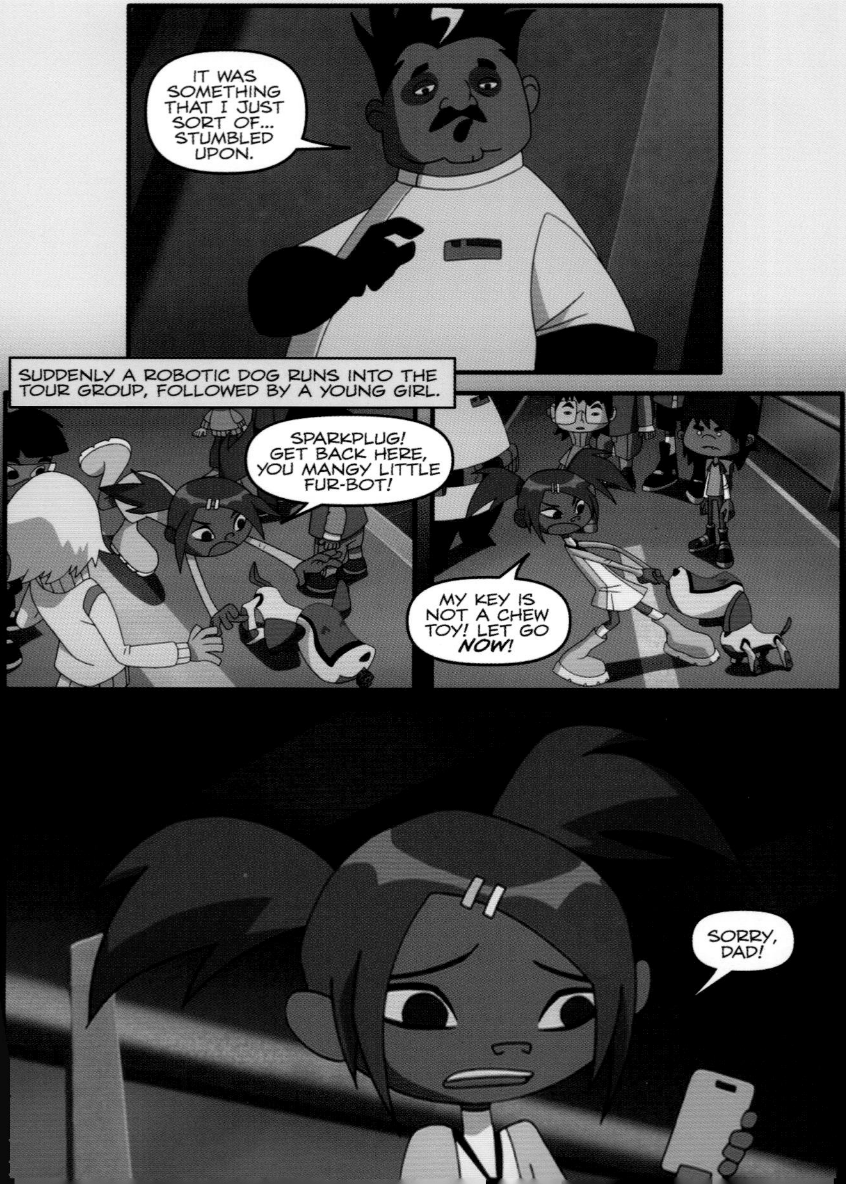
IT WAS SOMETHING THAT I JUST SORT OF... STUMBLED UPON.
SUDDENLY A ROBOTIC DOG RUNS INTO THE TOUR GROUP, FOLLOWED BY A YOUNG GIRL.
SPARKPLUG! GET BACK HERE, YOU MANGY LITTLE FUR-BOT!
MY KEY IS NOT A CHEW TOY! LET GO NOW!
SORRY, DAD!

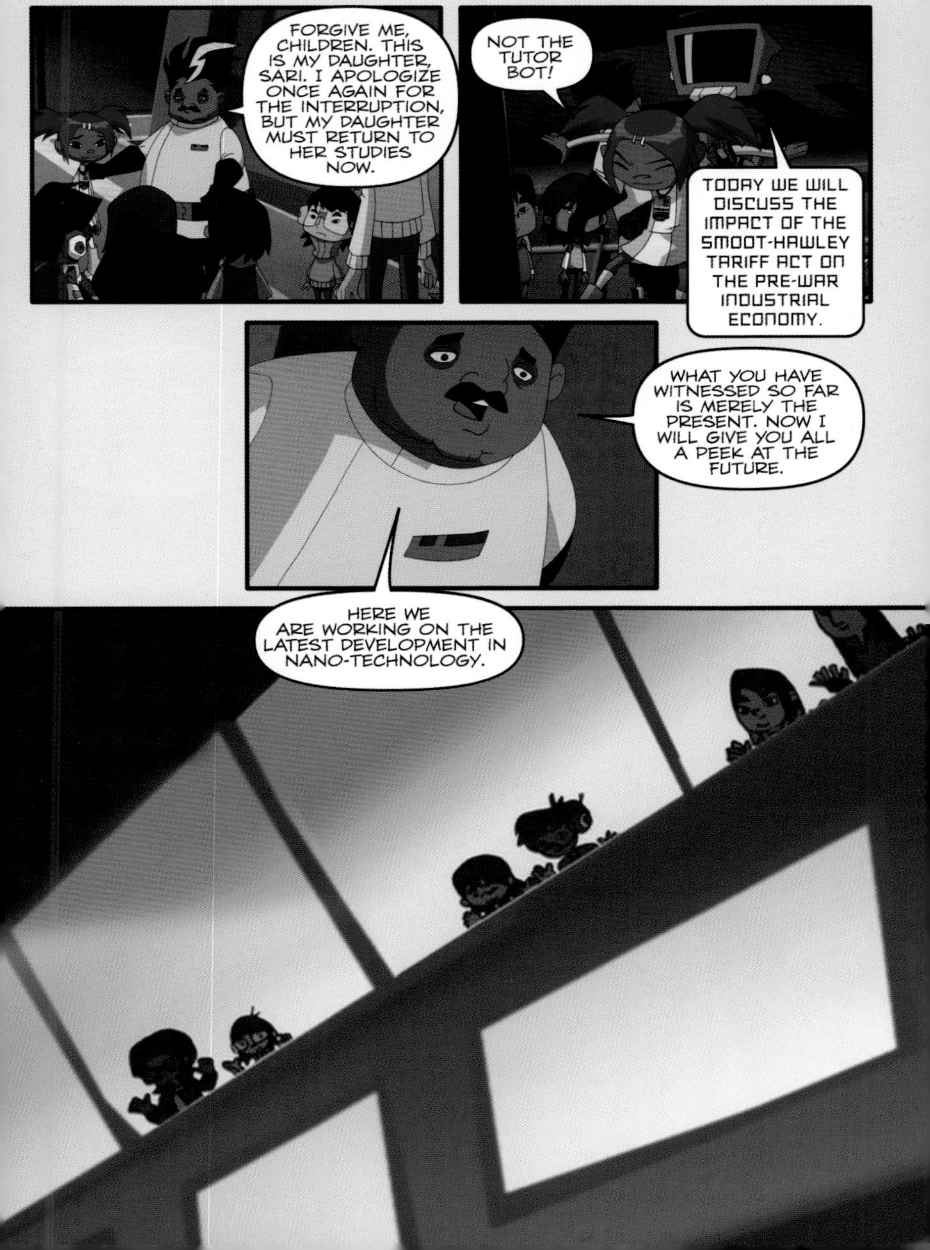
FORGIVE ME, CHILDREN. THIS IS MY DAUGHTER, SARI. I APOLOGIZE ONCE AGAIN FOR THE INTERRUPTION, BUT MY DAUGHTER MUST RETURN TO HER STUDIES NOW.
NOT THE TUTOR BOT!
TODAY WE WILL DISCUSS THE IMPACT OF THE SMOOT-HAWLEY TARIFF ACT ON THE PRE-WAR INDUSTRIAL ECONOMY.
WHAT YOU HAVE WITNESSED SO FAR IS MERELY THE PRESENT. NOW I WILL GIVE YOU ALL A PEEK AT THE FUTURE.
HERE WE ARE WORKING ON THE LATEST DEVELOPMENT IN NANO-TECHNOLOGY.

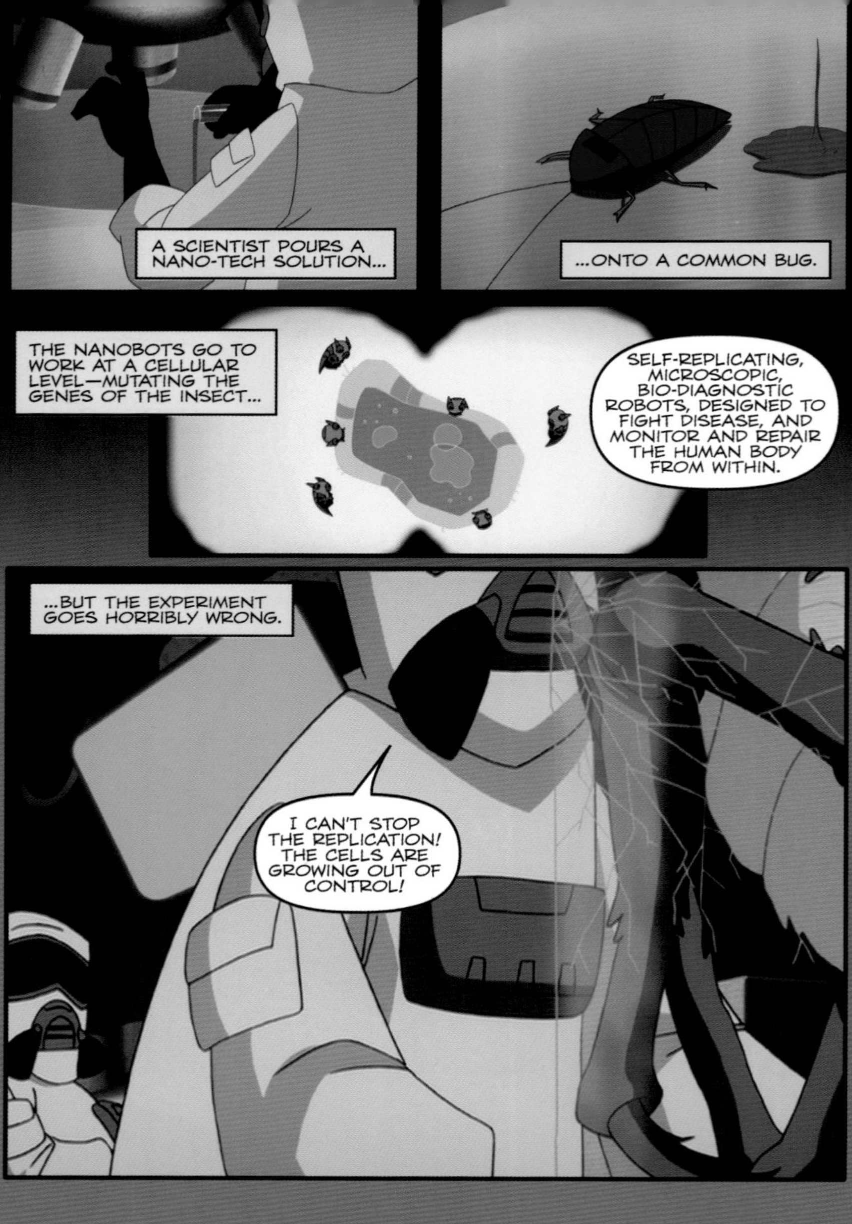
A SCIENTIST POURS A NANO-TECH SOLUTION...
...ONTO A COMMON BUG.
THE NANOBOTS GO TO WORK AT A CELLULAR LEVEL—MUTATING THE GENES OF THE INSECT...
SELF-REPLICATING, MICROSCOPIC, BIO-DIAGNOSTIC ROBOTS, DESIGNED TO FIGHT DISEASE, AND MONITOR AND REPAIR THE HUMAN BODY FROM WITHIN.
...BUT THE EXPERIMENT GOES HORRIBLY WRONG.
I CAN'T STOP THE REPLICATION! THE CELLS ARE GROWING OUT OF CONTROL!

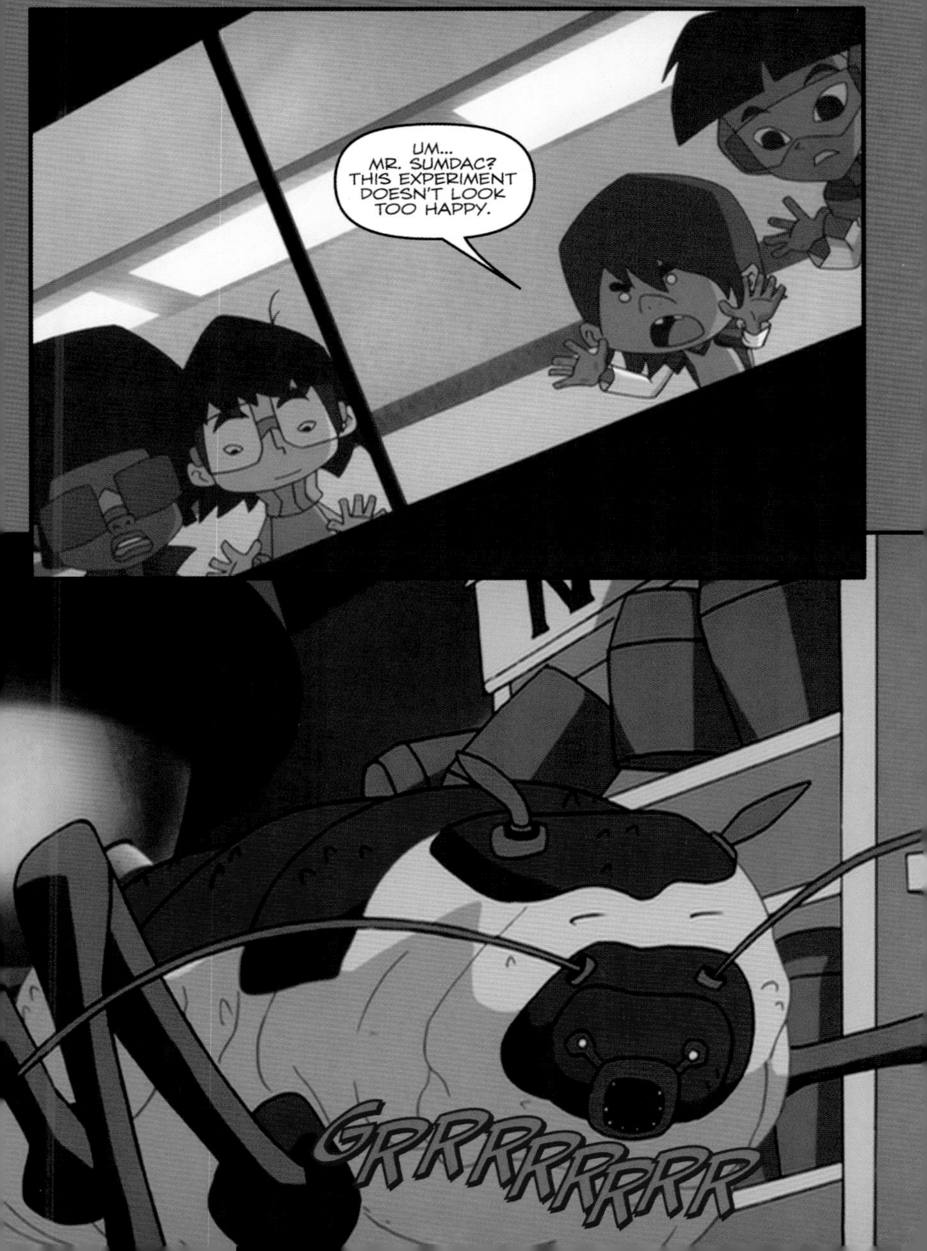
UM... MR. SUMDAC? THIS EXPERIMENT DOESN'T LOOK TOO HAPPY.
GRRRRRRRRR

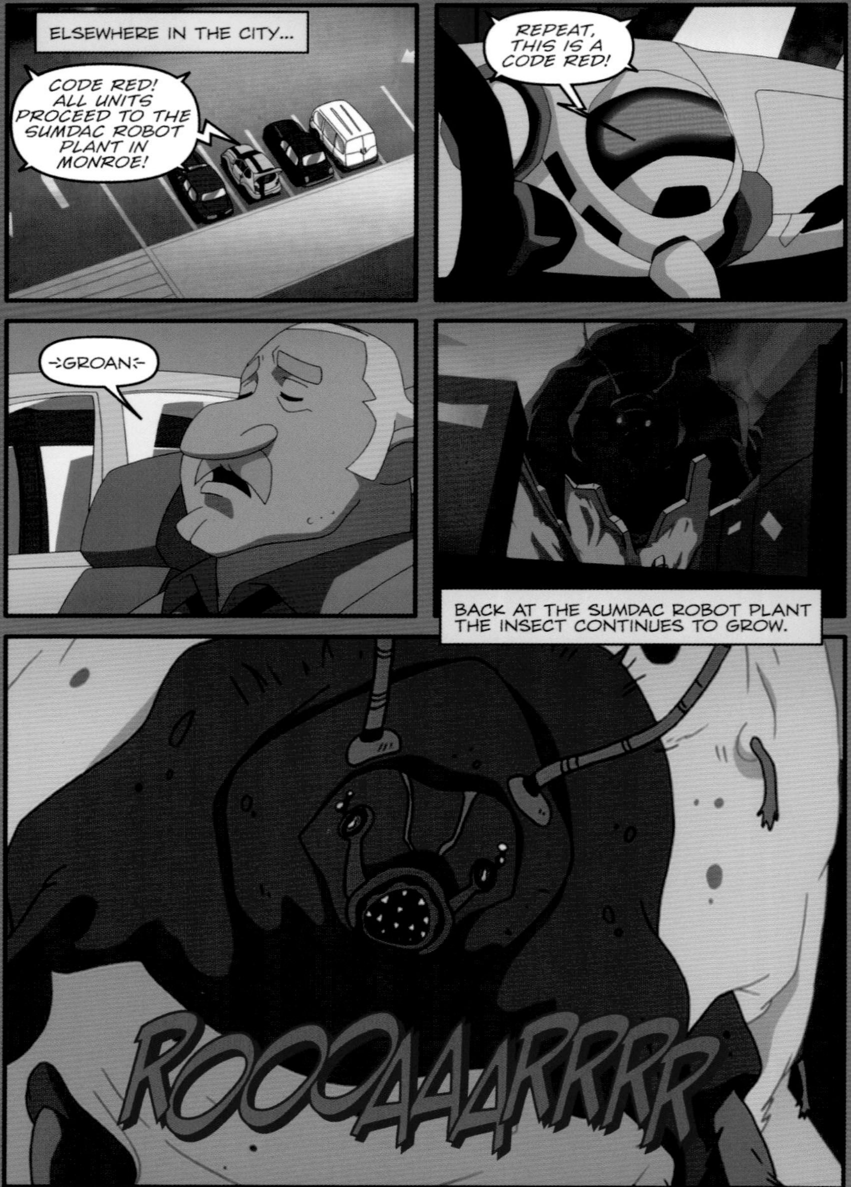
ELSEWHERE IN THE CITY...
CODE RED! ALL UNITS PROCEED TO THE SUMDAC ROBOT PLANT IN MONROE!
REPEAT, THIS IS A CODE RED!
GROAN
BACK AT THE SUMDAC ROBOT PLANT THE INSECT CONTINUES TO GROW.
ROOOAAARRRR

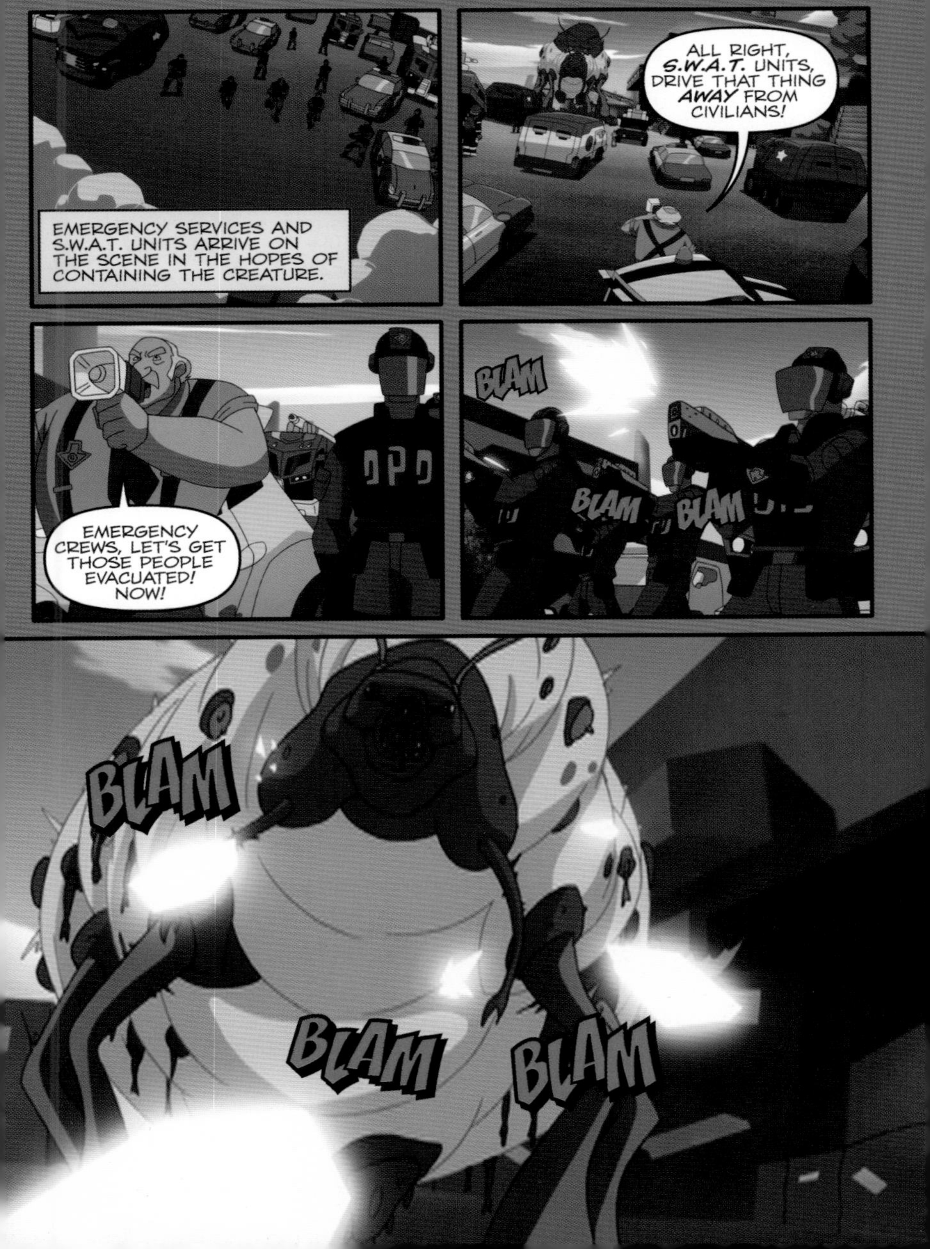
EMERGENCY SERVICES AND S.W.A.T. UNITS ARRIVE ON THE SCENE IN THE HOPES OF CONTAINING THE CREATURE.
ALL RIGHT, S.W.A.T. UNITS, DRIVE THAT THING AWAY FROM CIVILIANS!
EMERGENCY CREWS, LET'S GET THOSE PEOPLE EVACUATED! NOW!
DPD
BLAM
BLAM
BLAM
BLAM
BLAM
BLAM

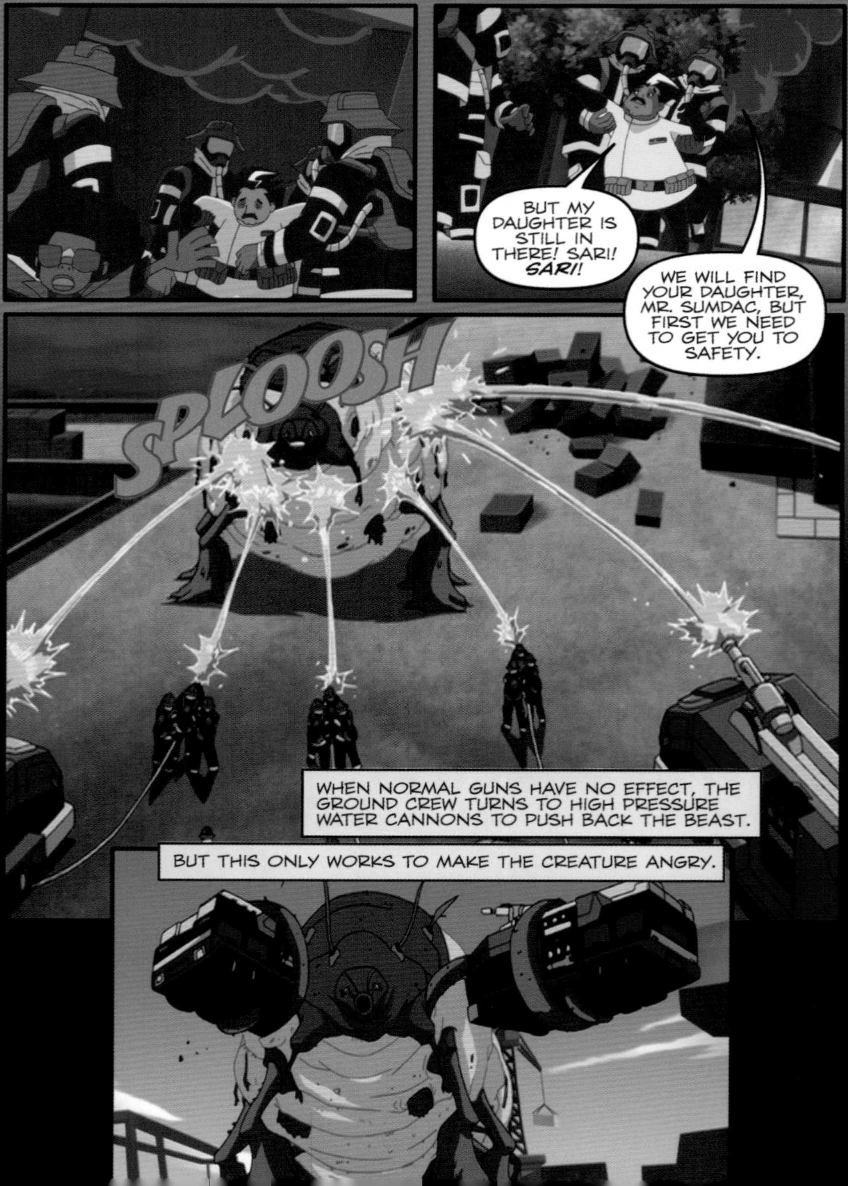
BUT MY DAUGHTER IS STILL IN THERE! SARI! SARI!
WE WILL FIND YOUR DAUGHTER, MR. SUMDAC, BUT FIRST WE NEED TO GET YOU TO SAFETY.
SPLOOSH
WHEN NORMAL GUNS HAVE NO EFFECT, THE GROUND CREW TURNS TO HIGH PRESSURE WATER CANNONS TO PUSH BACK THE BEAST.
BUT THIS ONLY WORKS TO MAKE THE CREATURE ANGRY.

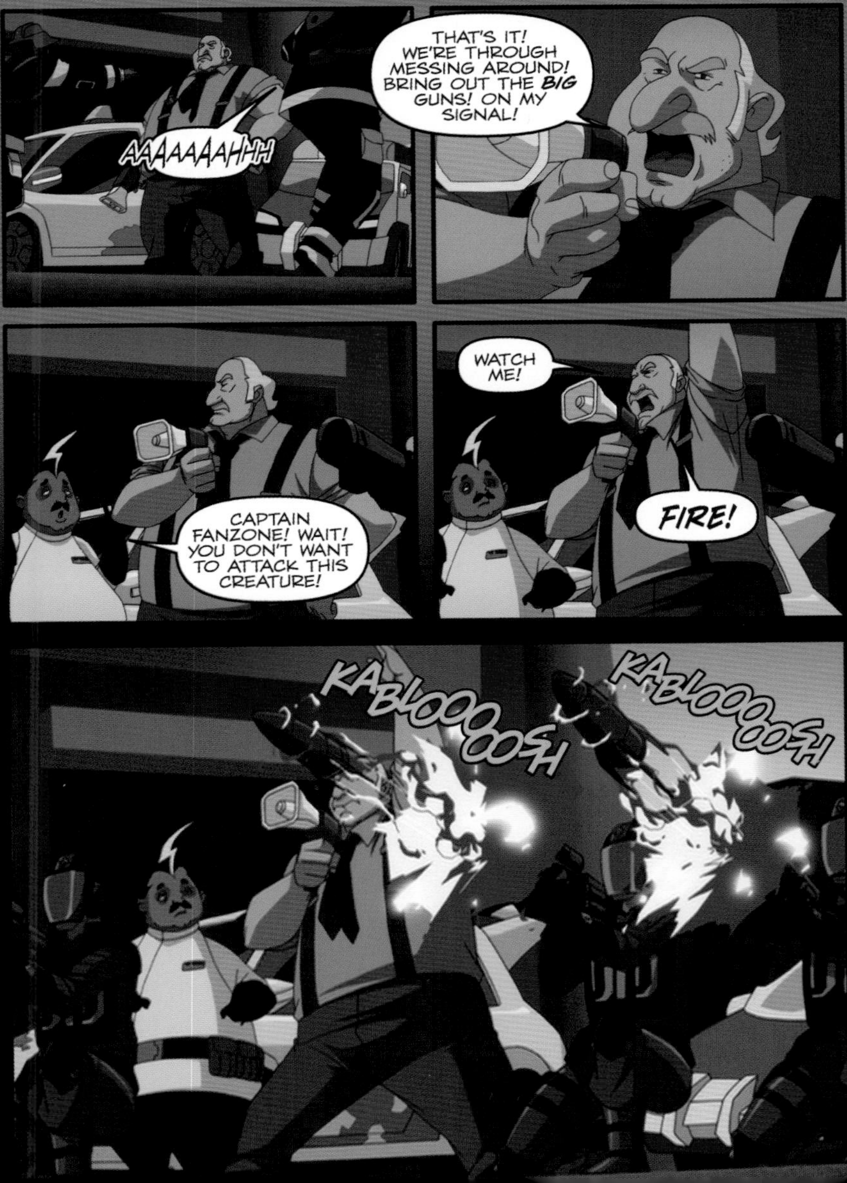

AAAAAAAHHH
THAT'S IT! WE'RE THROUGH MESSING AROUND! BRING OUT THE BIG GUNS! ON MY SIGNAL!
CAPTAIN FANZONE! WAIT! YOU DON'T WANT TO ATTACK THIS CREATURE!
WATCH ME!
FIRE!
KABLOOOOOOSH
KABLOOOOOOSH

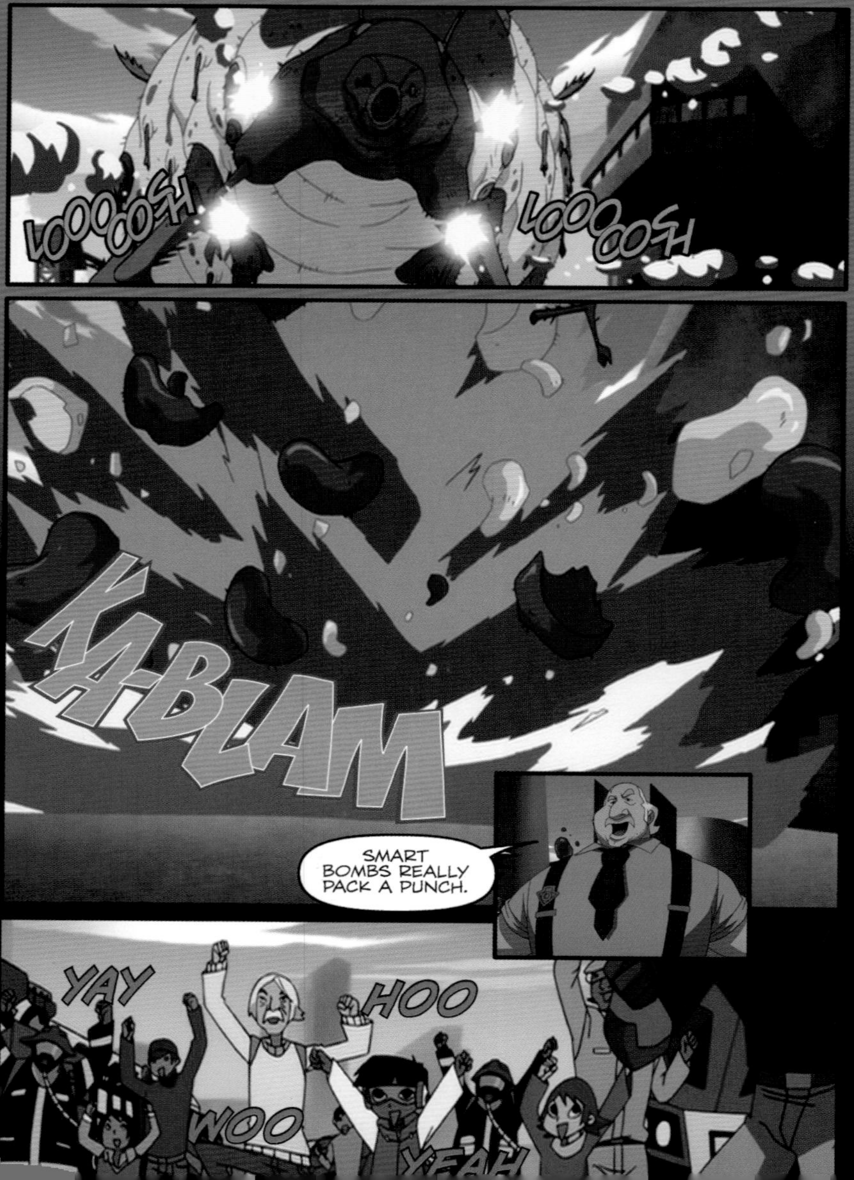
VOOOOOSH
VOOOOOSH
KA-BLAM
SMART BOMBS REALLY PACK A PUNCH.
YAY
HOO
WOO
YEAH

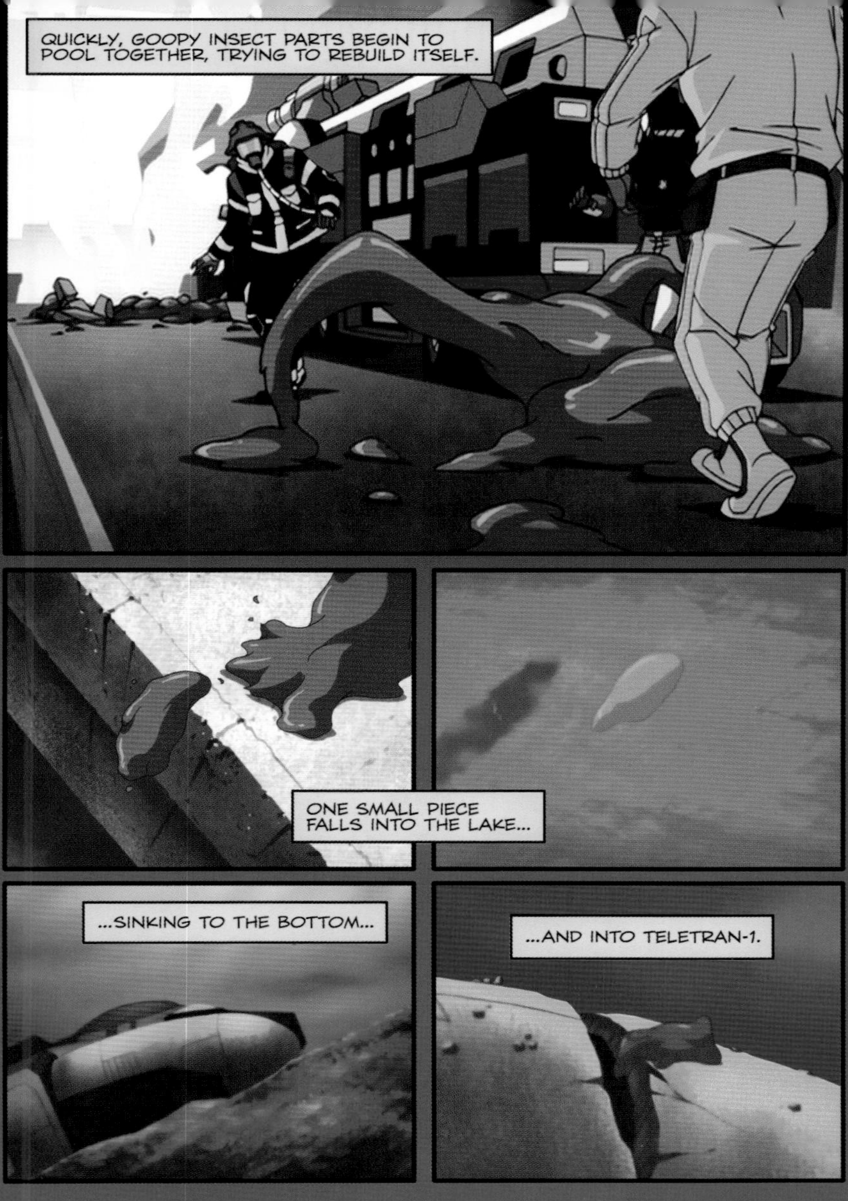
QUICKLY, GOOPY INSECT PARTS BEGIN TO POOL TOGETHER, TRYING TO REBUILD ITSELF.
ONE SMALL PIECE FALLS INTO THE LAKE...
...SINKING TO THE BOTTOM...
...AND INTO TELETRAN-1.

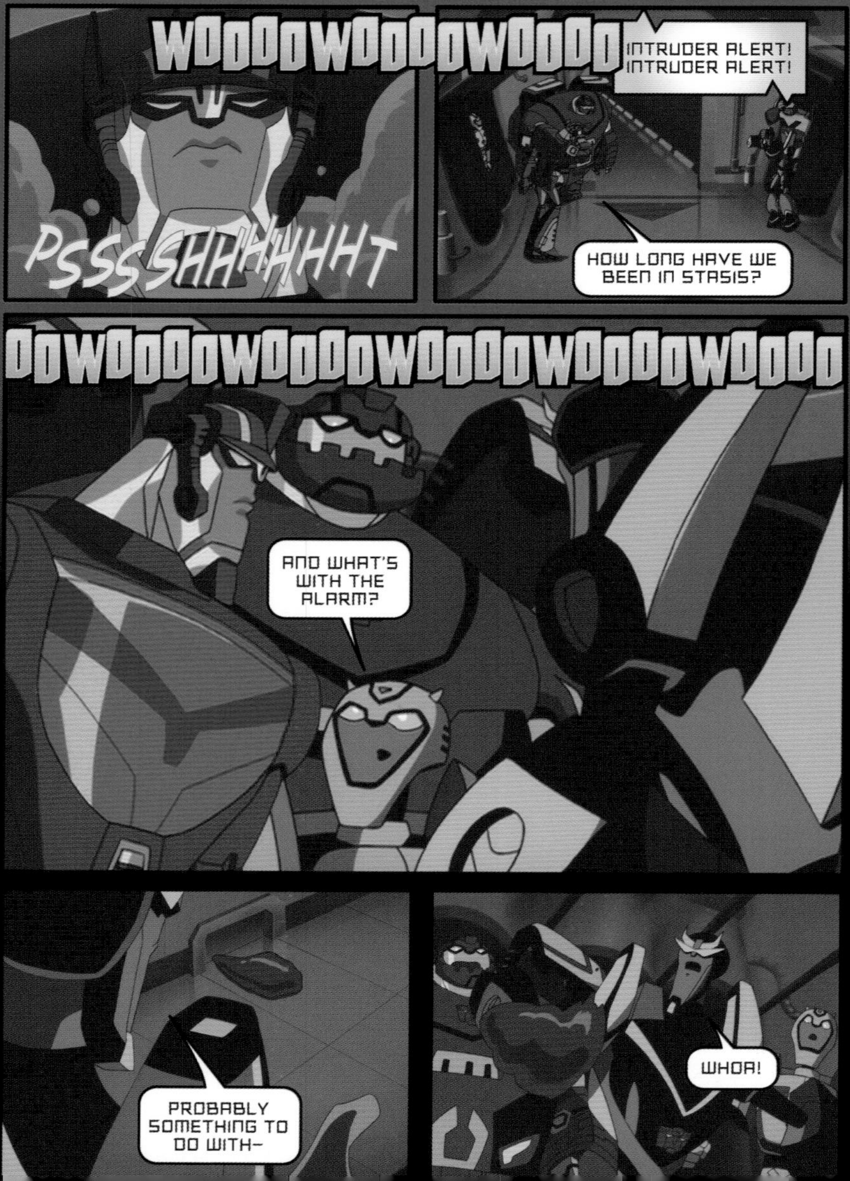
WOOOOWOOOOOWOOOO
PSSSSHHHHHHT
INTRUDER ALERT! INTRUDER ALERT!
HOW LONG HAVE WE BEEN IN STASIS?
OOWOOOOWOOOOOWOOOOOWOOOOOWOOOO
AND WHAT'S WITH THE ALARM?
PROBABLY SOMETHING TO DO WITH–
WHOA!

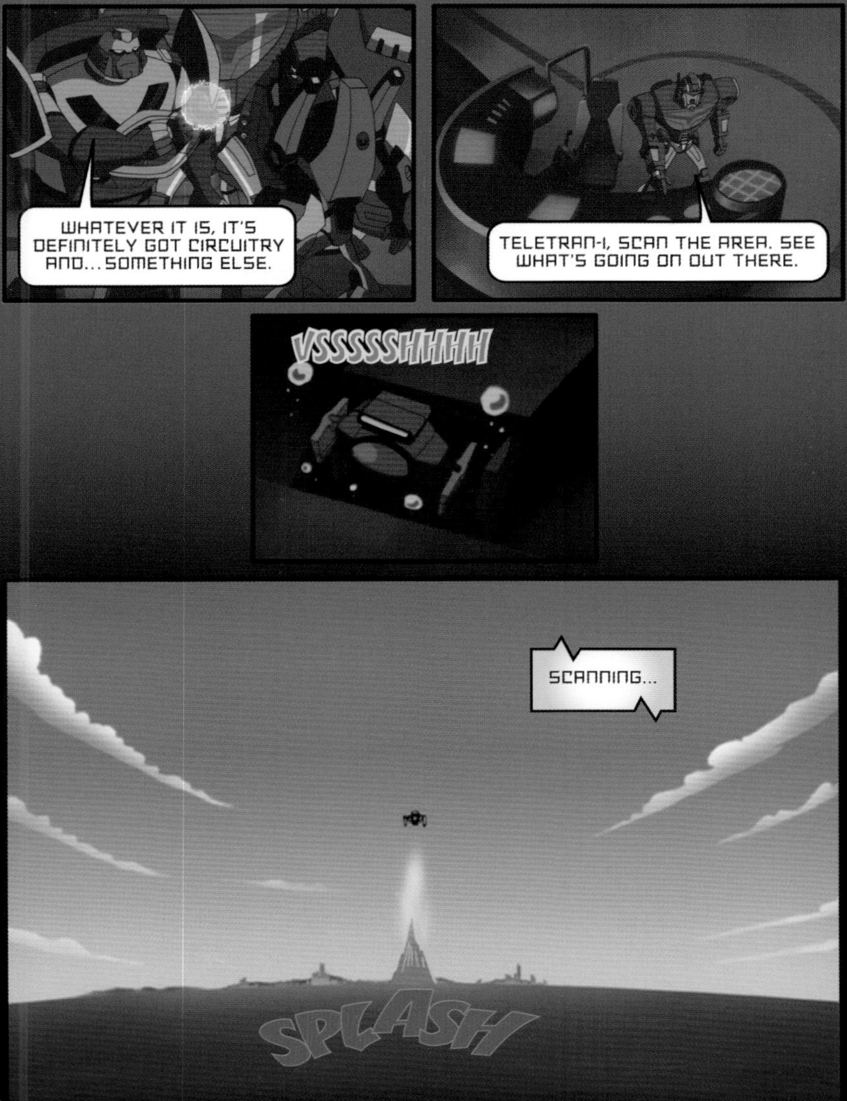
WHATEVER IT IS, IT'S DEFINITELY GOT CIRCUITRY AND... SOMETHING ELSE.
TELETRAN-1, SCAN THE AREA. SEE WHAT'S GOING ON OUT THERE.
VSSSSSHHHHH
SCANNING...
SPLASH

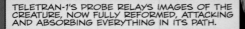

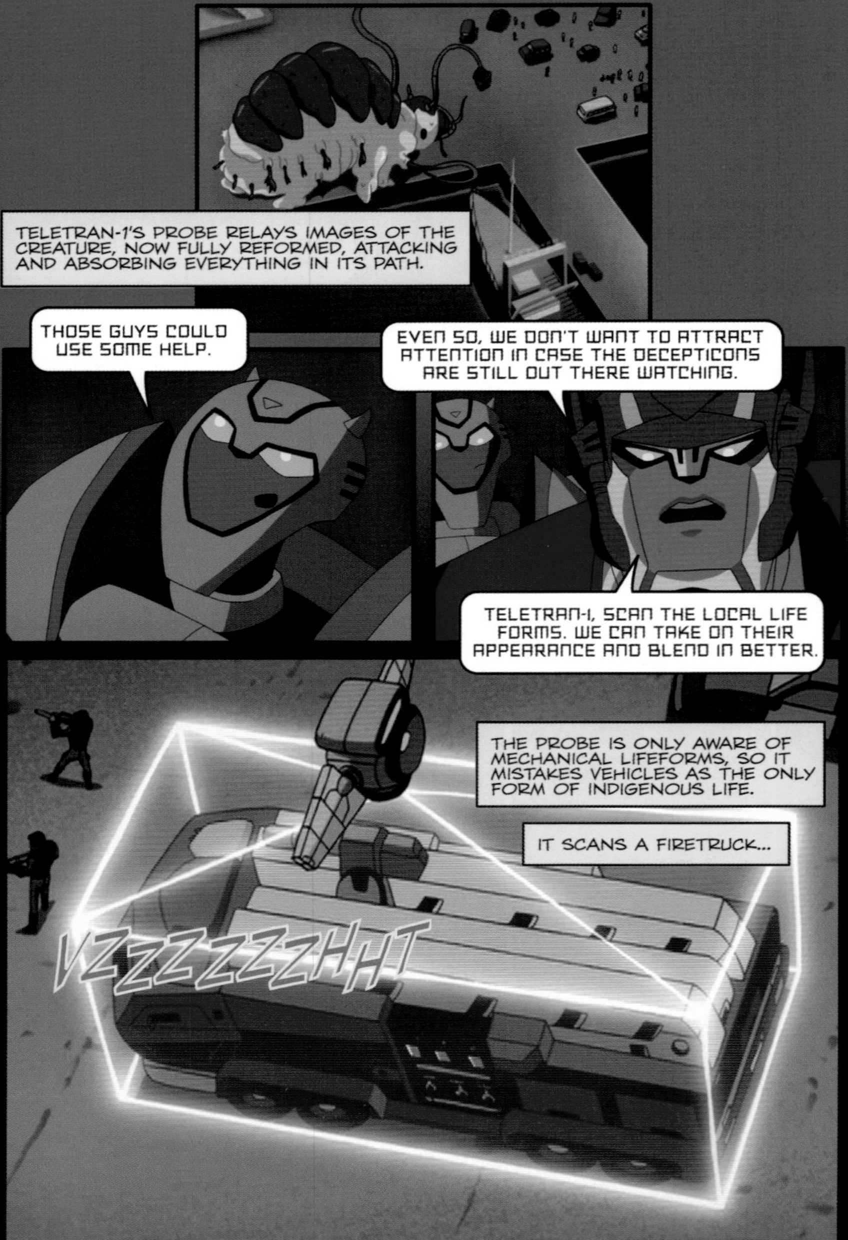

TELETRAN-1'S PROBE RELAYS IMAGES OF THE CREATURE, NOW FULLY REFORMED, ATTACKING AND ABSORBING EVERYTHING IN ITS PATH.

THOSE GUYS COULD USE SOME HELP.

EVEN SO, WE DON'T WANT TO ATTRACT ATTENTION IN CASE THE DECEPTICONS ARE STILL OUT THERE WATCHING.

TELETRAN-1, SCAN THE LOCAL LIFE FORMS. WE CAN TAKE ON THEIR APPEARANCE AND BLEND IN BETTER.

THE PROBE IS ONLY AWARE OF MECHANICAL LIFEFORMS, SO IT MISTAKES VEHICLES AS THE ONLY FORM OF INDIGENOUS LIFE.

IT SCANS A FIRETRUCK...

VZZZZZZHHT

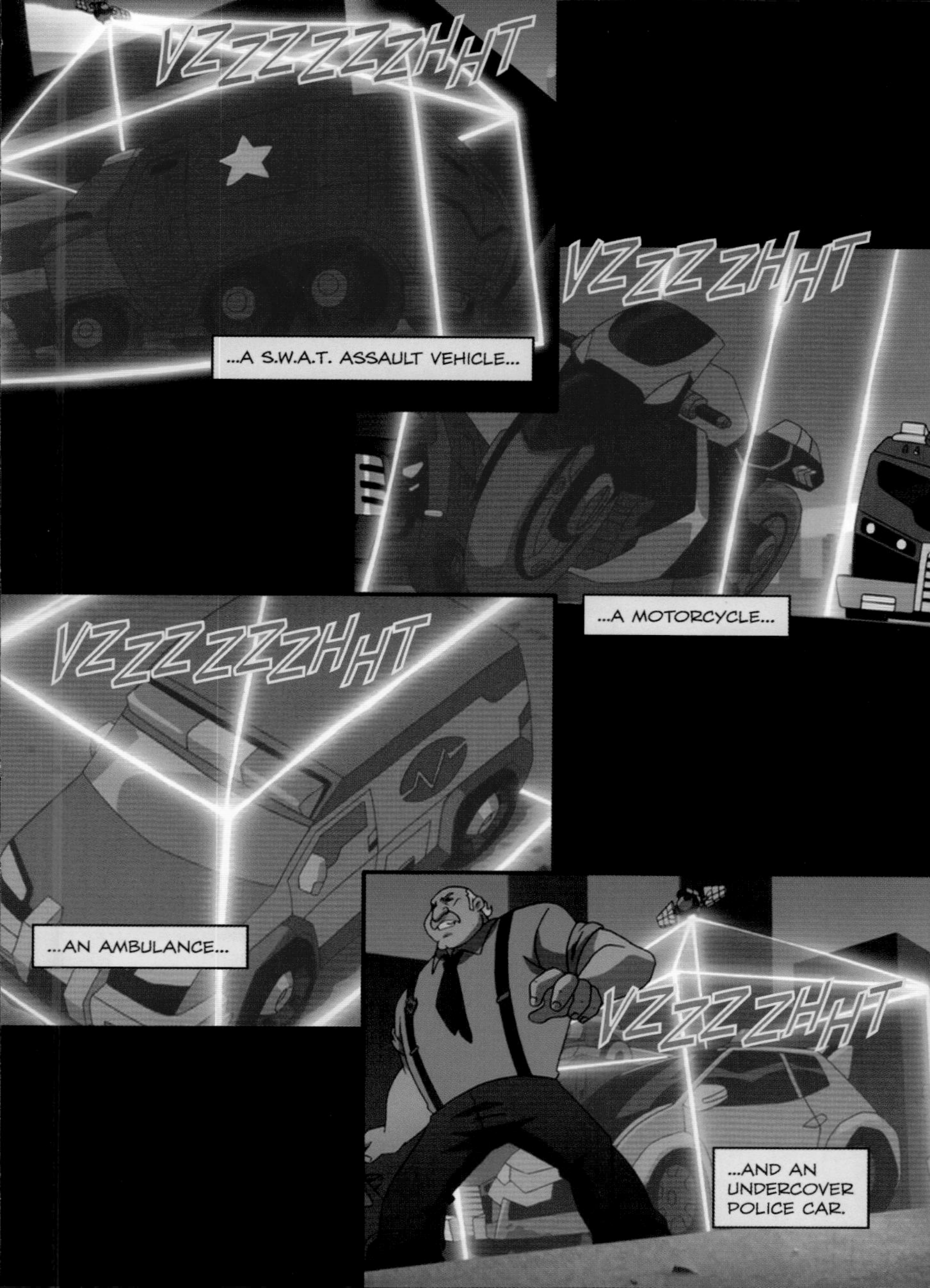
VZZZZZZHHT
...A S.W.A.T. ASSAULT VEHICLE...
VZZZ ZHHT
...A MOTORCYCLE...
VZZZZZZHHT
...AN AMBULANCE...
VZZZ ZHHT
...AND AN UNDERCOVER POLICE CAR.

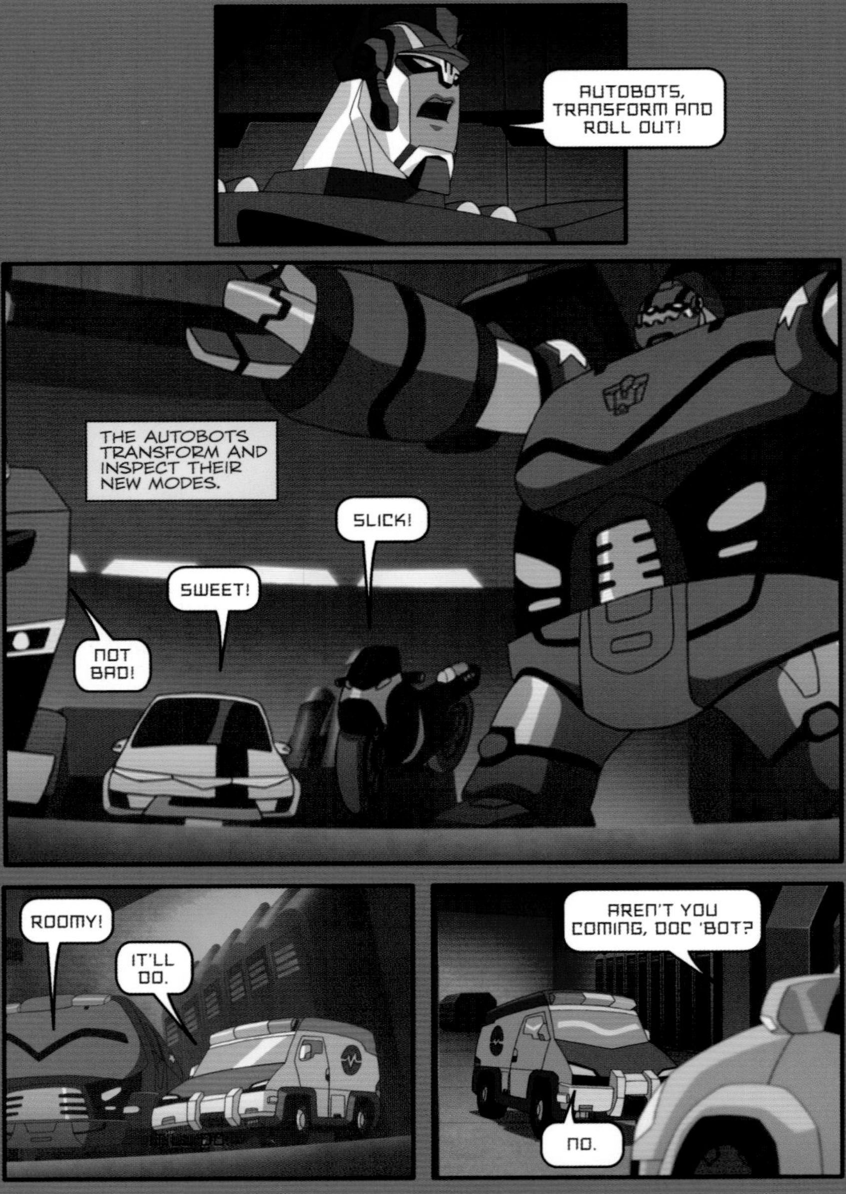
AUTOBOTS, TRANSFORM AND ROLL OUT!
THE AUTOBOTS TRANSFORM AND INSPECT THEIR NEW MODES.
SLICK!
SWEET!
NOT BAD!
ROOMY!
IT'LL DO.
AREN'T YOU COMING, DOC 'BOT?
NO.

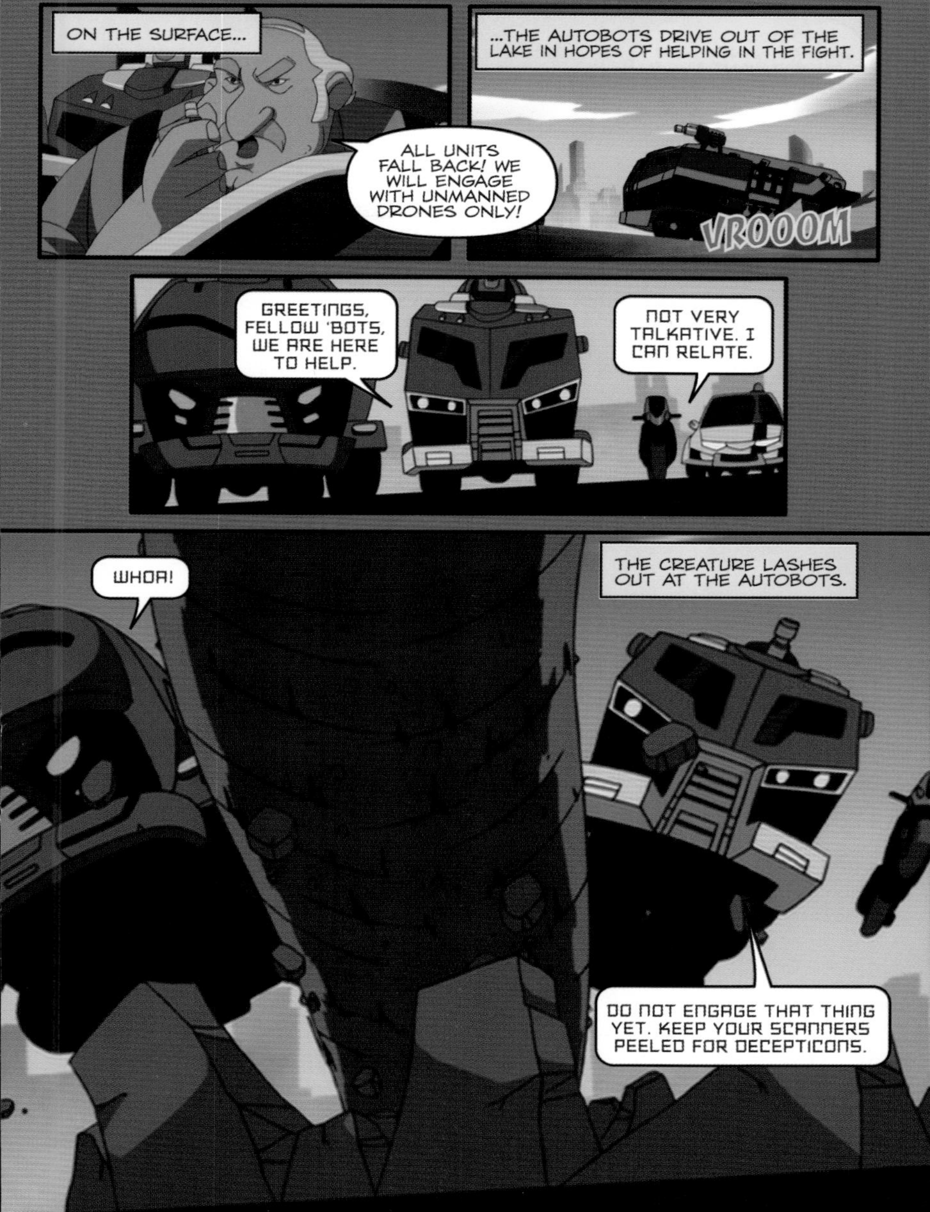
ON THE SURFACE...
ALL UNITS FALL BACK! WE WILL ENGAGE WITH UNMANNED DRONES ONLY!
...THE AUTOBOTS DRIVE OUT OF THE LAKE IN HOPES OF HELPING IN THE FIGHT.
VROOOM
GREETINGS, FELLOW 'BOTS, WE ARE HERE TO HELP.
NOT VERY TALKATIVE. I CAN RELATE.
WHOA!
THE CREATURE LASHES OUT AT THE AUTOBOTS.
DO NOT ENGAGE THAT THING YET. KEEP YOUR SCANNERS PEELED FOR DECEPTICONS.

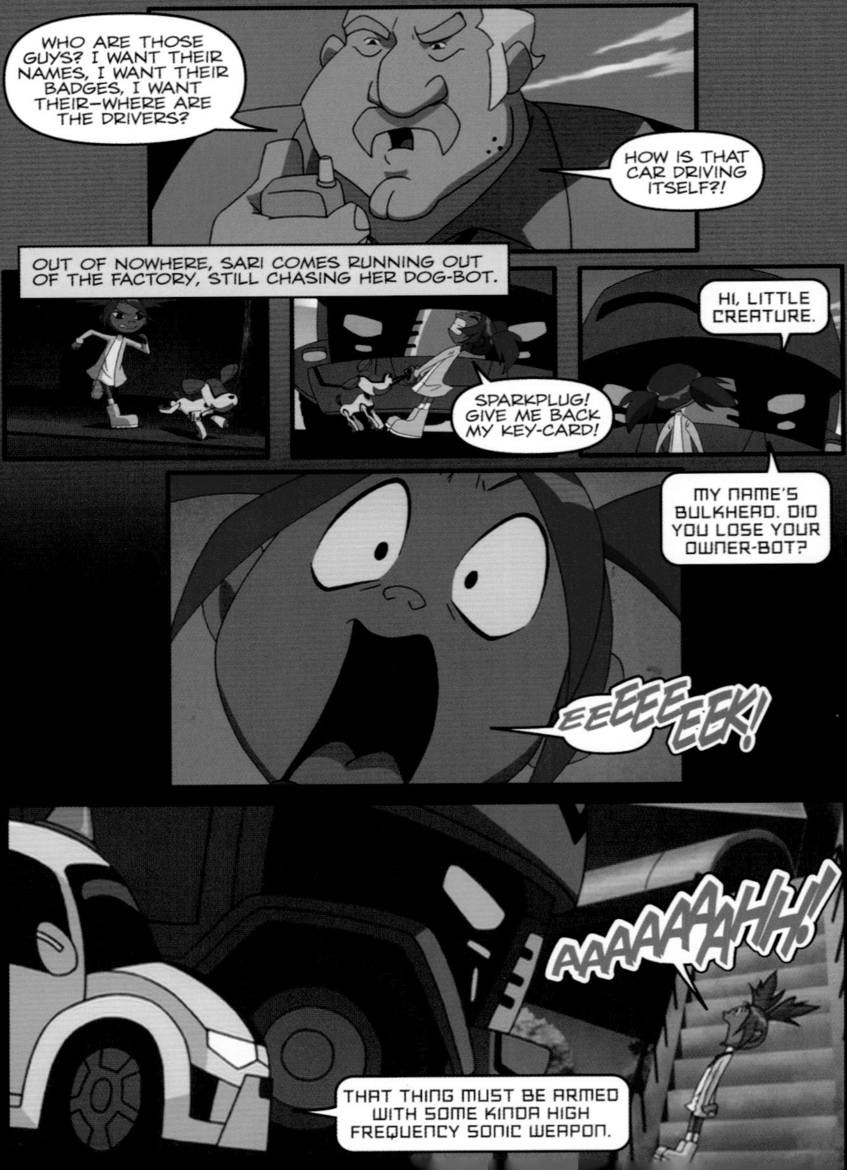
WHO ARE THOSE GUYS? I WANT THEIR NAMES, I WANT THEIR BADGES, I WANT THEIR—WHERE ARE THE DRIVERS?
HOW IS THAT CAR DRIVING ITSELF?!
OUT OF NOWHERE, SARI COMES RUNNING OUT OF THE FACTORY, STILL CHASING HER DOG-BOT.
SPARKPLUG! GIVE ME BACK MY KEY-CARD!
HI, LITTLE CREATURE.
MY NAME'S BULKHEAD. DID YOU LOSE YOUR OWNER-BOT?
EEEEEEEEK!
AAAAAAAAHH!!
THAT THING MUST BE ARMED WITH SOME KINDA HIGH FREQUENCY SONIC WEAPON.

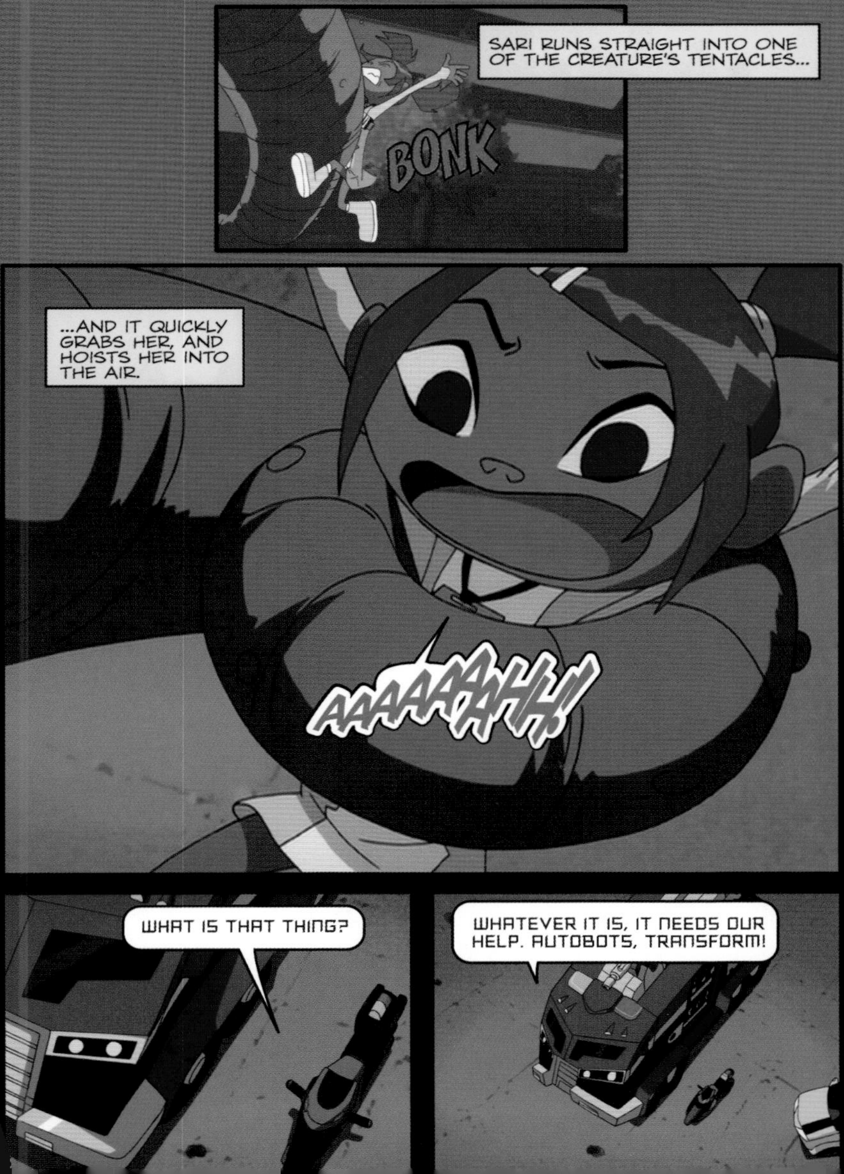
SARI RUNS STRAIGHT INTO ONE OF THE CREATURE'S TENTACLES...
BONK
...AND IT QUICKLY GRABS HER, AND HOISTS HER INTO THE AIR.
AAAAAAAHH!!
WHAT IS THAT THING?
WHATEVER IT IS, IT NEEDS OUR HELP. AUTOBOTS, TRANSFORM!

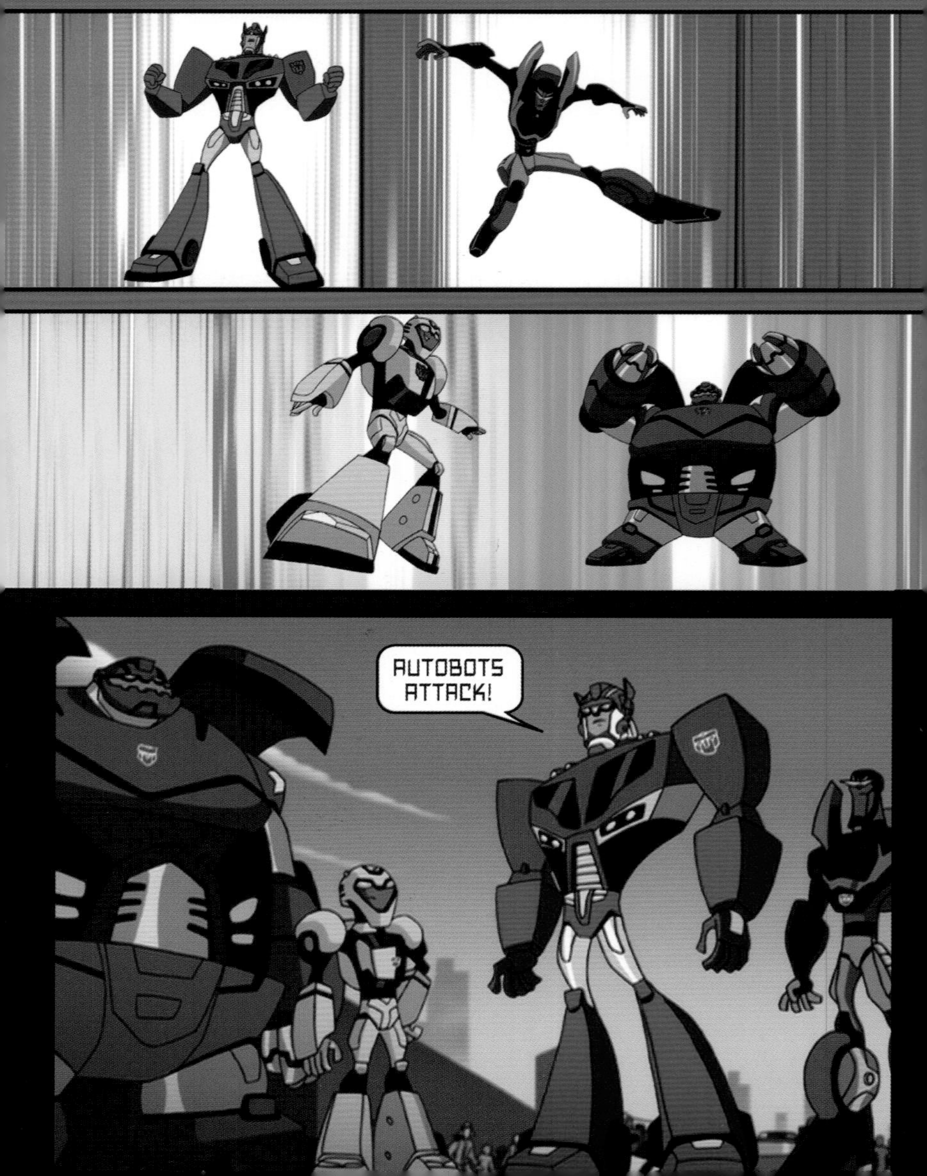
AUTOBOTS ATTACK!

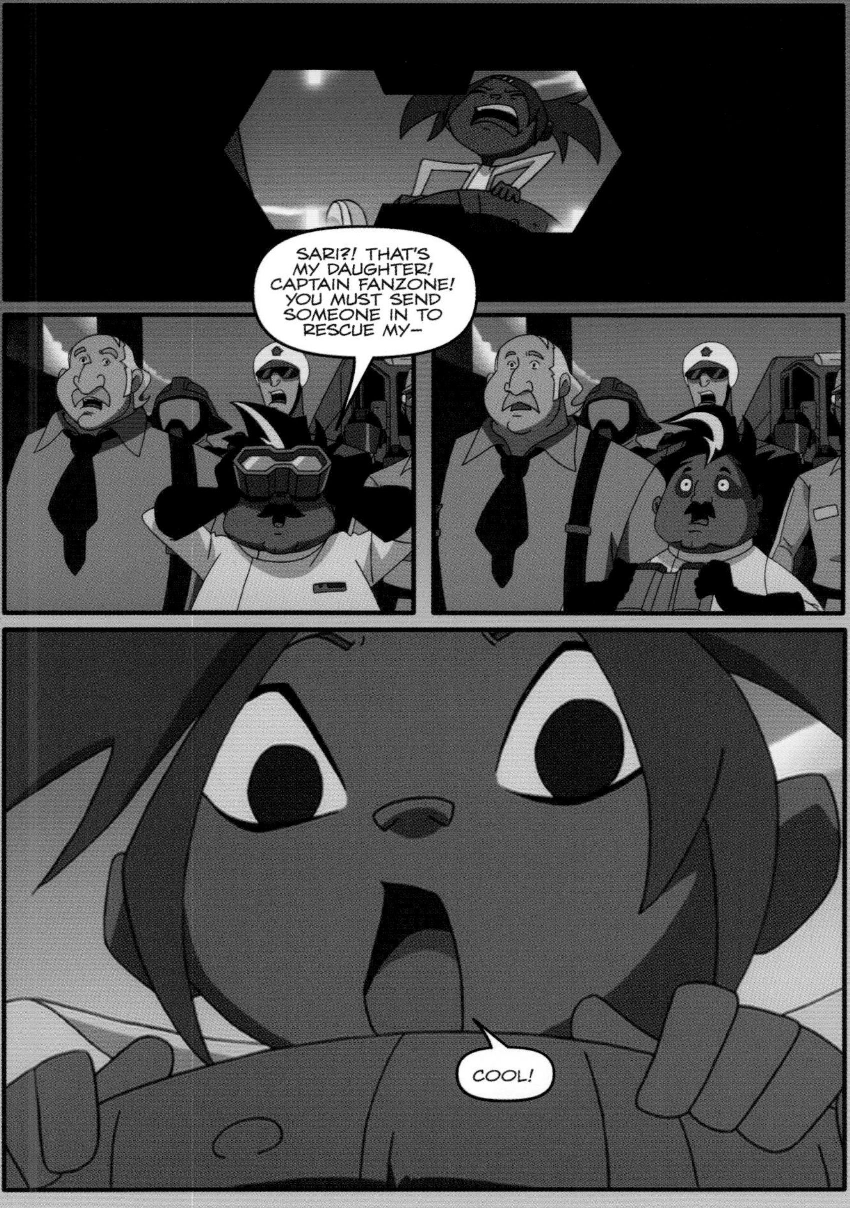
SARI?! THAT'S MY DAUGHTER! CAPTAIN FANZONE! YOU MUST SEND SOMEONE IN TO RESCUE MY–
COOL!

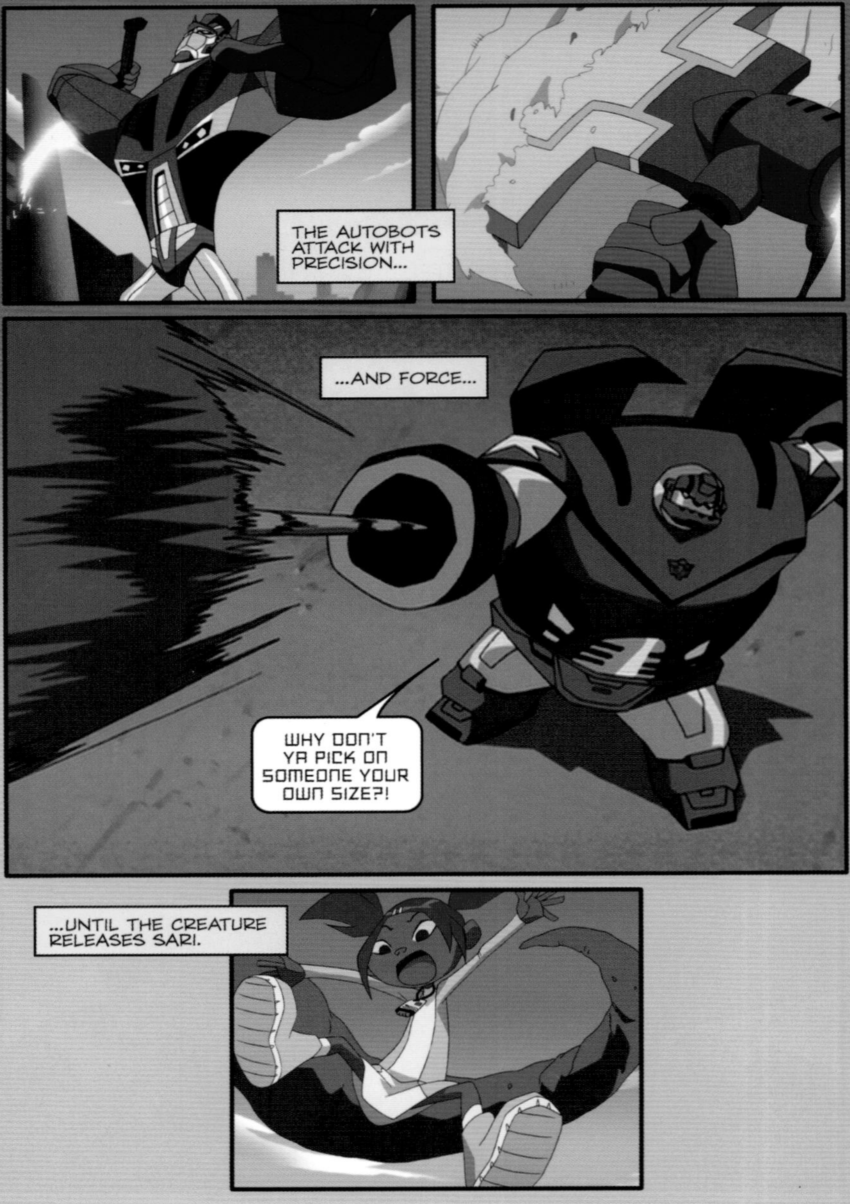
THE AUTOBOTS ATTACK WITH PRECISION...
...AND FORCE...
WHY DON'T YA PICK ON SOMEONE YOUR OWN SIZE?!
...UNTIL THE CREATURE RELEASES SARI.

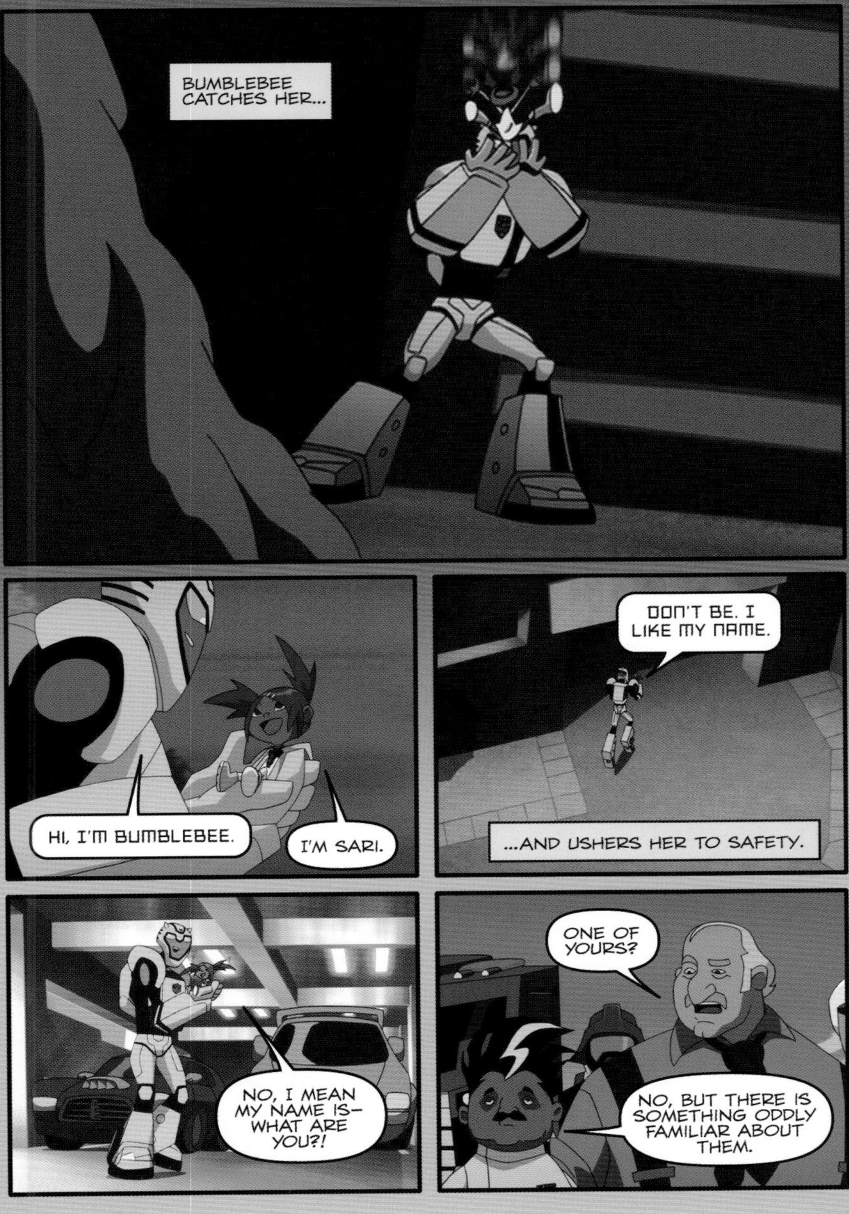
BUMBLEBEE CATCHES HER...
HI, I'M BUMBLEBEE.
I'M SARI.
DON'T BE. I LIKE MY NAME.
...AND USHERS HER TO SAFETY.
NO, I MEAN MY NAME IS— WHAT ARE YOU?!
ONE OF YOURS?
NO, BUT THERE IS SOMETHING ODDLY FAMILIAR ABOUT THEM.

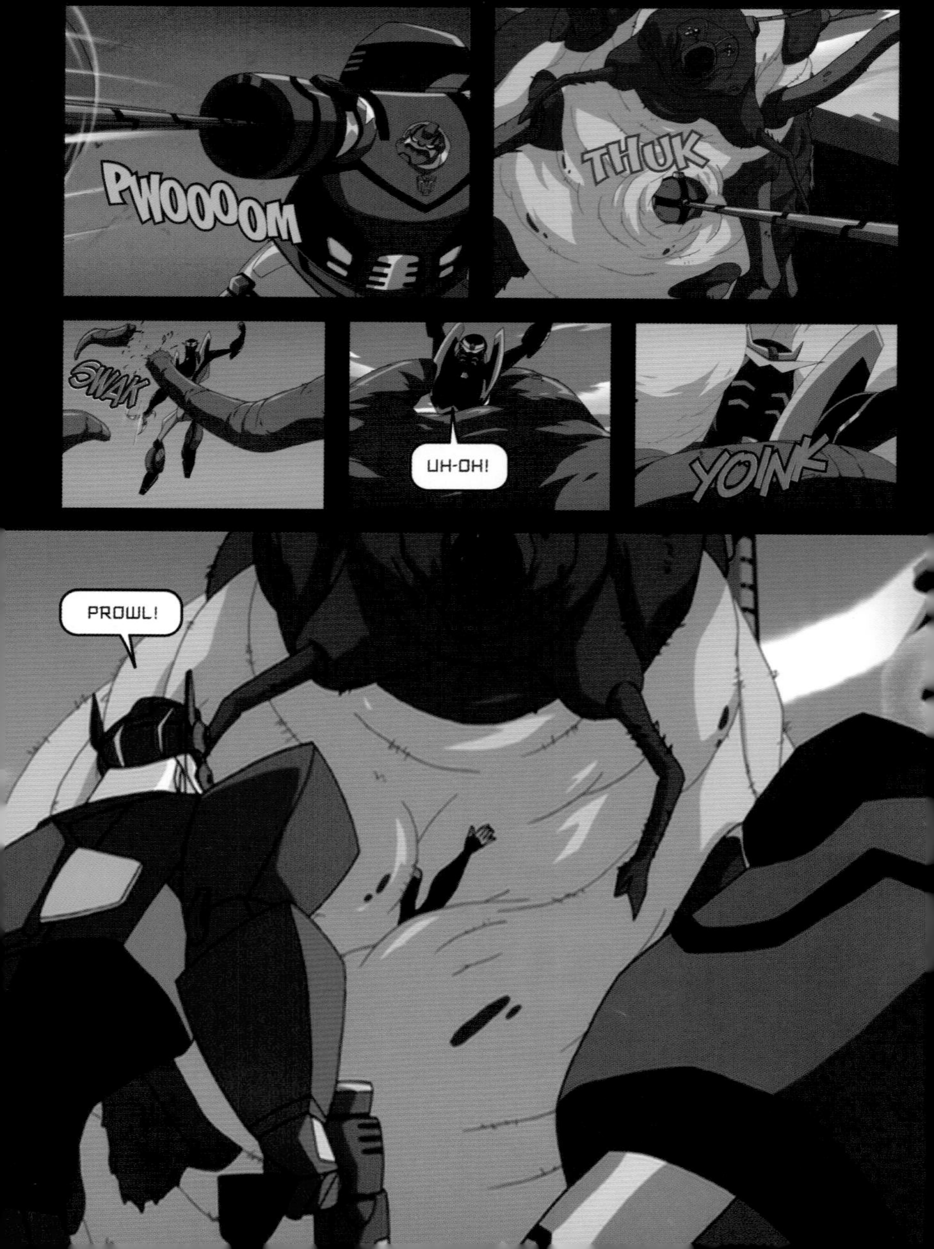
PWOOOOM
THUK
SWAK
UH-OH!
YOINK
PROWL!

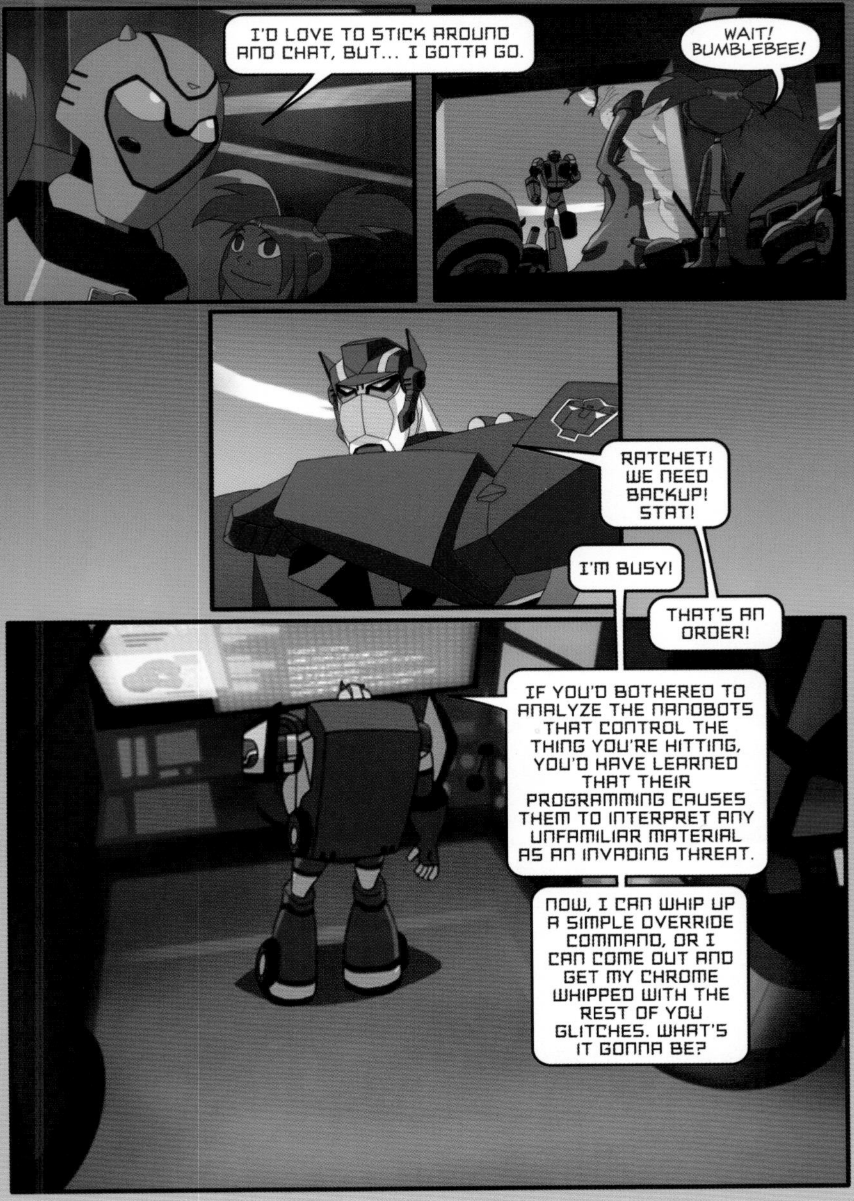
I'D LOVE TO STICK AROUND AND CHAT, BUT... I GOTTA GO.
WAIT! BUMBLEBEE!
RATCHET! WE NEED BACKUP! STAT!
I'M BUSY!
THAT'S AN ORDER!
IF YOU'D BOTHERED TO ANALYZE THE NANOBOTS THAT CONTROL THE THING YOU'RE HITTING, YOU'D HAVE LEARNED THAT THEIR PROGRAMMING CAUSES THEM TO INTERPRET ANY UNFAMILIAR MATERIAL AS AN INVADING THREAT.
NOW, I CAN WHIP UP A SIMPLE OVERRIDE COMMAND, OR I CAN COME OUT AND GET MY CHROME WHIPPED WITH THE REST OF YOU GLITCHES. WHAT'S IT GONNA BE?

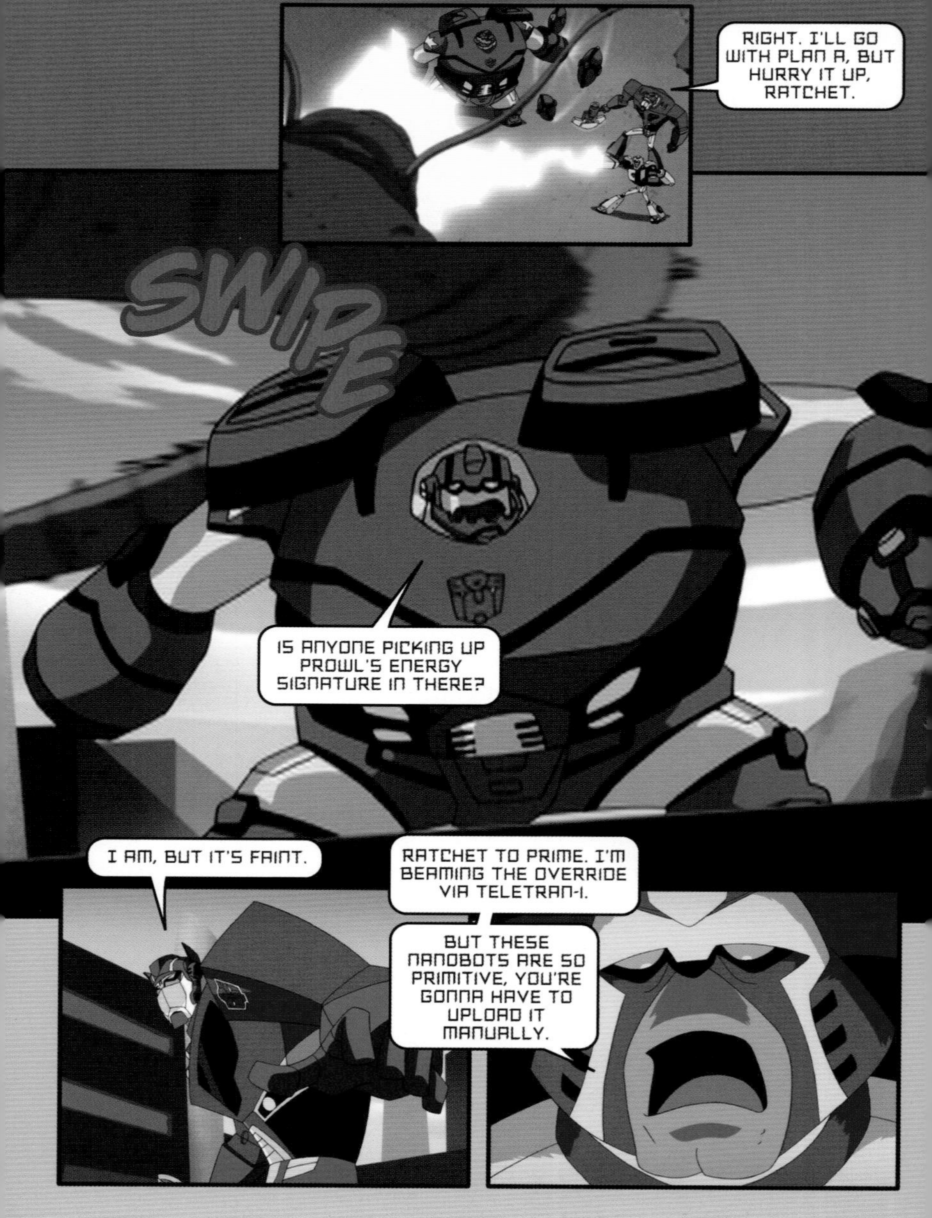

RIGHT. I'LL GO WITH PLAN A, BUT HURRY IT UP, RATCHET.
SWIPE
IS ANYONE PICKING UP PROWL'S ENERGY SIGNATURE IN THERE?
I AM, BUT IT'S FAINT.
RATCHET TO PRIME. I'M BEAMING THE OVERRIDE VIA TELETRAN-1.
BUT THESE NANOBOTS ARE SO PRIMITIVE, YOU'RE GONNA HAVE TO UPLOAD IT MANUALLY.

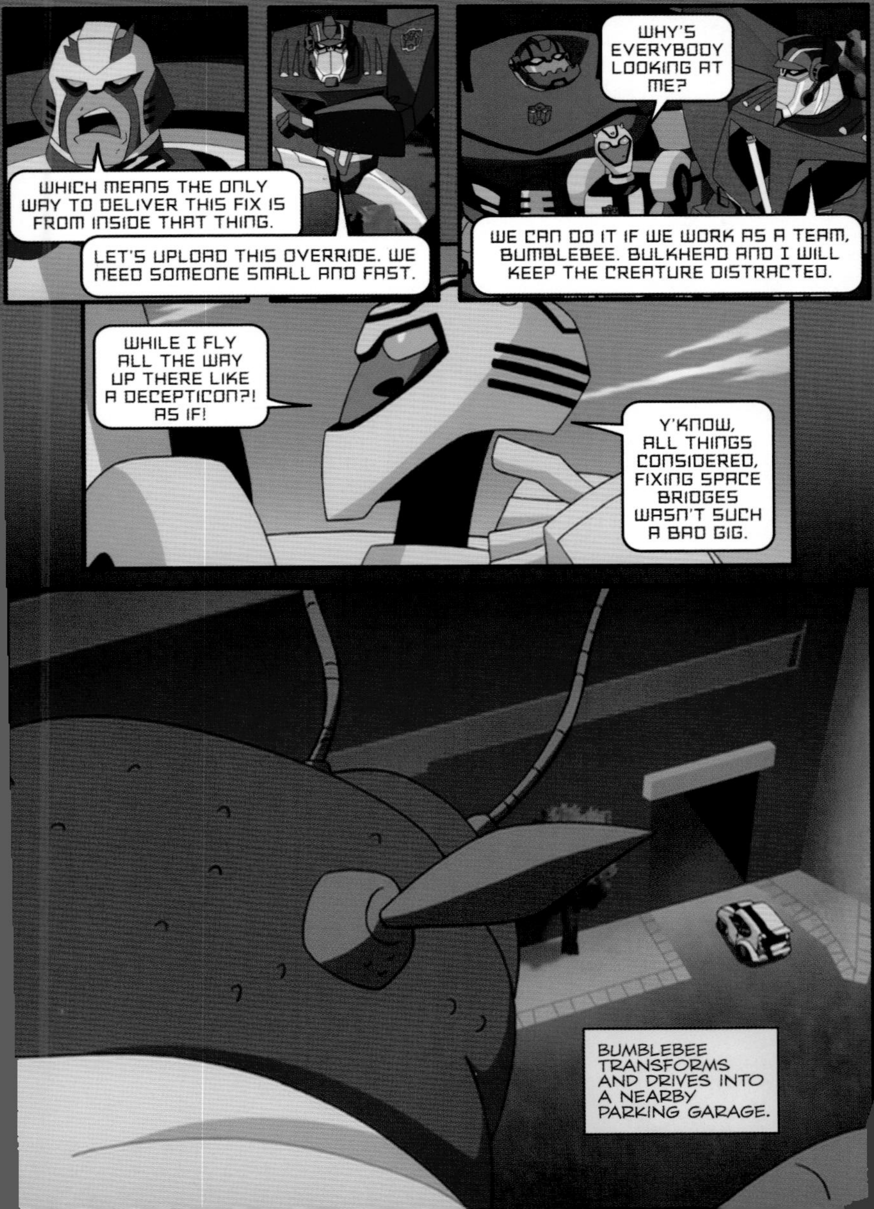
WHICH MEANS THE ONLY WAY TO DELIVER THIS FIX IS FROM INSIDE THAT THING.
LET'S UPLOAD THIS OVERRIDE. WE NEED SOMEONE SMALL AND FAST.
WHY'S EVERYBODY LOOKING AT ME?
WE CAN DO IT IF WE WORK AS A TEAM, BUMBLEBEE. BULKHEAD AND I WILL KEEP THE CREATURE DISTRACTED.
WHILE I FLY ALL THE WAY UP THERE LIKE A DECEPTICON?! AS IF!
Y'KNOW, ALL THINGS CONSIDERED, FIXING SPACE BRIDGES WASN'T SUCH A BAD GIG.
BUMBLEBEE TRANSFORMS AND DRIVES INTO A NEARBY PARKING GARAGE.

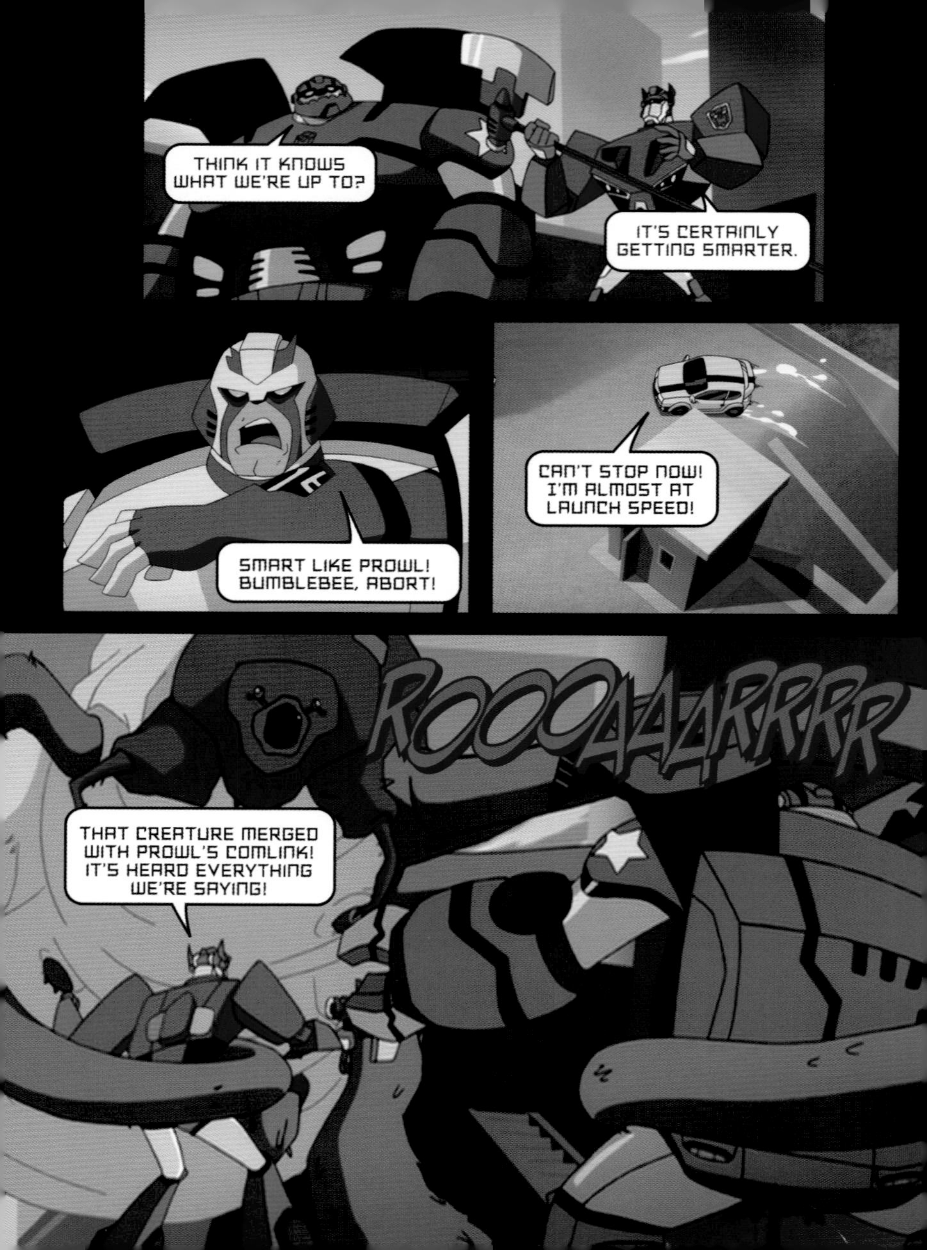
THINK IT KNOWS WHAT WE'RE UP TO?
IT'S CERTAINLY GETTING SMARTER.
SMART LIKE PROWL! BUMBLEBEE, ABORT!
CAN'T STOP NOW! I'M ALMOST AT LAUNCH SPEED!
ROOOAAARRRR
THAT CREATURE MERGED WITH PROWL'S COMLINK! IT'S HEARD EVERYTHING WE'RE SAYING!

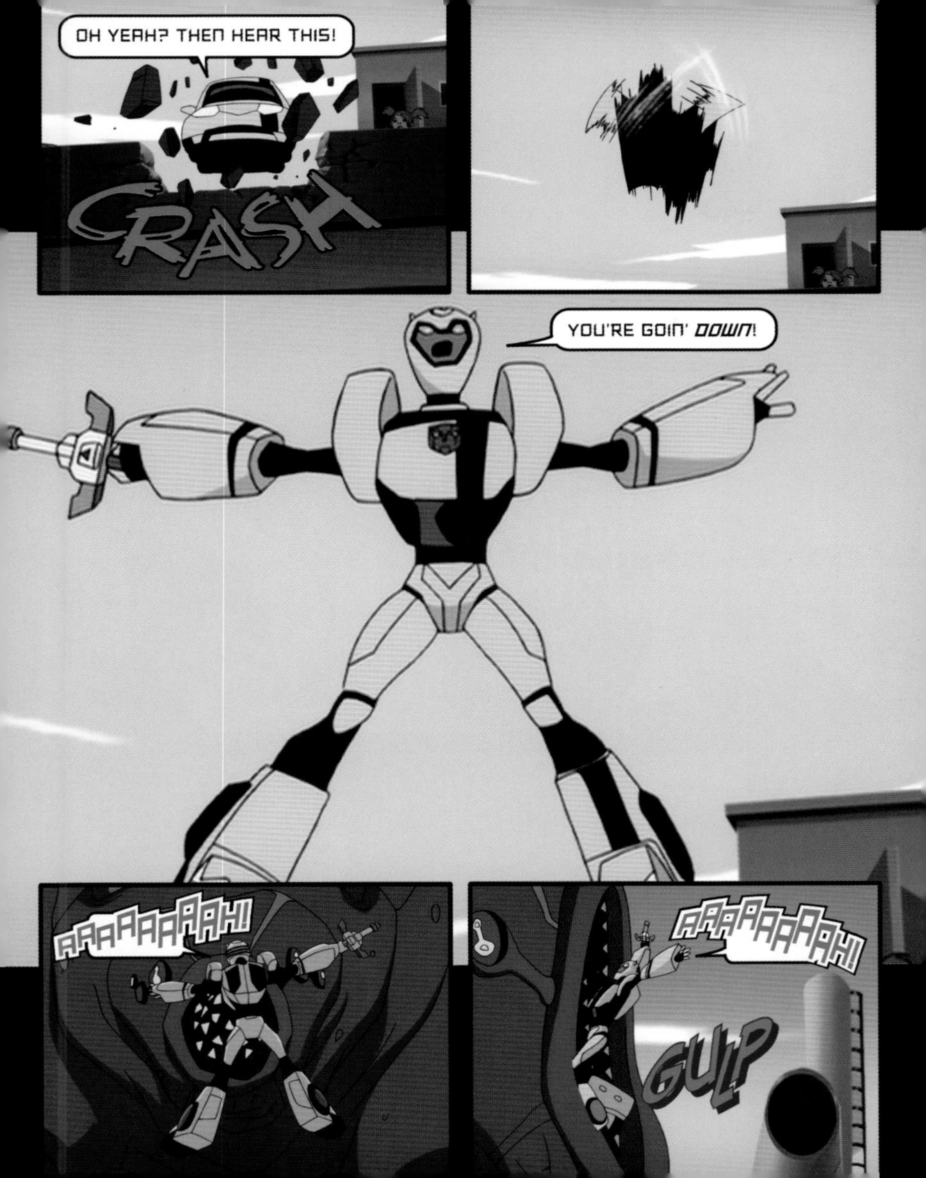
OH YEAH? THEN HEAR THIS!
CRASH
YOU'RE GOIN' *DOWN*!
AAAAAAAAAH!
AAAAAAAAAAH!
GULP

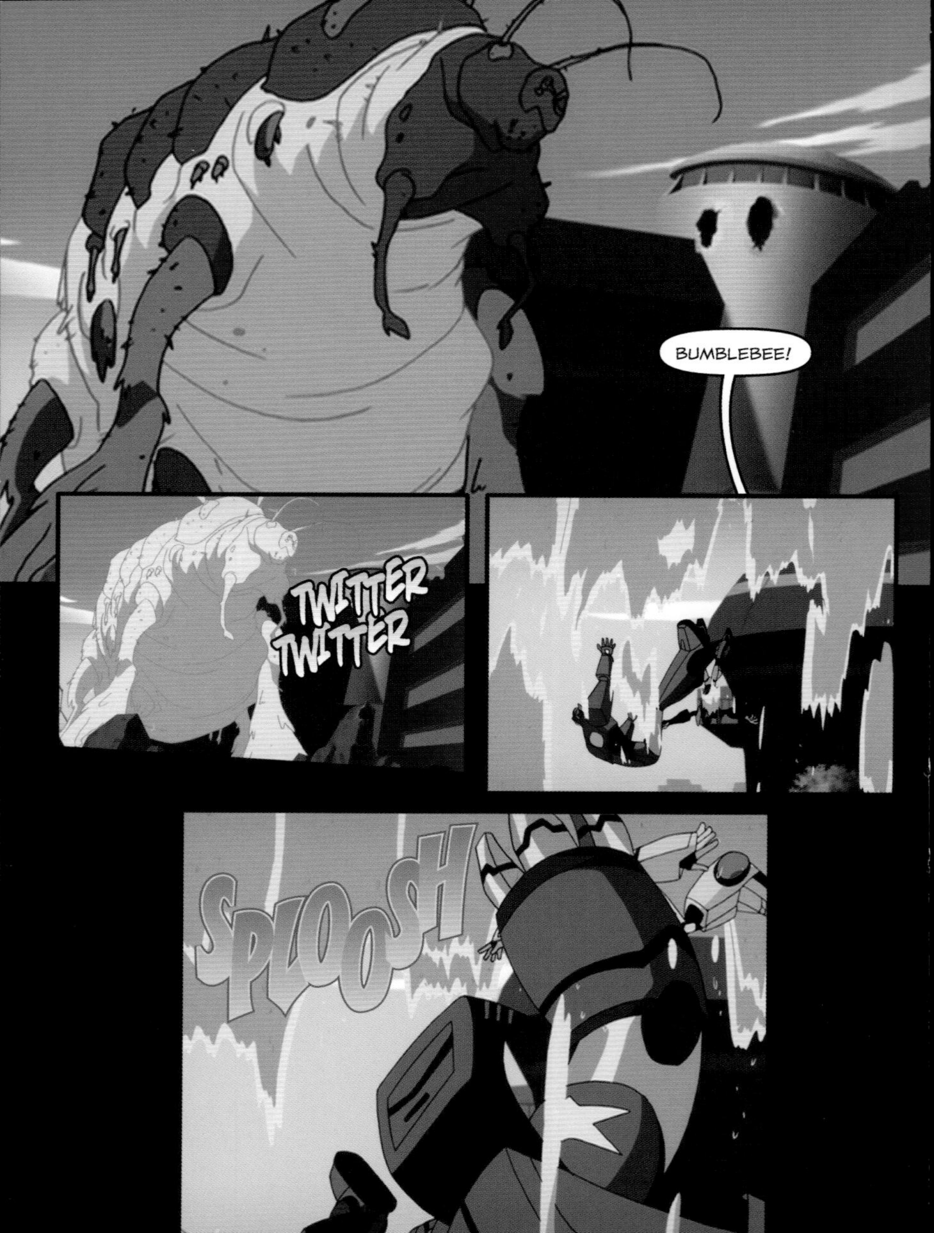
BUMBLEBEE!
TWITTER
TWITTER
SPLOOSH

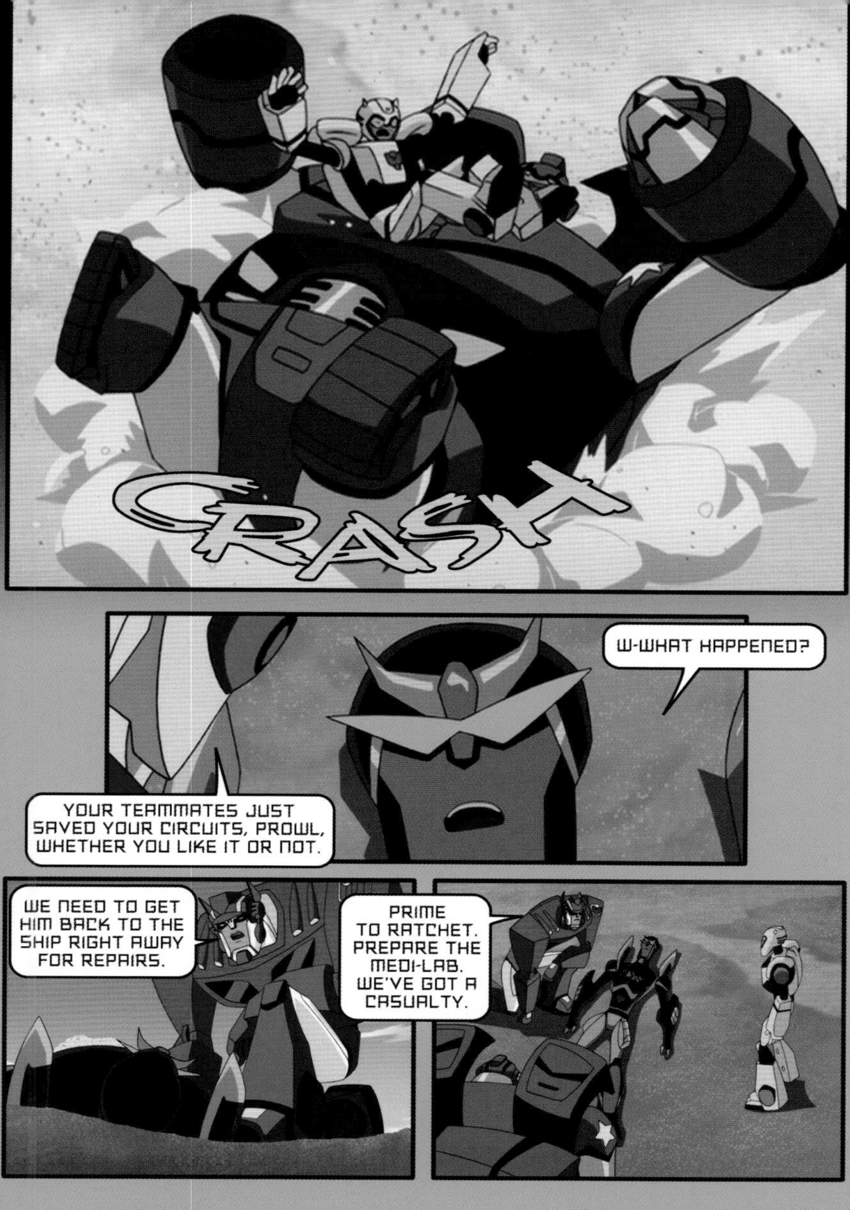
CRASH
W-WHAT HAPPENED?
YOUR TEAMMATES JUST SAVED YOUR CIRCUITS, PROWL, WHETHER YOU LIKE IT OR NOT.
WE NEED TO GET HIM BACK TO THE SHIP RIGHT AWAY FOR REPAIRS.
PRIME TO RATCHET. PREPARE THE MEDI-LAB. WE'VE GOT A CASUALTY.

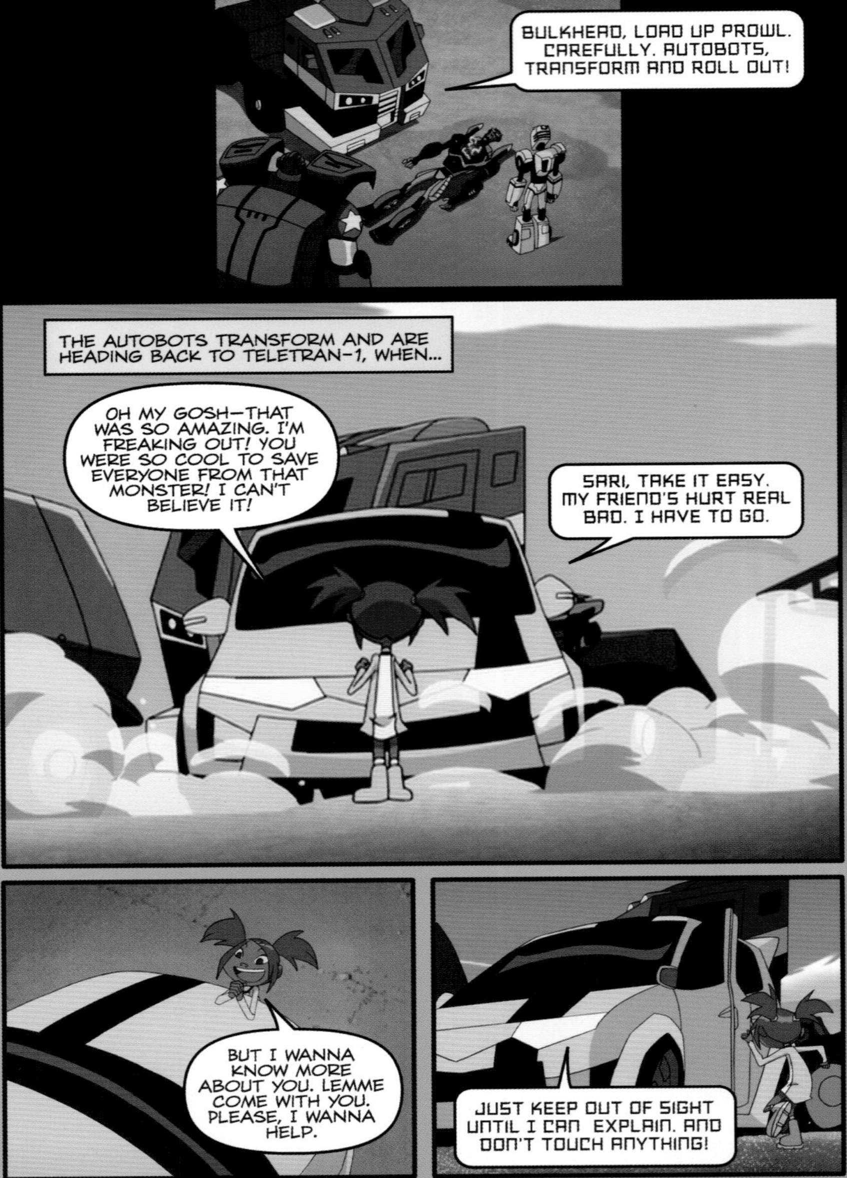
BULKHEAD, LOAD UP PROWL. CAREFULLY. AUTOBOTS, TRANSFORM AND ROLL OUT!
THE AUTOBOTS TRANSFORM AND ARE HEADING BACK TO TELETRAN-1, WHEN...
OH MY GOSH—THAT WAS SO AMAZING. I'M FREAKING OUT! YOU WERE SO COOL TO SAVE EVERYONE FROM THAT MONSTER! I CAN'T BELIEVE IT!
SARI, TAKE IT EASY. MY FRIEND'S HURT REAL BAD. I HAVE TO GO.
BUT I WANNA KNOW MORE ABOUT YOU. LEMME COME WITH YOU. PLEASE, I WANNA HELP.
JUST KEEP OUT OF SIGHT UNTIL I CAN EXPLAIN. AND DON'T TOUCH ANYTHING!

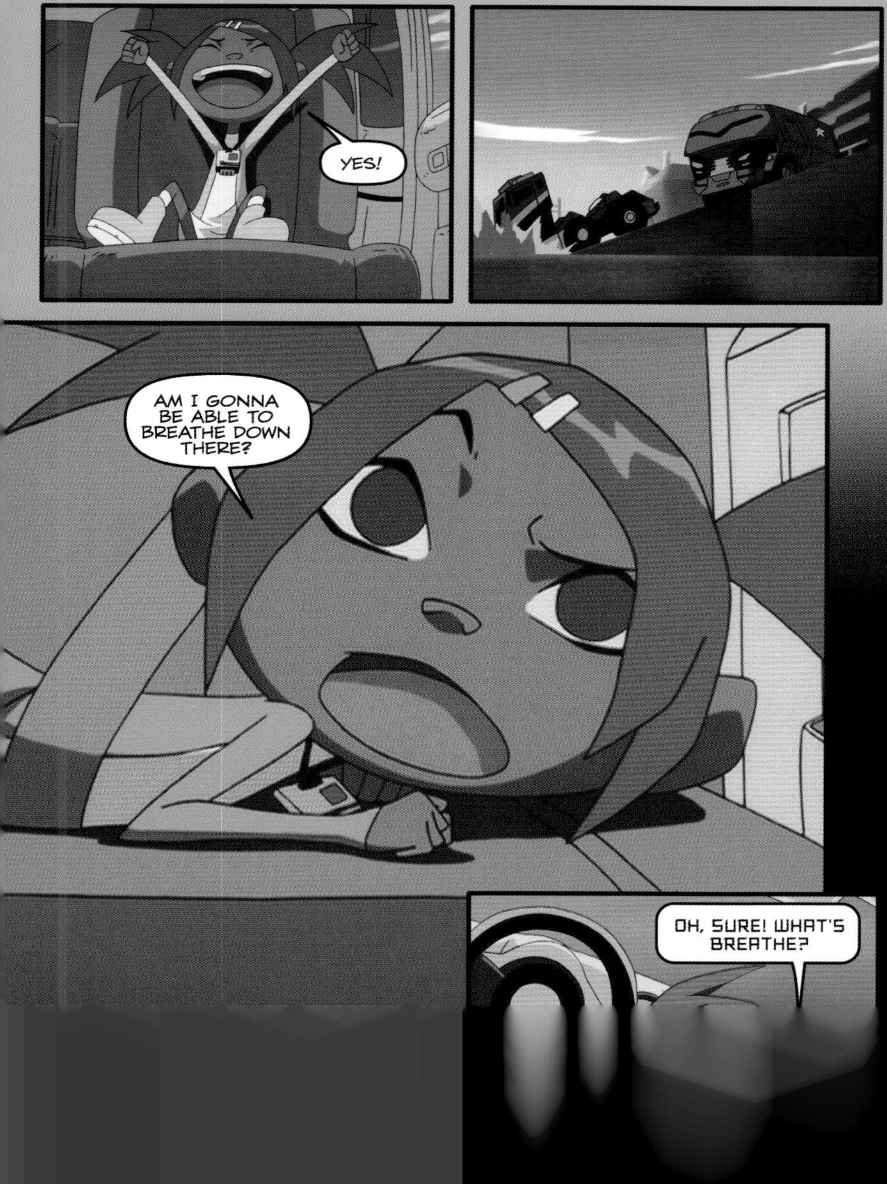
YES!
AM I GONNA BE ABLE TO BREATHE DOWN THERE?
OH, SURE! WHAT'S BREATHE?

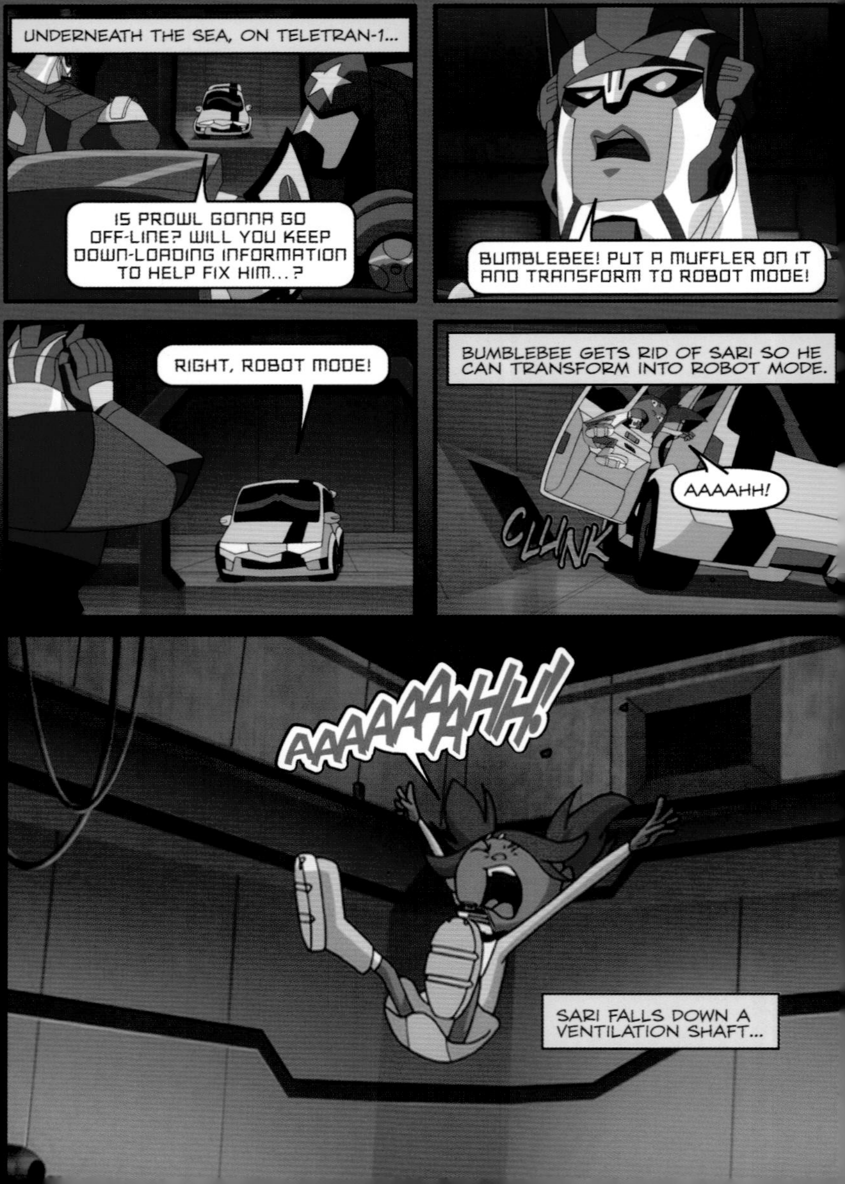

UNDERNEATH THE SEA, ON TELETRAN-1...
IS PROWL GONNA GO OFF-LINE? WILL YOU KEEP DOWN-LOADING INFORMATION TO HELP FIX HIM...?
BUMBLEBEE! PUT A MUFFLER ON IT AND TRANSFORM TO ROBOT MODE!
RIGHT, ROBOT MODE!
BUMBLEBEE GETS RID OF SARI SO HE CAN TRANSFORM INTO ROBOT MODE.
AAAAHH!
CLUNK
AAAAAAAHH!!
SARI FALLS DOWN A VENTILATION SHAFT...

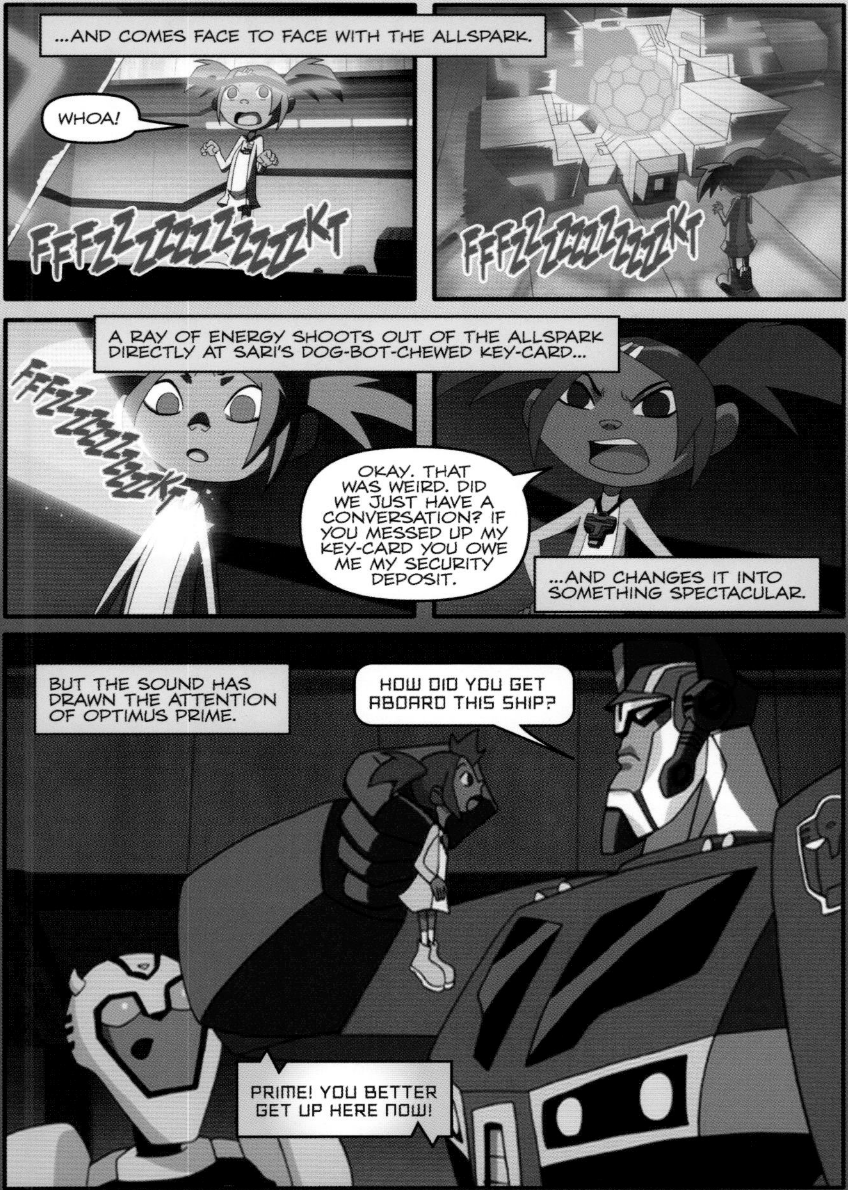
...AND COMES FACE TO FACE WITH THE ALLSPARK.
WHOA!
FFFZZZZZZZZZZZZKT
FFFZZZZZZZZZZZZKT
A RAY OF ENERGY SHOOTS OUT OF THE ALLSPARK DIRECTLY AT SARI'S DOG-BOT-CHEWED KEY-CARD...
FFFZZZZZZZZZZZKT
OKAY. THAT WAS WEIRD. DID WE JUST HAVE A CONVERSATION? IF YOU MESSED UP MY KEY-CARD YOU OWE ME MY SECURITY DEPOSIT.
...AND CHANGES IT INTO SOMETHING SPECTACULAR.
BUT THE SOUND HAS DRAWN THE ATTENTION OF OPTIMUS PRIME.
HOW DID YOU GET ABOARD THIS SHIP?
PRIME! YOU BETTER GET UP HERE NOW!

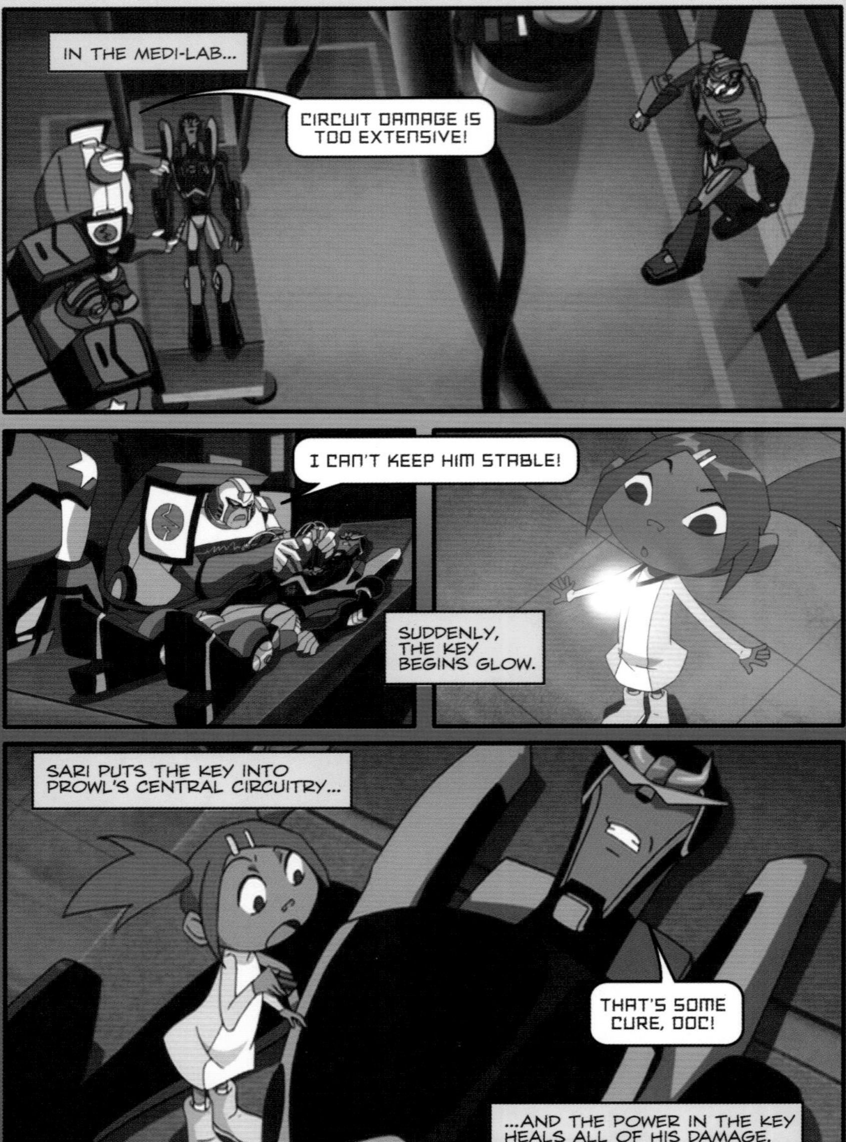
IN THE MEDI-LAB...
CIRCUIT DAMAGE IS TOO EXTENSIVE!
I CAN'T KEEP HIM STABLE!
SUDDENLY, THE KEY BEGINS GLOW.
SARI PUTS THE KEY INTO PROWL'S CENTRAL CIRCUITRY...
THAT'S SOME CURE, DOC!
...AND THE POWER IN THE KEY HEALS ALL OF HIS DAMAGE.

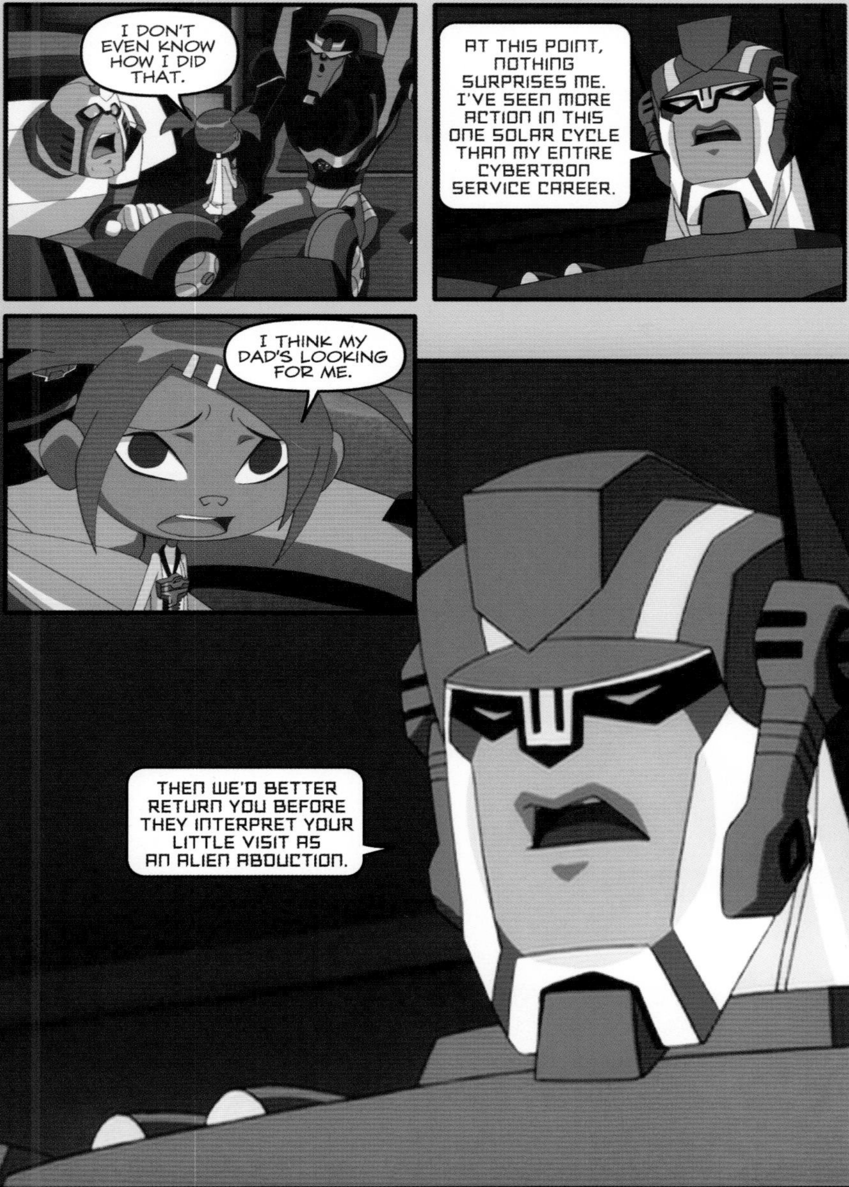
I DON'T EVEN KNOW HOW I DID THAT.
AT THIS POINT, NOTHING SURPRISES ME. I'VE SEEN MORE ACTION IN THIS ONE SOLAR CYCLE THAN MY ENTIRE CYBERTRON SERVICE CAREER.
I THINK MY DAD'S LOOKING FOR ME.
THEN WE'D BETTER RETURN YOU BEFORE THEY INTERPRET YOUR LITTLE VISIT AS AN ALIEN ABDUCTION.

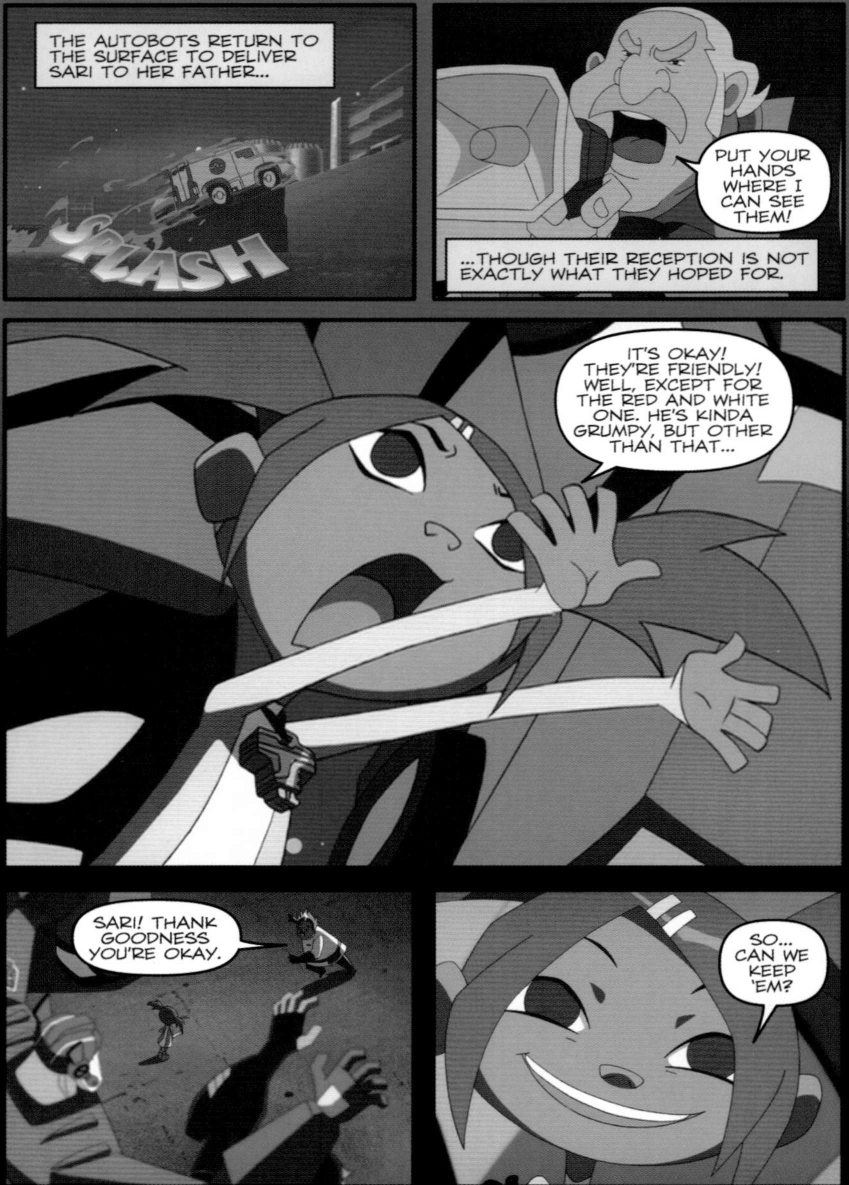
THE AUTOBOTS RETURN TO THE SURFACE TO DELIVER SARI TO HER FATHER...
SPLASH
PUT YOUR HANDS WHERE I CAN SEE THEM!
...THOUGH THEIR RECEPTION IS NOT EXACTLY WHAT THEY HOPED FOR.
IT'S OKAY! THEY'RE FRIENDLY! WELL, EXCEPT FOR THE RED AND WHITE ONE. HE'S KINDA GRUMPY, BUT OTHER THAN THAT...
SARI! THANK GOODNESS YOU'RE OKAY.
SO... CAN WE KEEP 'EM?

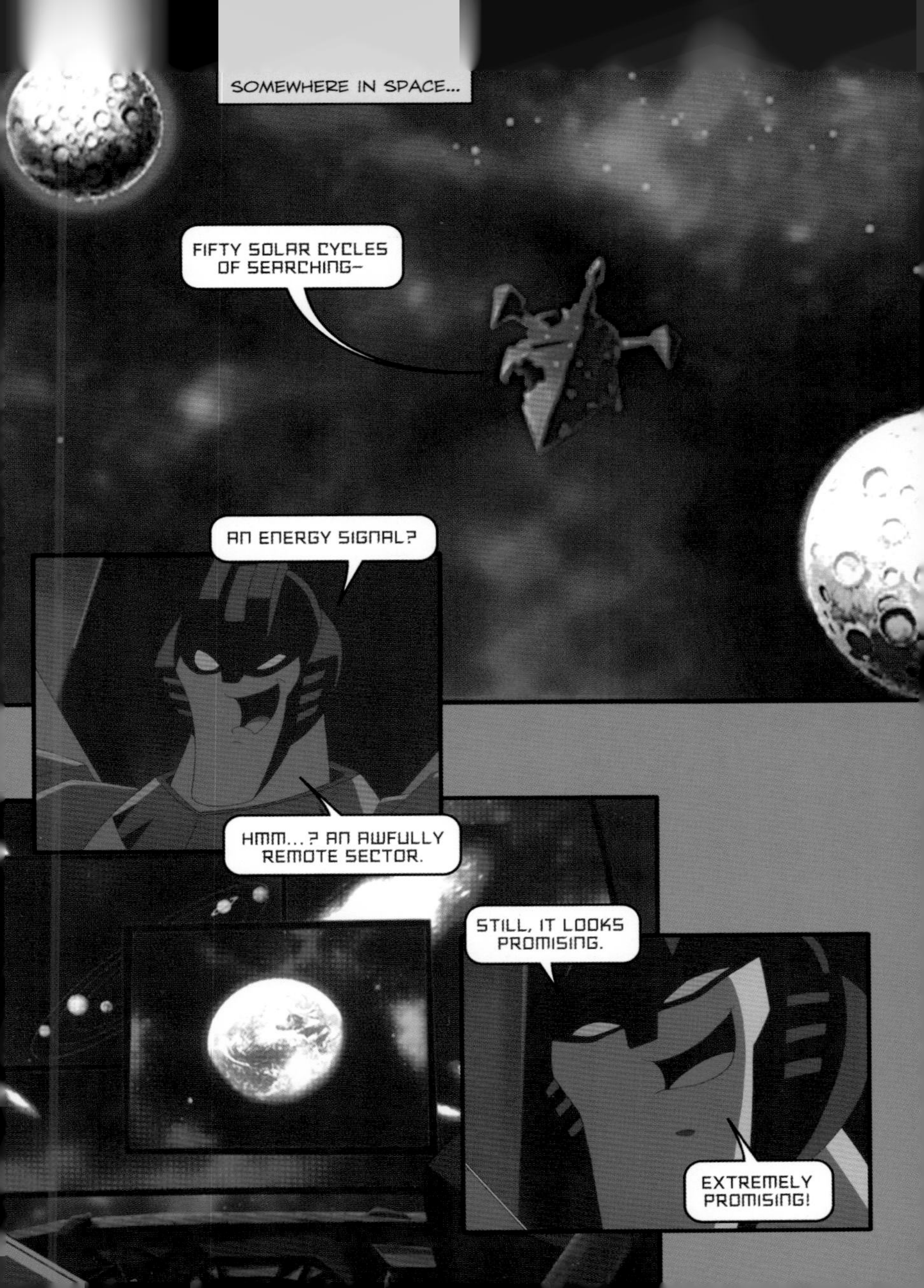
SOMEWHERE IN SPACE...
FIFTY SOLAR CYCLES OF SEARCHING–
AN ENERGY SIGNAL?
HMM...? AN AWFULLY REMOTE SECTOR.
STILL, IT LOOKS PROMISING.
EXTREMELY PROMISING!

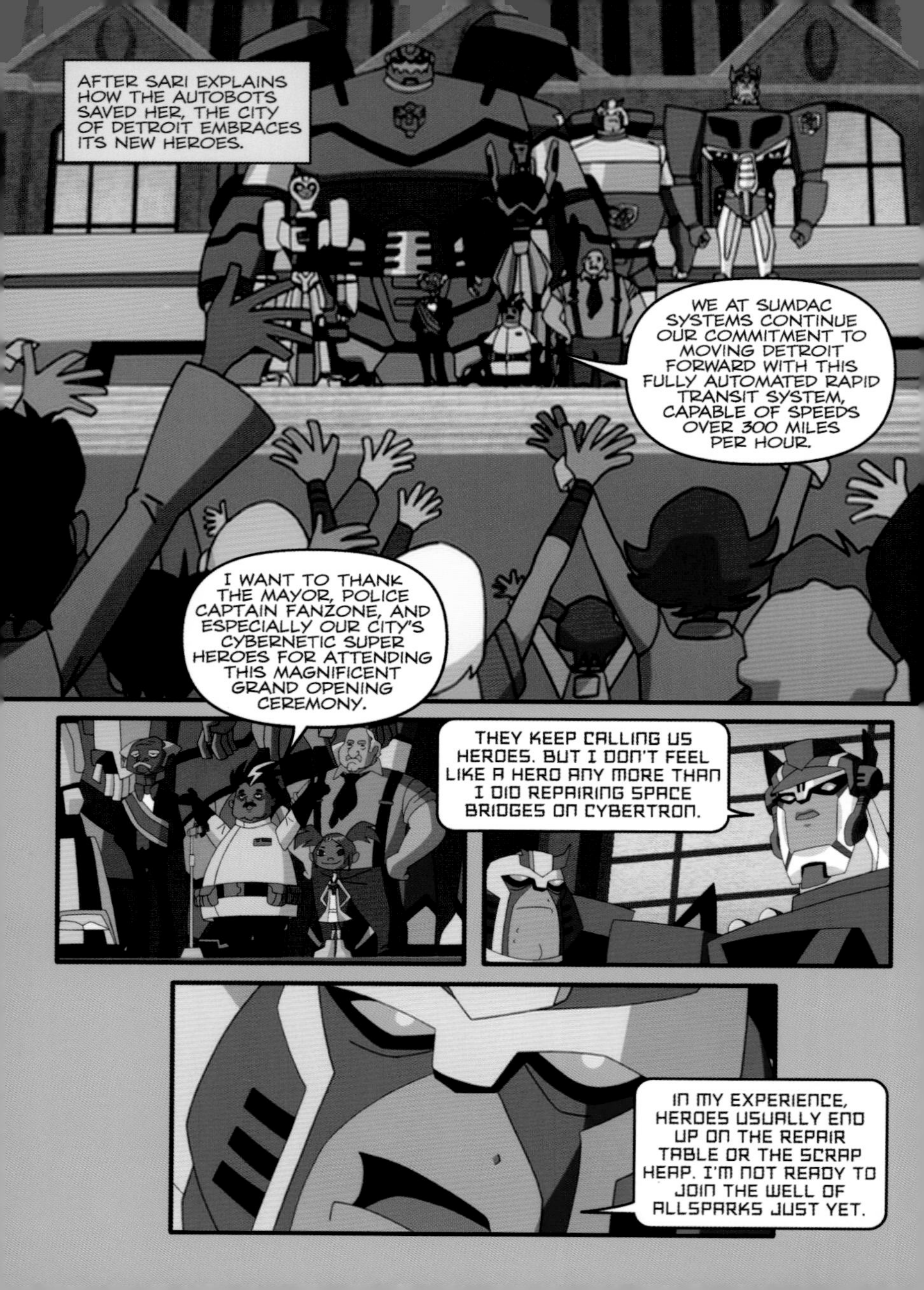
AFTER SARI EXPLAINS HOW THE AUTOBOTS SAVED HER, THE CITY OF DETROIT EMBRACES ITS NEW HEROES.
WE AT SUMDAC SYSTEMS CONTINUE OUR COMMITMENT TO MOVING DETROIT FORWARD WITH THIS FULLY AUTOMATED RAPID TRANSIT SYSTEM, CAPABLE OF SPEEDS OVER 300 MILES PER HOUR.
I WANT TO THANK THE MAYOR, POLICE CAPTAIN FANZONE, AND ESPECIALLY OUR CITY'S CYBERNETIC SUPER HEROES FOR ATTENDING THIS MAGNIFICENT GRAND OPENING CEREMONY.
THEY KEEP CALLING US HEROES. BUT I DON'T FEEL LIKE A HERO ANY MORE THAN I DID REPAIRING SPACE BRIDGES ON CYBERTRON.
IN MY EXPERIENCE, HEROES USUALLY END UP ON THE REPAIR TABLE OR THE SCRAP HEAP. I'M NOT READY TO JOIN THE WELL OF ALLSPARKS JUST YET.

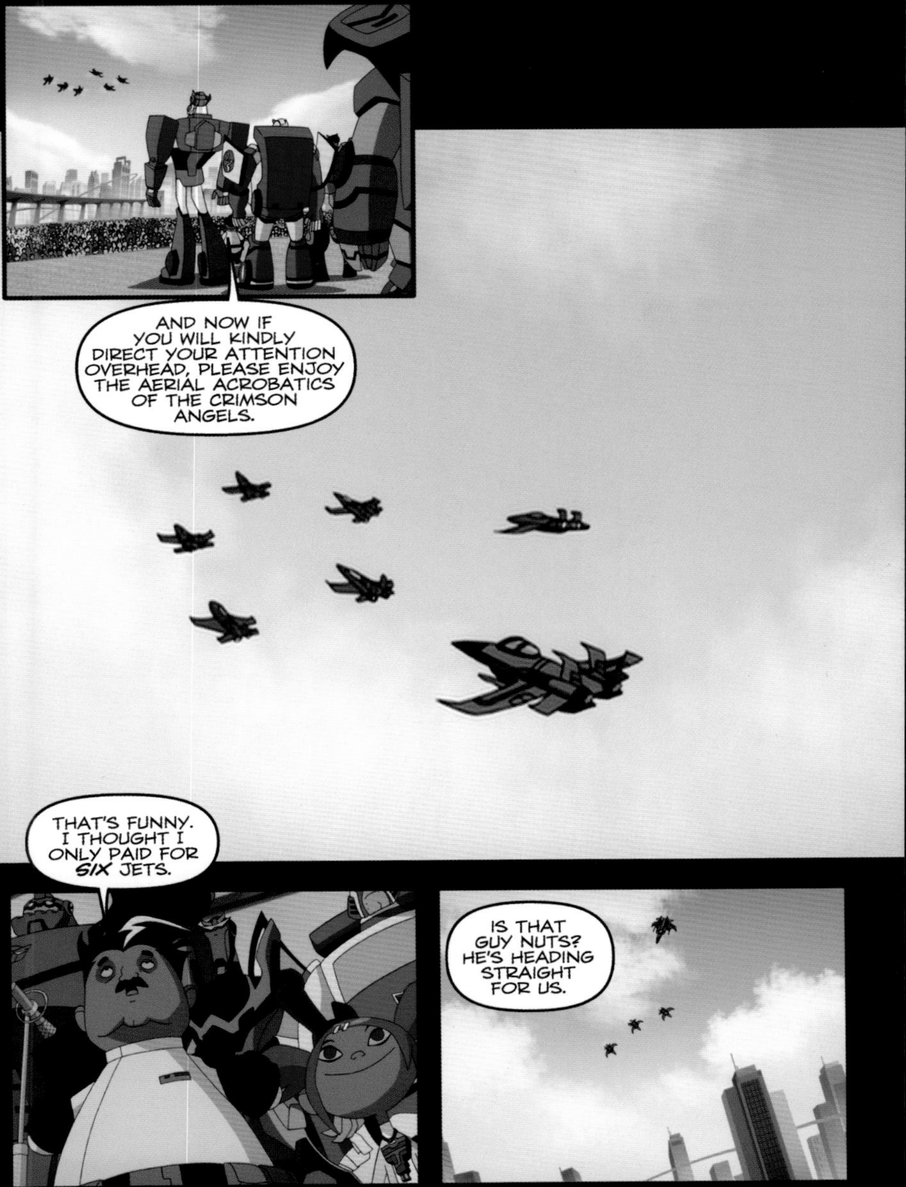
AND NOW IF YOU WILL KINDLY DIRECT YOUR ATTENTION OVERHEAD, PLEASE ENJOY THE AERIAL ACROBATICS OF THE CRIMSON ANGELS.
THAT'S FUNNY. I THOUGHT I ONLY PAID FOR SIX JETS.
IS THAT GUY NUTS? HE'S HEADING STRAIGHT FOR US.

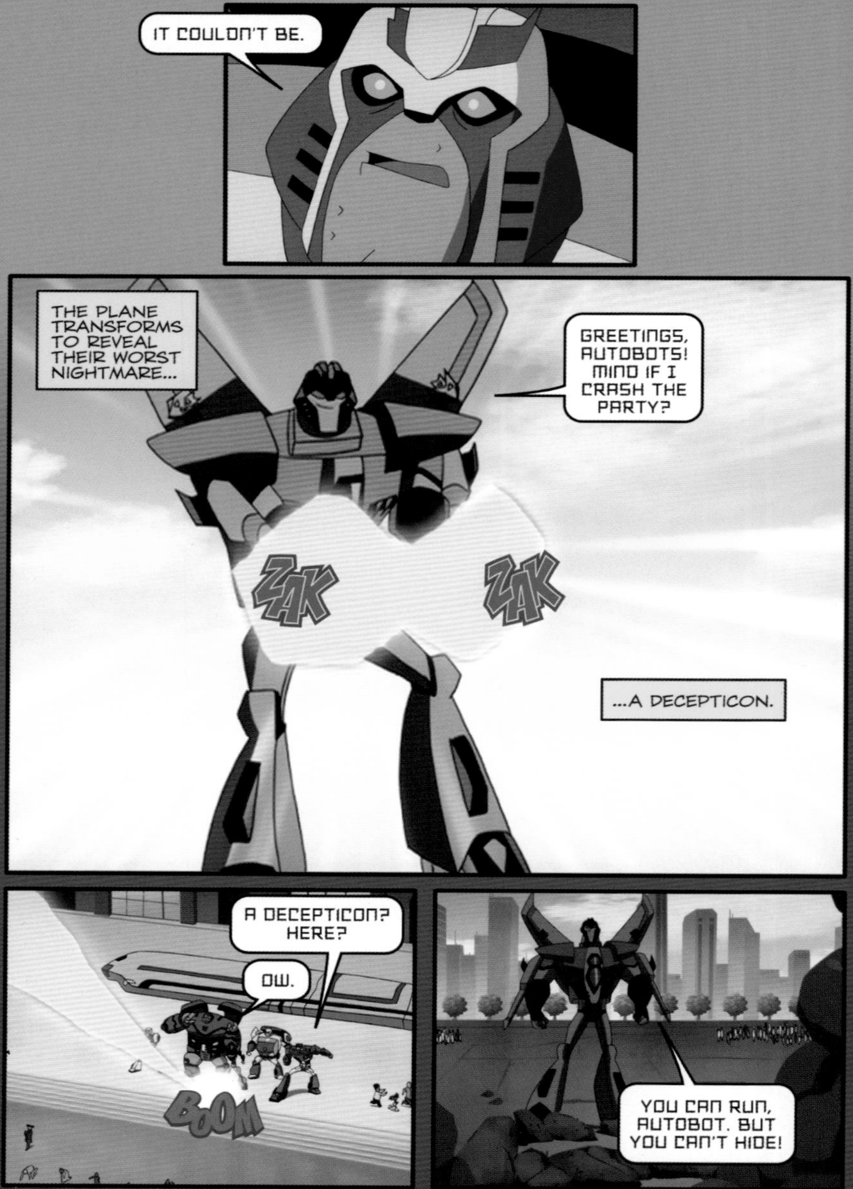
IT COULDN'T BE.
THE PLANE TRANSFORMS TO REVEAL THEIR WORST NIGHTMARE...
GREETINGS, AUTOBOTS! MIND IF I CRASH THE PARTY?
ZAK
ZAK
...A DECEPTICON.
A DECEPTICON? HERE?
OW.
BOOM
YOU CAN RUN, AUTOBOT. BUT YOU CAN'T HIDE!

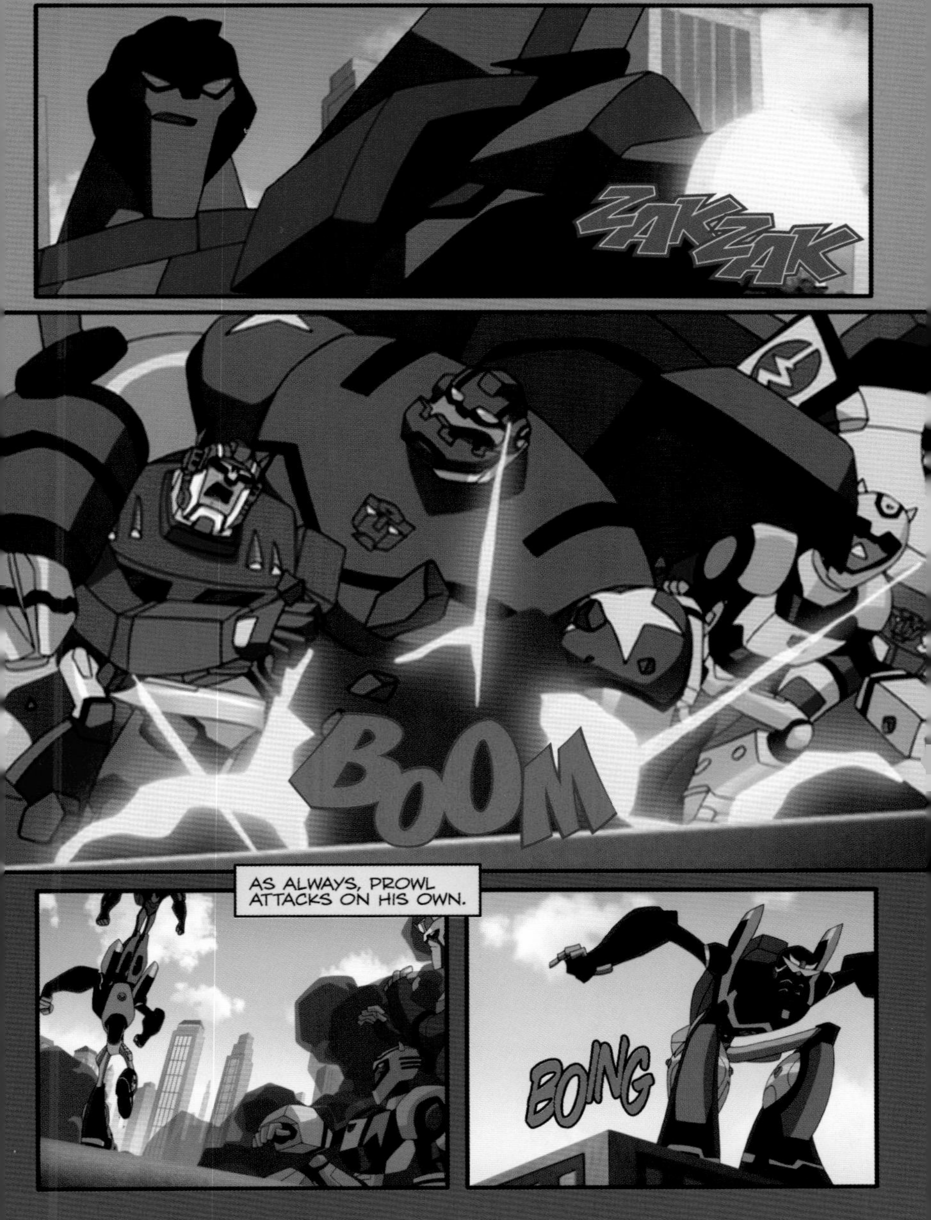
ZAK ZAK
BOOM
AS ALWAYS, PROWL ATTACKS ON HIS OWN.
BOING

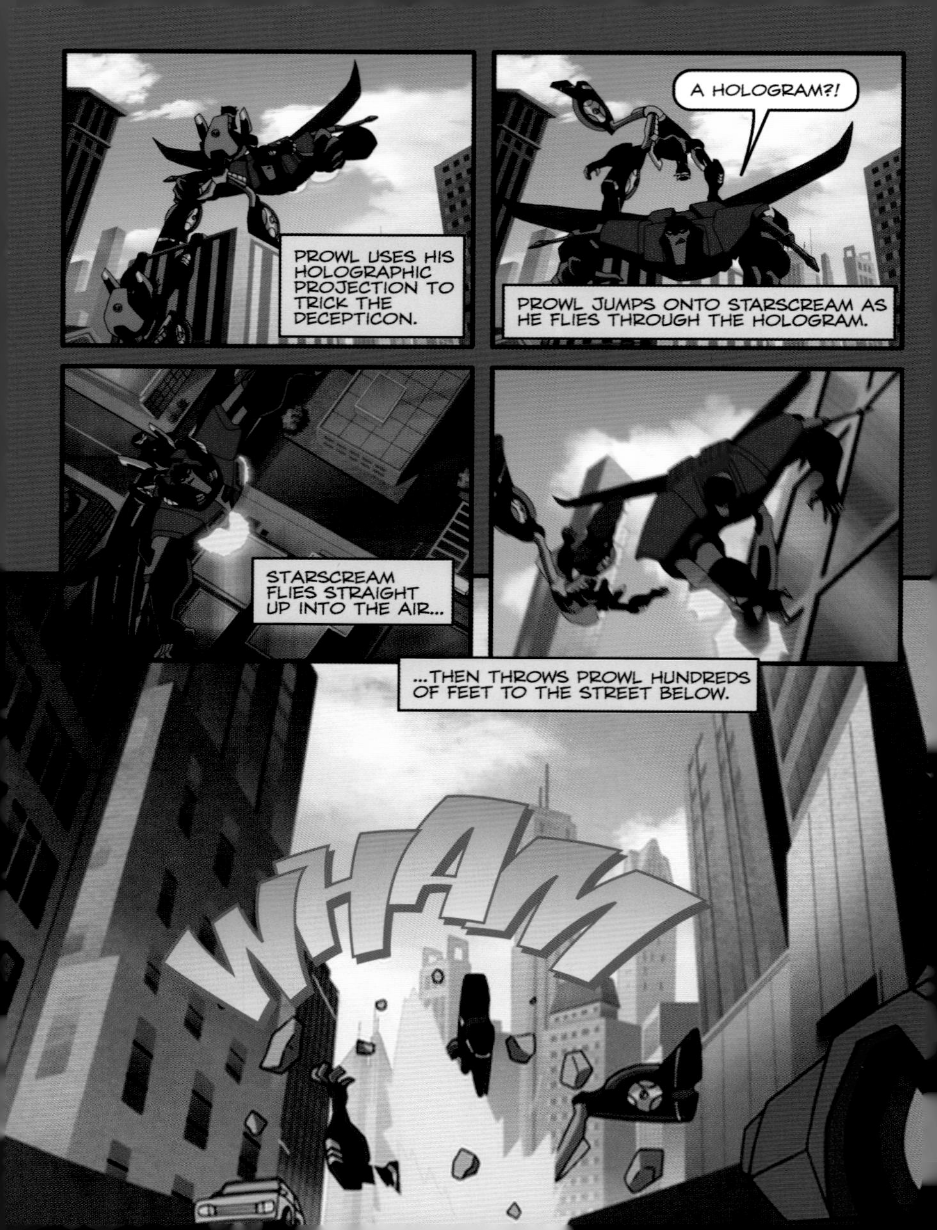
PROWL USES HIS HOLOGRAPHIC PROJECTION TO TRICK THE DECEPTICON.
A HOLOGRAM?!
PROWL JUMPS ONTO STARSCREAM AS HE FLIES THROUGH THE HOLOGRAM.
STARSCREAM FLIES STRAIGHT UP INTO THE AIR...
...THEN THROWS PROWL HUNDREDS OF FEET TO THE STREET BELOW.
WHAM

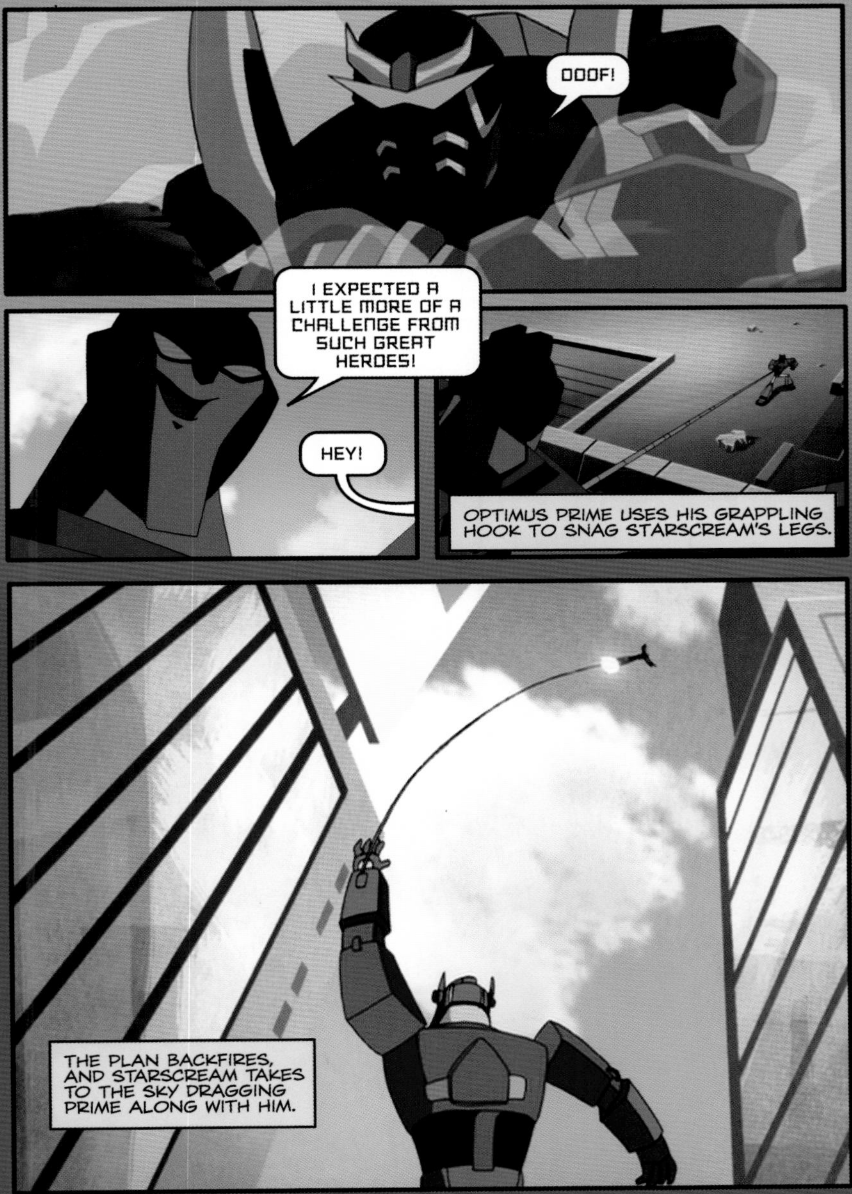
OOOF!
I EXPECTED A LITTLE MORE OF A CHALLENGE FROM SUCH GREAT HEROES!
HEY!
OPTIMUS PRIME USES HIS GRAPPLING HOOK TO SNAG STARSCREAM'S LEGS.
THE PLAN BACKFIRES, AND STARSCREAM TAKES TO THE SKY DRAGGING PRIME ALONG WITH HIM.

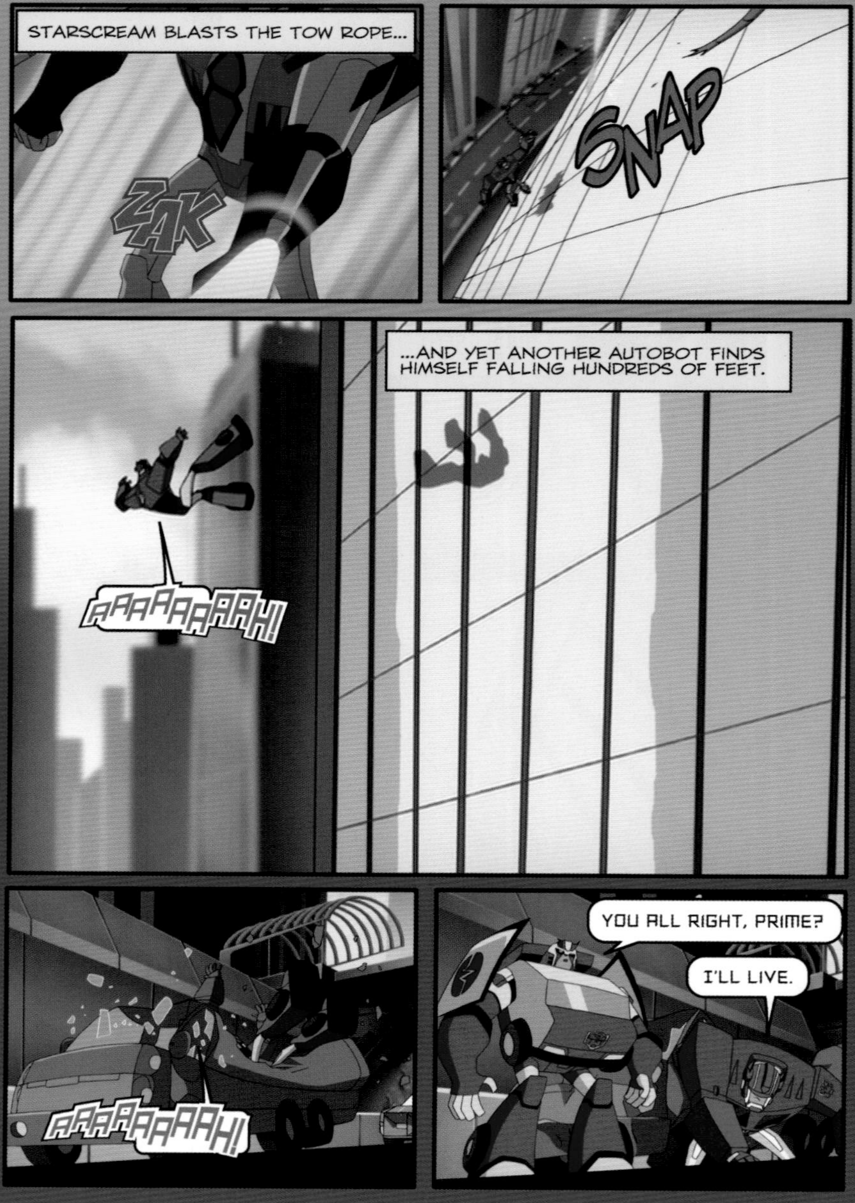
STARSCREAM BLASTS THE TOW ROPE...
ZAK
SNAP
...AND YET ANOTHER AUTOBOT FINDS HIMSELF FALLING HUNDREDS OF FEET.
AAAAAAAAAH!
AAAAAAAAAH!
YOU ALL RIGHT, PRIME?
I'LL LIVE.

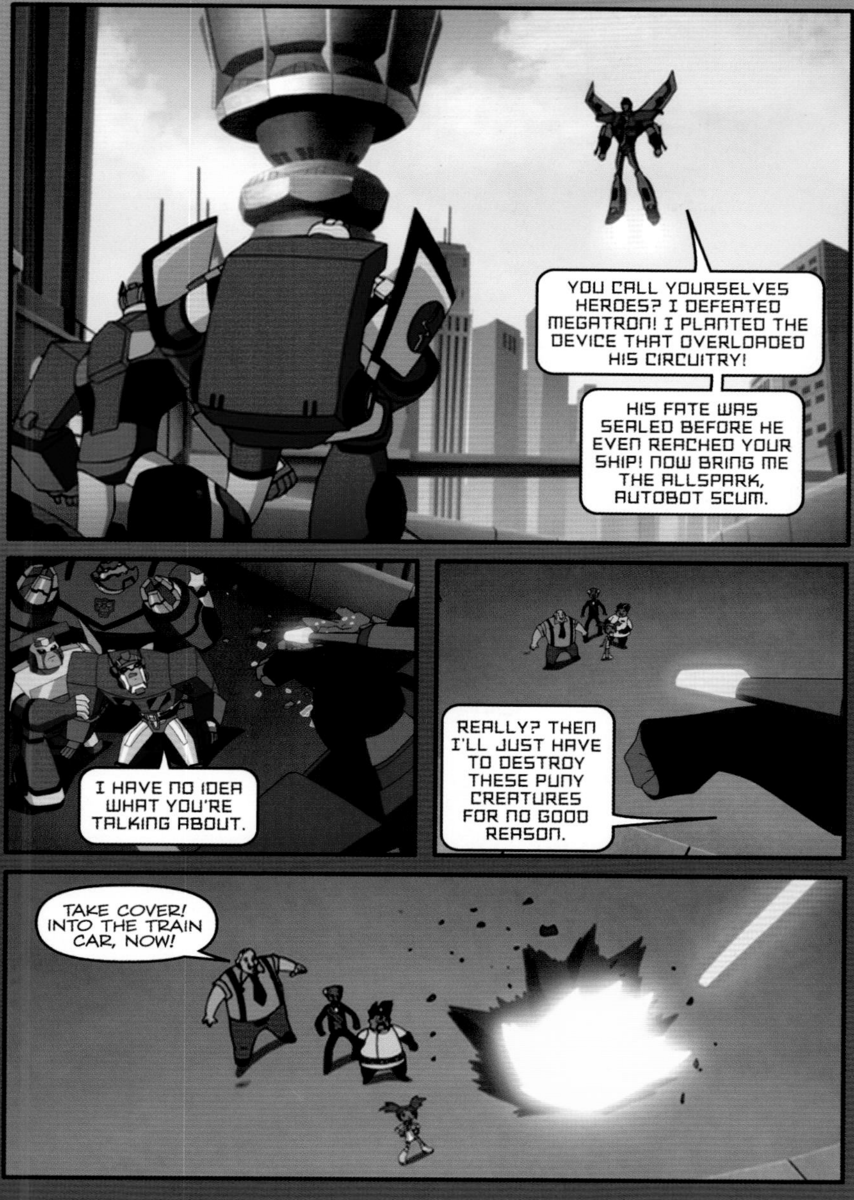
YOU CALL YOURSELVES HEROES? I DEFEATED MEGATRON! I PLANTED THE DEVICE THAT OVERLOADED HIS CIRCUITRY!
HIS FATE WAS SEALED BEFORE HE EVEN REACHED YOUR SHIP! NOW BRING ME THE ALLSPARK, AUTOBOT SCUM.
I HAVE NO IDEA WHAT YOU'RE TALKING ABOUT.
REALLY? THEN I'LL JUST HAVE TO DESTROY THESE PUNY CREATURES FOR NO GOOD REASON.
TAKE COVER! INTO THE TRAIN CAR, NOW!

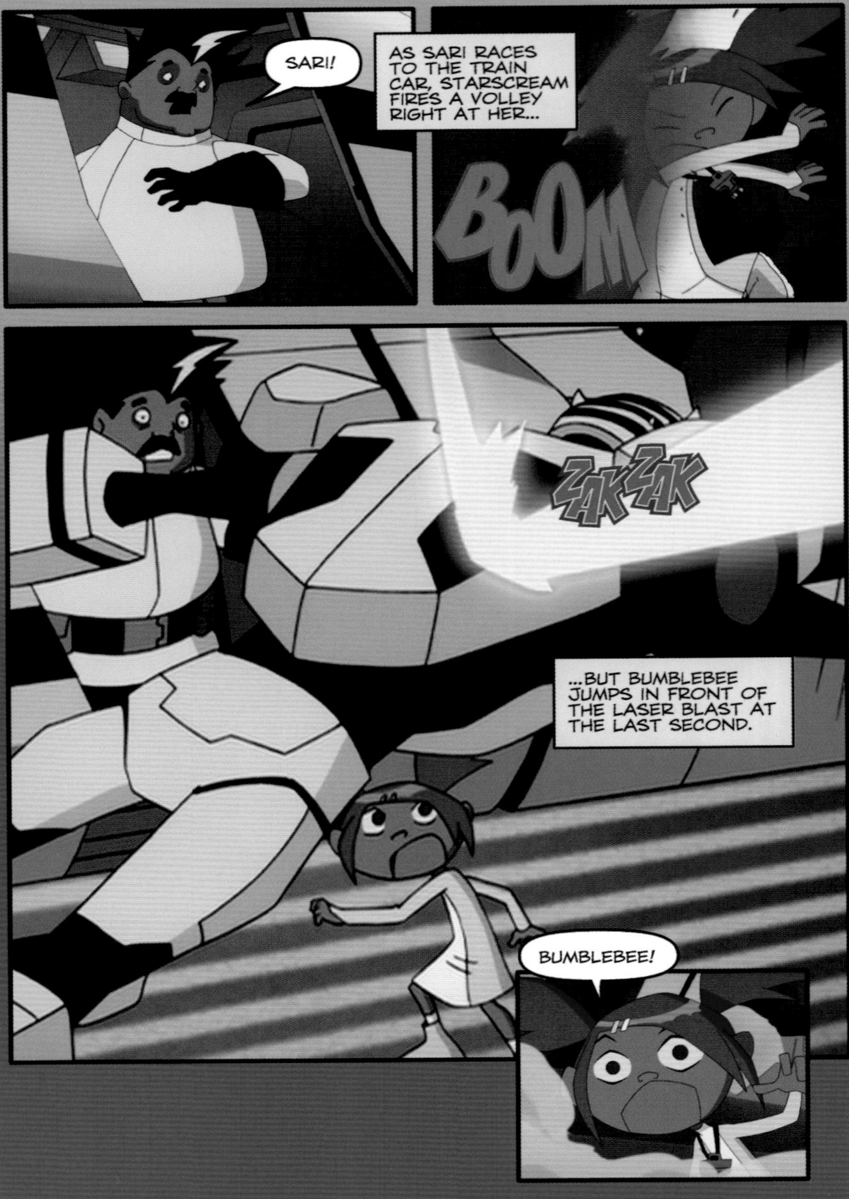
SARI!
AS SARI RACES TO THE TRAIN CAR, STARSCREAM FIRES A VOLLEY RIGHT AT HER...
BOOM
ZAK ZAK
...BUT BUMBLEBEE JUMPS IN FRONT OF THE LASER BLAST AT THE LAST SECOND.
BUMBLEBEE!

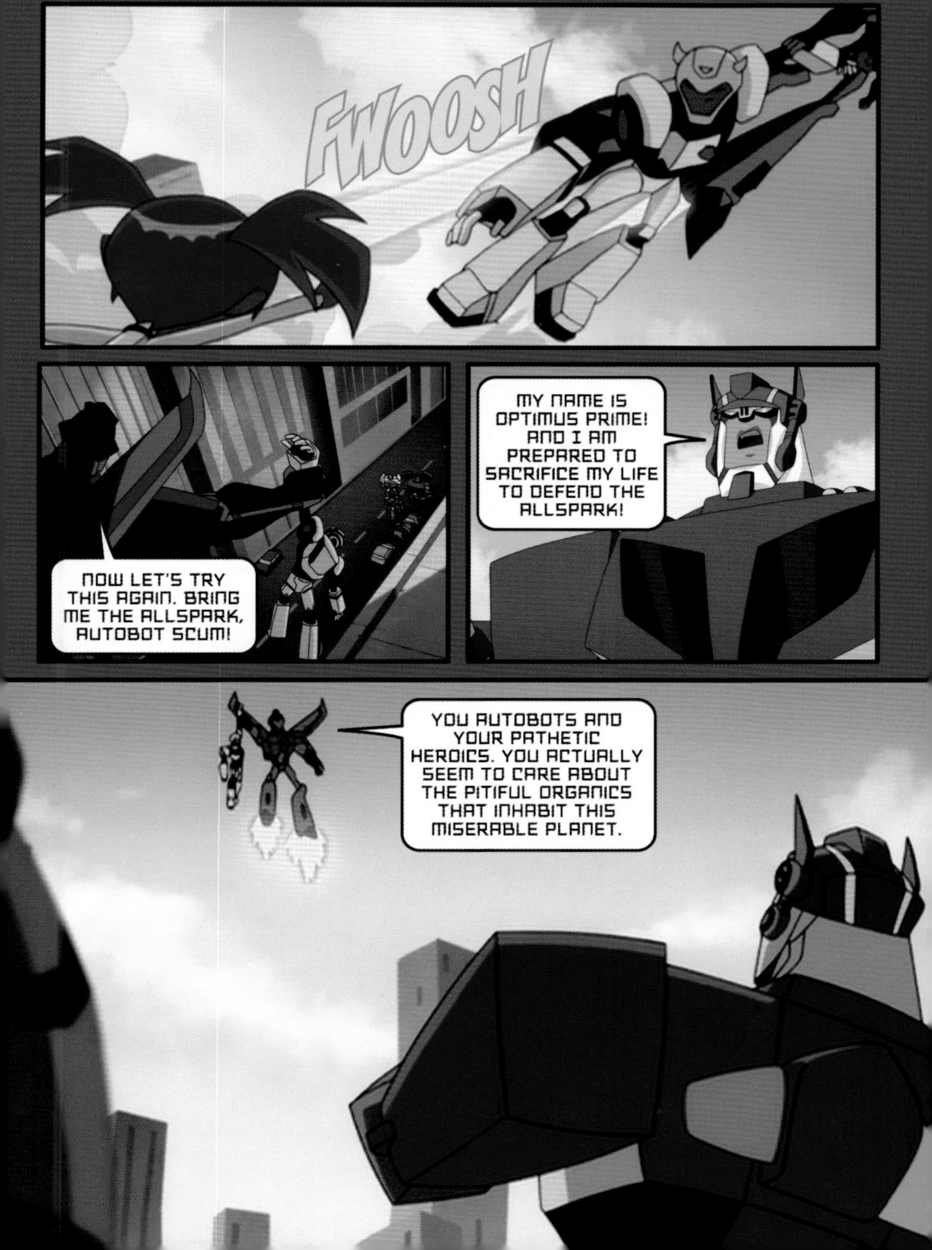
FWOOSH
NOW LET'S TRY THIS AGAIN. BRING ME THE ALLSPARK, AUTOBOT SCUM!
MY NAME IS OPTIMUS PRIME! AND I AM PREPARED TO SACRIFICE MY LIFE TO DEFEND THE ALLSPARK!
YOU AUTOBOTS AND YOUR PATHETIC HEROICS. YOU ACTUALLY SEEM TO CARE ABOUT THE PITIFUL ORGANICS THAT INHABIT THIS MISERABLE PLANET.

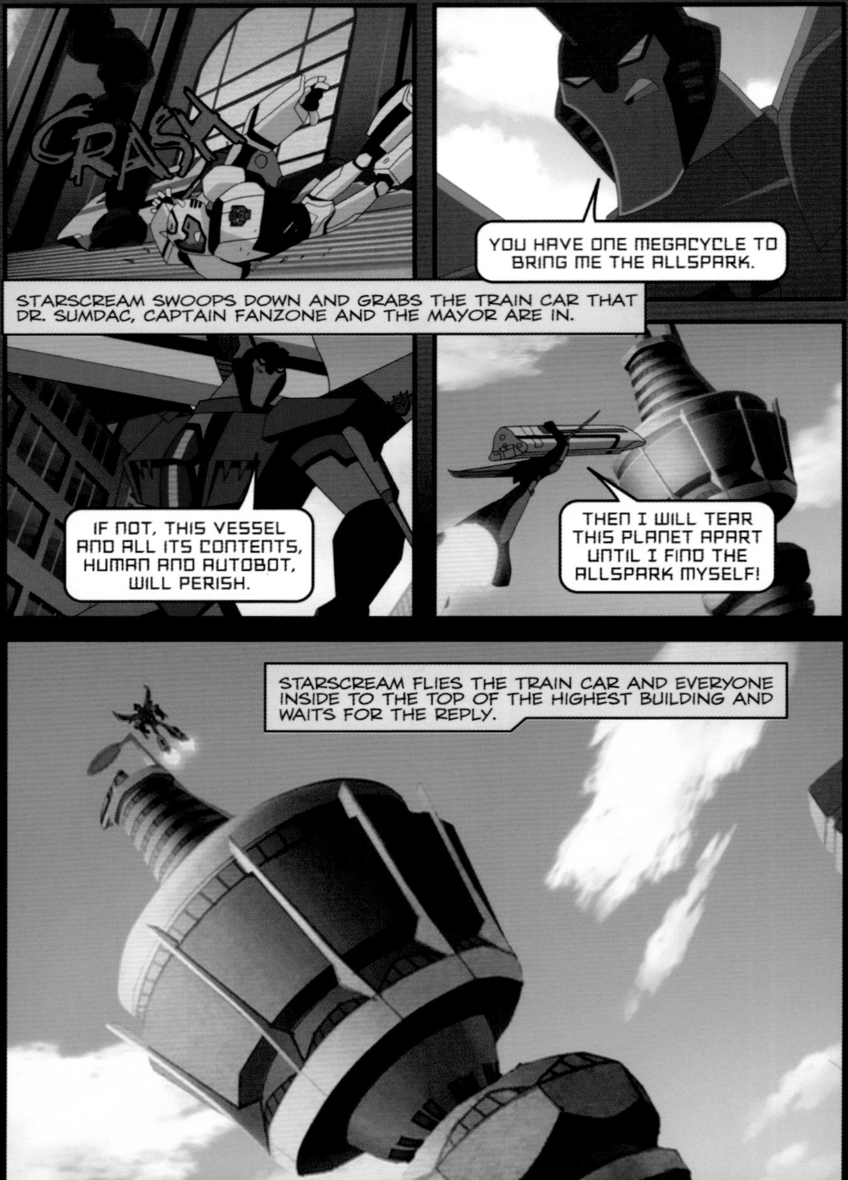
CRASH
YOU HAVE ONE MEGACYCLE TO BRING ME THE ALLSPARK.
STARSCREAM SWOOPS DOWN AND GRABS THE TRAIN CAR THAT DR. SUMDAC, CAPTAIN FANZONE AND THE MAYOR ARE IN.
IF NOT, THIS VESSEL AND ALL ITS CONTENTS, HUMAN AND AUTOBOT, WILL PERISH.
THEN I WILL TEAR THIS PLANET APART UNTIL I FIND THE ALLSPARK MYSELF!
STARSCREAM FLIES THE TRAIN CAR AND EVERYONE INSIDE TO THE TOP OF THE HIGHEST BUILDING AND WAITS FOR THE REPLY.

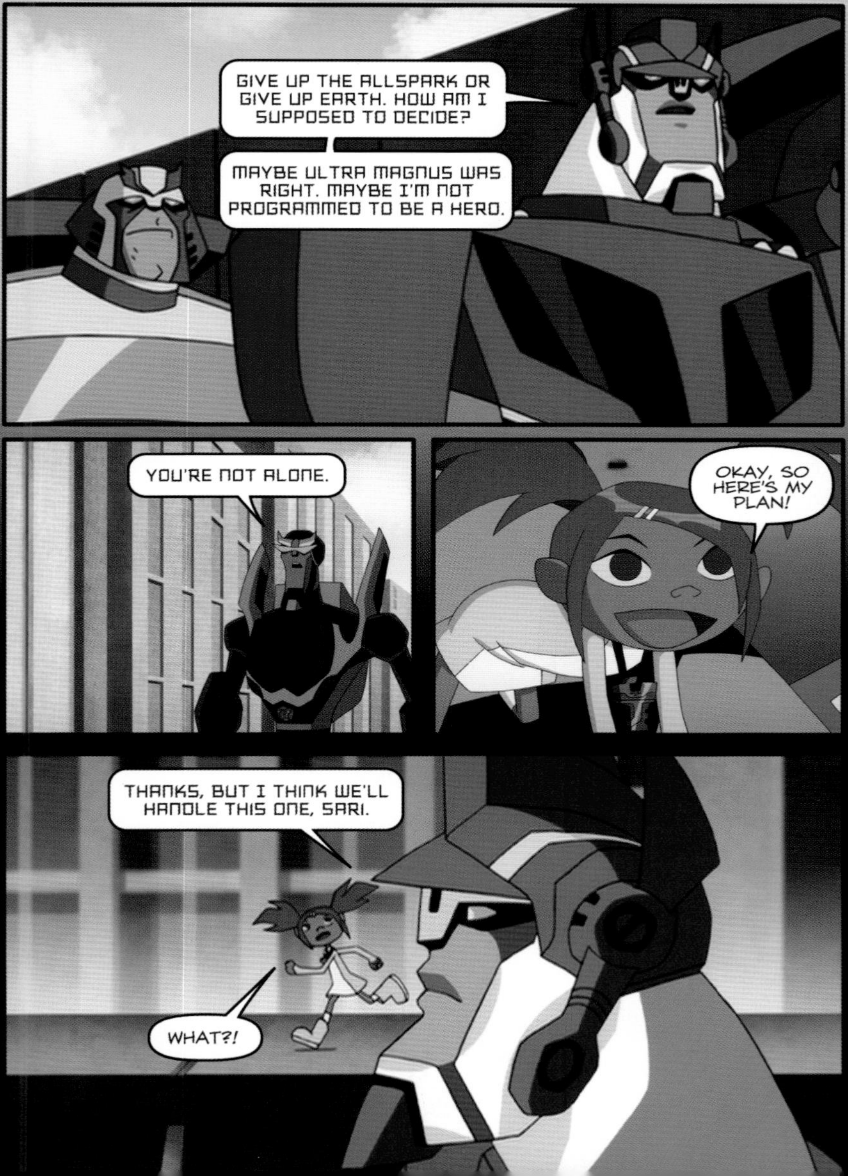
GIVE UP THE ALLSPARK OR GIVE UP EARTH. HOW AM I SUPPOSED TO DECIDE?
MAYBE ULTRA MAGNUS WAS RIGHT. MAYBE I'M NOT PROGRAMMED TO BE A HERO.
YOU'RE NOT ALONE.
OKAY, SO HERE'S MY PLAN!
THANKS, BUT I THINK WE'LL HANDLE THIS ONE, SARI.
WHAT?!

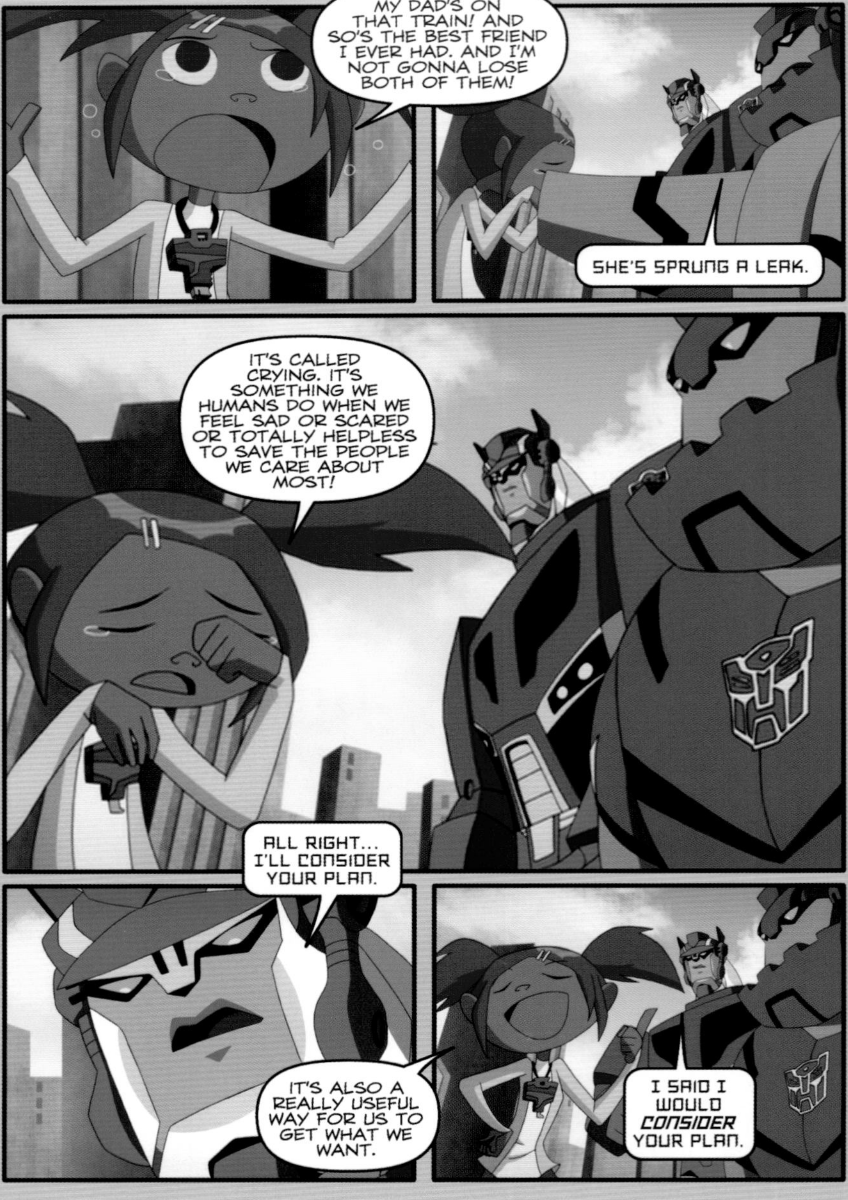
MY DAD'S ON THAT TRAIN! AND SO'S THE BEST FRIEND I EVER HAD. AND I'M NOT GONNA LOSE BOTH OF THEM!
SHE'S SPRUNG A LEAK.
IT'S CALLED CRYING. IT'S SOMETHING WE HUMANS DO WHEN WE FEEL SAD OR SCARED OR TOTALLY HELPLESS TO SAVE THE PEOPLE WE CARE ABOUT MOST!
ALL RIGHT... I'LL CONSIDER YOUR PLAN.
IT'S ALSO A REALLY USEFUL WAY FOR US TO GET WHAT WE WANT.
I SAID I WOULD *CONSIDER* YOUR PLAN.

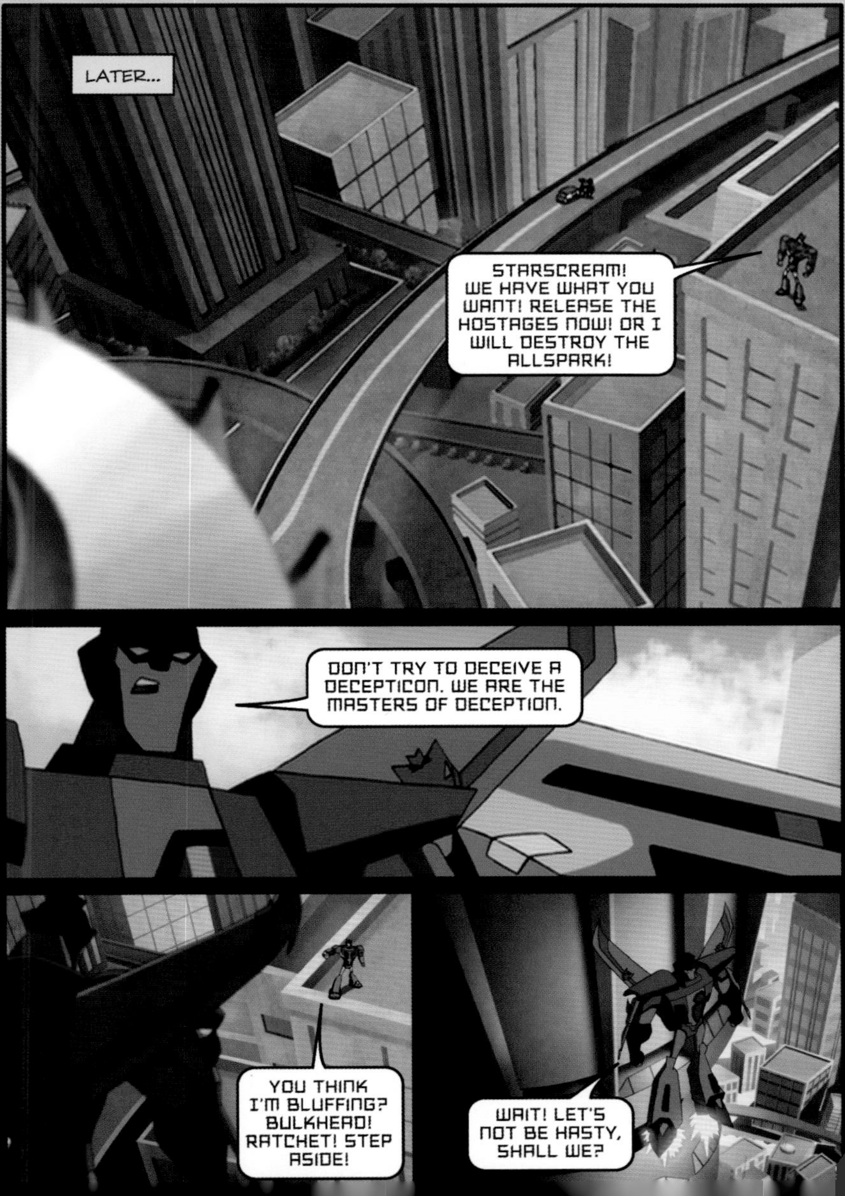
LATER...
STARSCREAM! WE HAVE WHAT YOU WANT! RELEASE THE HOSTAGES NOW! OR I WILL DESTROY THE ALLSPARK!
DON'T TRY TO DECEIVE A DECEPTICON. WE ARE THE MASTERS OF DECEPTION.
YOU THINK I'M BLUFFING? BULKHEAD! RATCHET! STEP ASIDE!
WAIT! LET'S NOT BE HASTY, SHALL WE?

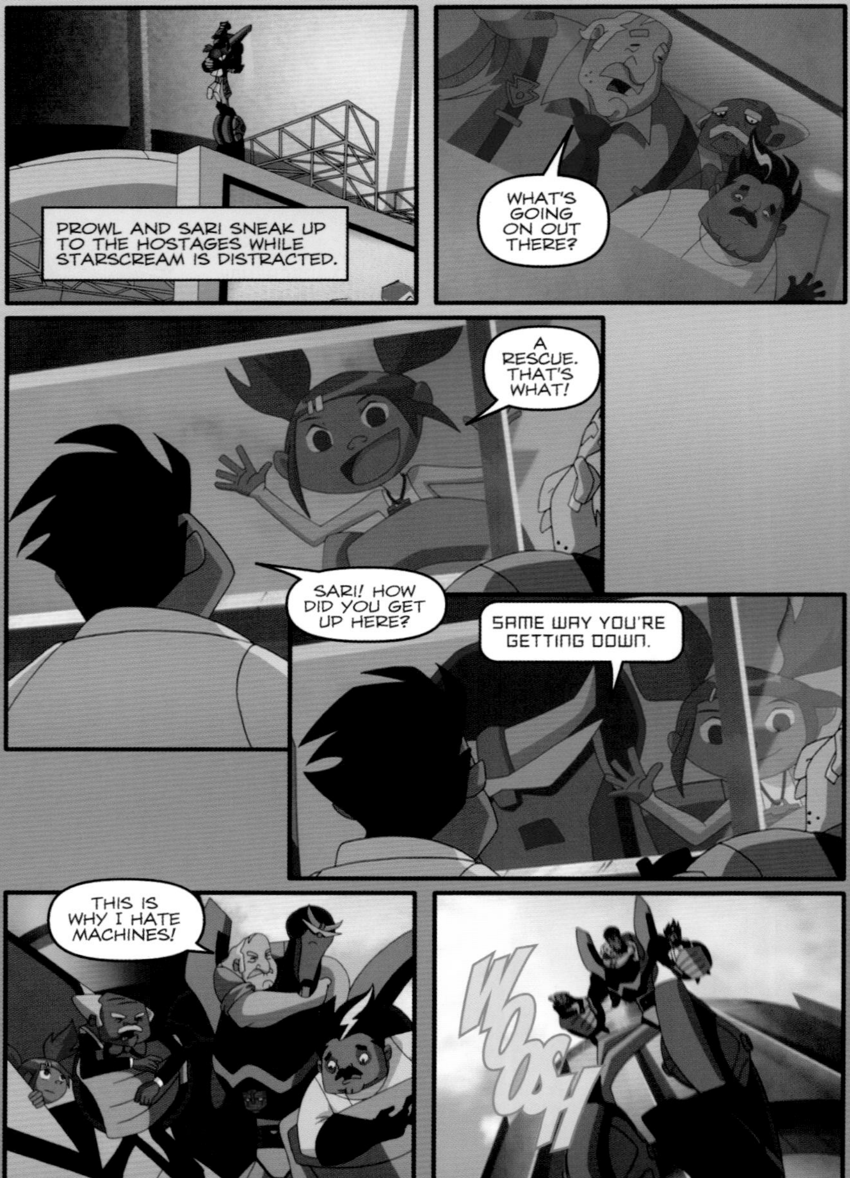
PROWL AND SARI SNEAK UP TO THE HOSTAGES WHILE STARSCREAM IS DISTRACTED.
WHAT'S GOING ON OUT THERE?
A RESCUE. THAT'S WHAT!
SARI! HOW DID YOU GET UP HERE?
SAME WAY YOU'RE GETTING DOWN.
THIS IS WHY I HATE MACHINES!
WOOSH

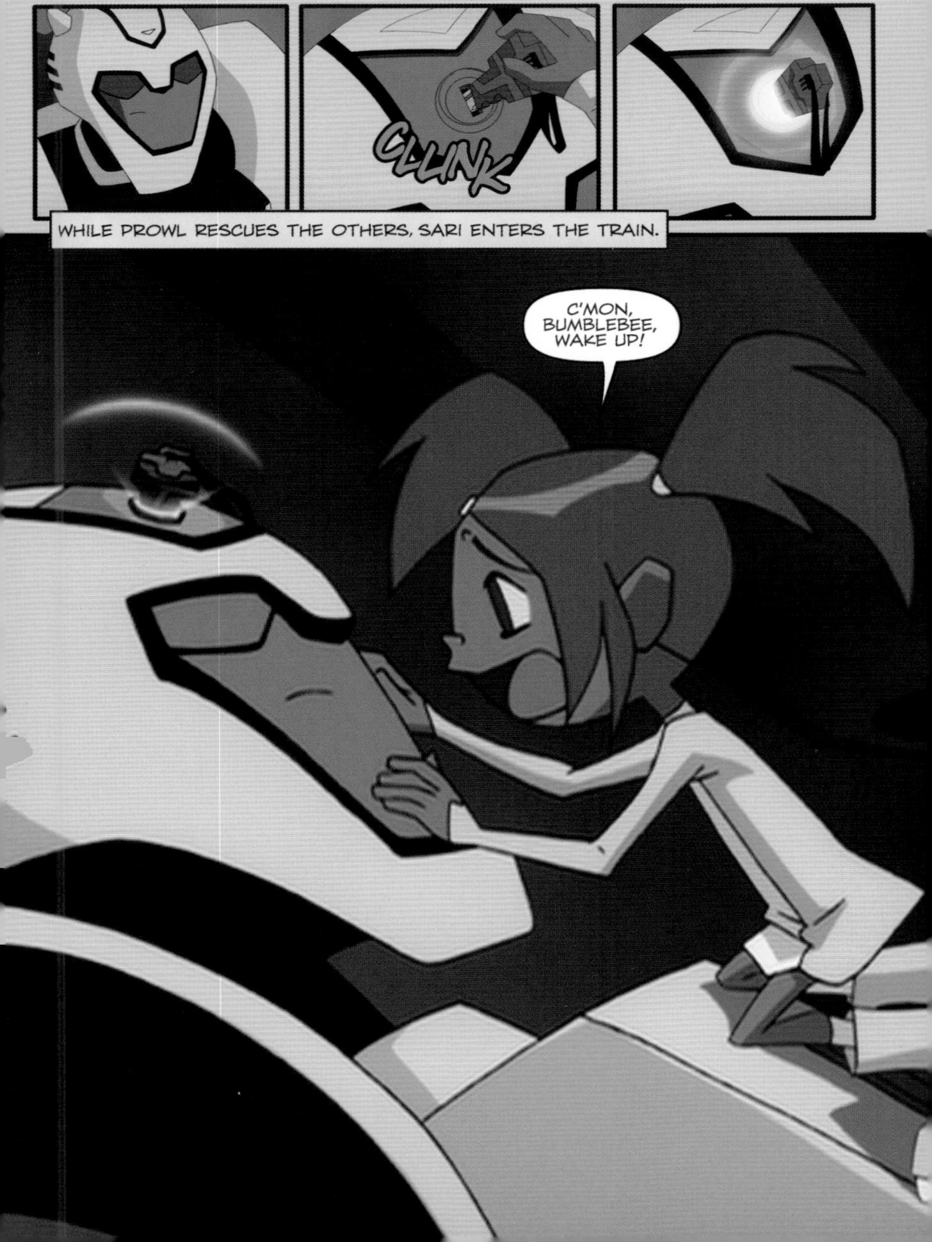
CLLINK
WHILE PROWL RESCUES THE OTHERS, SARI ENTERS THE TRAIN.
C'MON, BUMBLEBEE, WAKE UP!

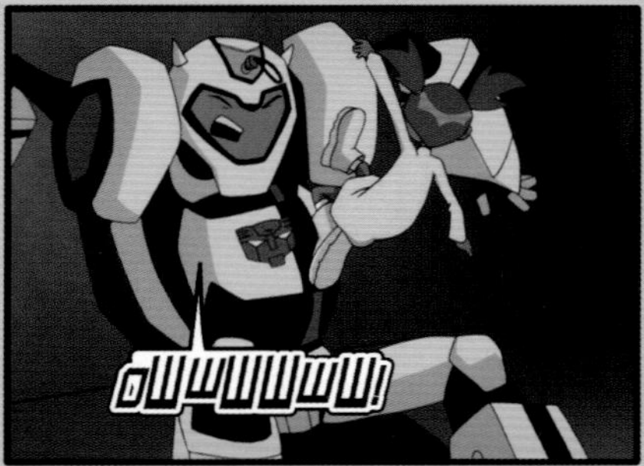
OWWWWWW!

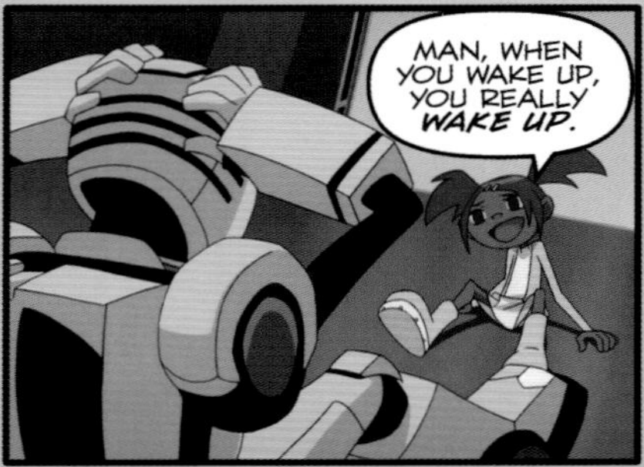
MAN, WHEN YOU WAKE UP, YOU REALLY WAKE UP.

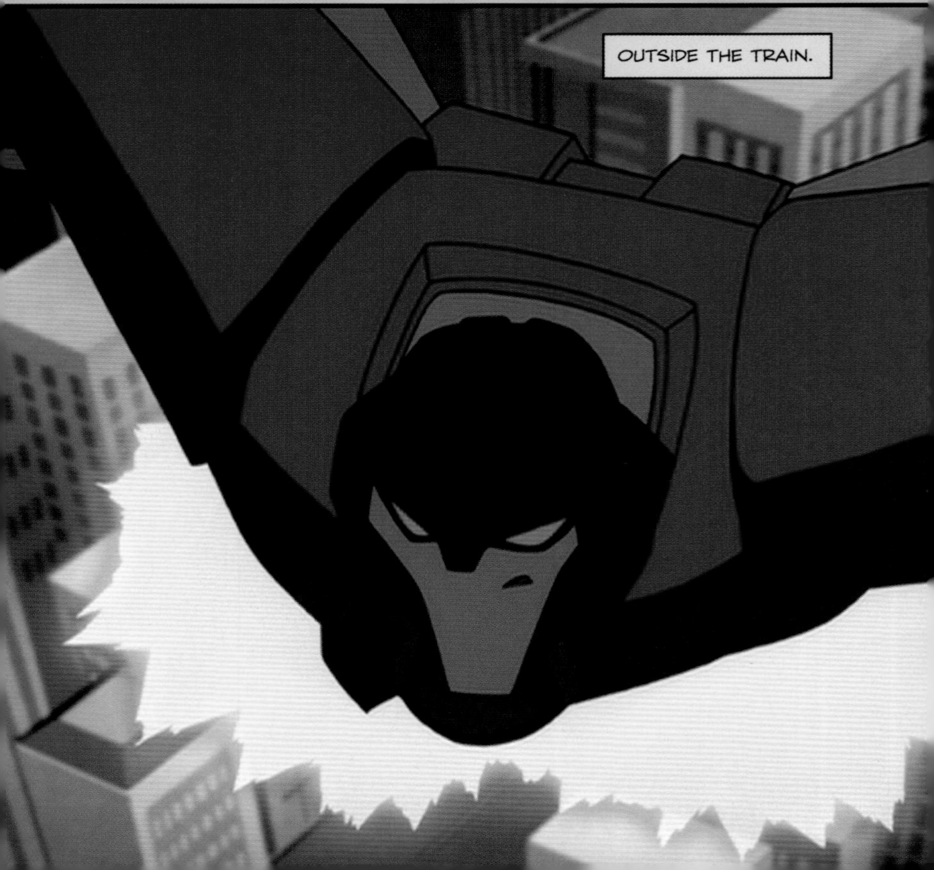
OUTSIDE THE TRAIN.

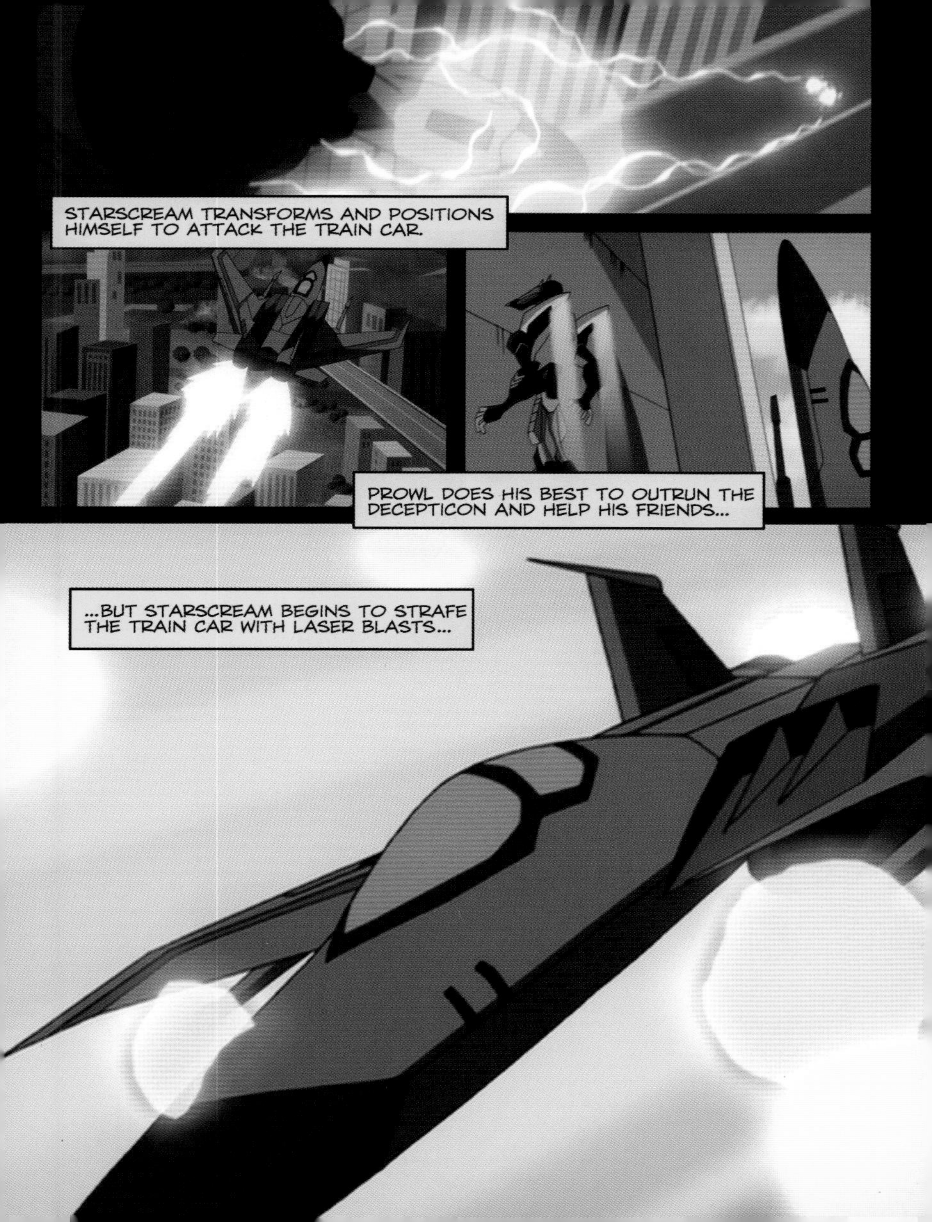
STARSCREAM TRANSFORMS AND POSITIONS HIMSELF TO ATTACK THE TRAIN CAR.
PROWL DOES HIS BEST TO OUTRUN THE DECEPTICON AND HELP HIS FRIENDS...
...BUT STARSCREAM BEGINS TO STRAFE THE TRAIN CAR WITH LASER BLASTS...

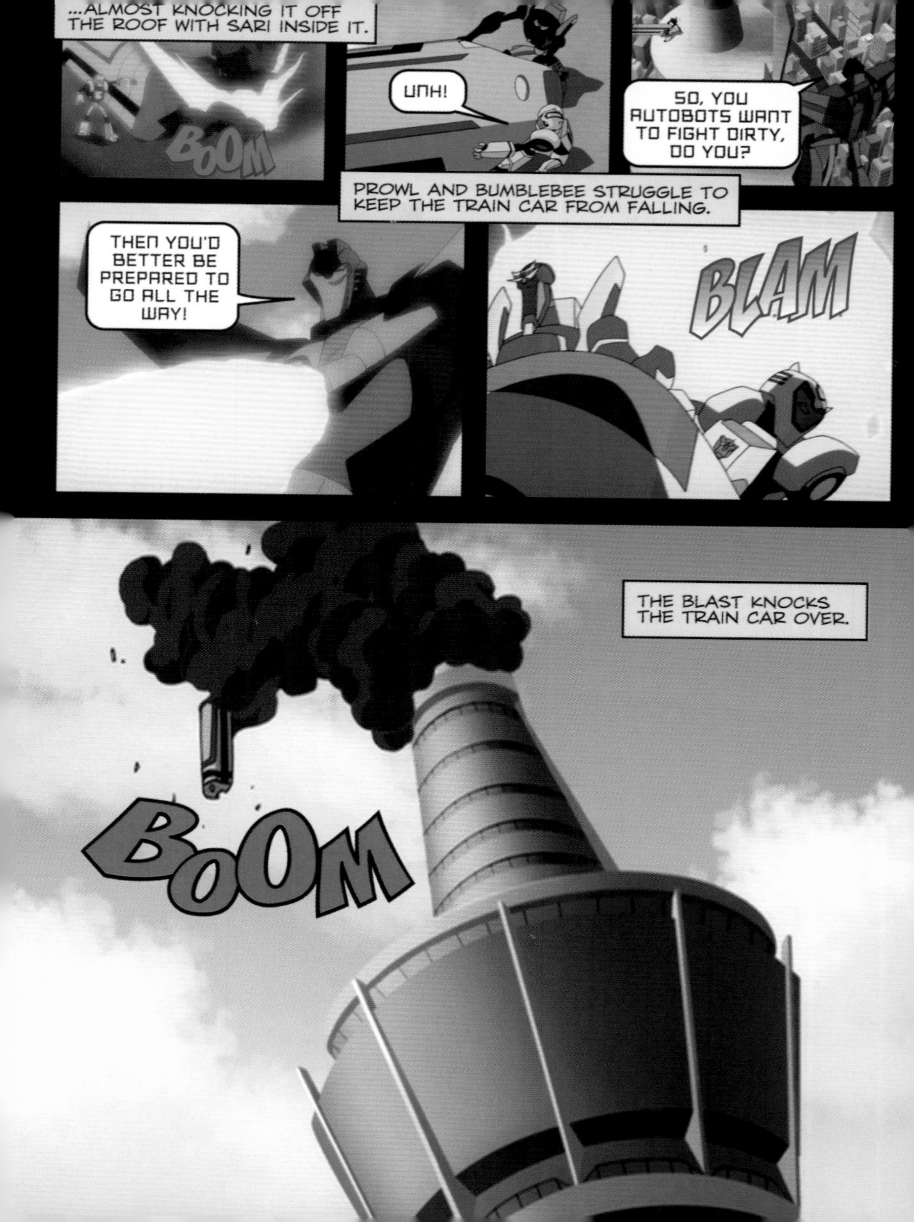
...ALMOST KNOCKING IT OFF THE ROOF WITH SARI INSIDE IT.
BOOM
UNH!
SO, YOU AUTOBOTS WANT TO FIGHT DIRTY, DO YOU?
PROWL AND BUMBLEBEE STRUGGLE TO KEEP THE TRAIN CAR FROM FALLING.
THEN YOU'D BETTER BE PREPARED TO GO ALL THE WAY!
BLAM
THE BLAST KNOCKS THE TRAIN CAR OVER.
BOOM

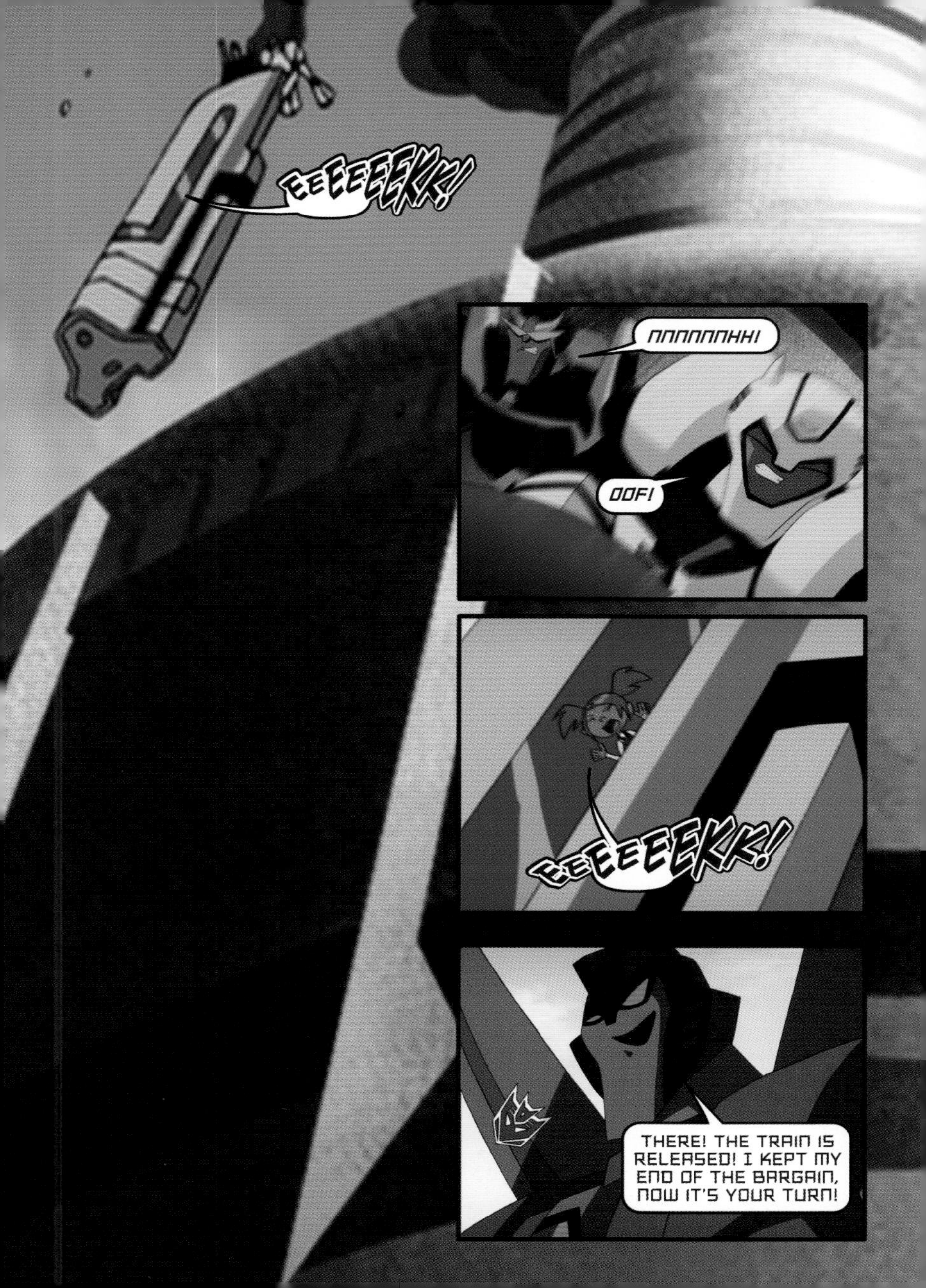
EEEEEEKK!
NNNNNNHH!
OOF!
EEEEEEKK!
THERE! THE TRAIN IS RELEASED! I KEPT MY END OF THE BARGAIN, NOW IT'S YOUR TURN!

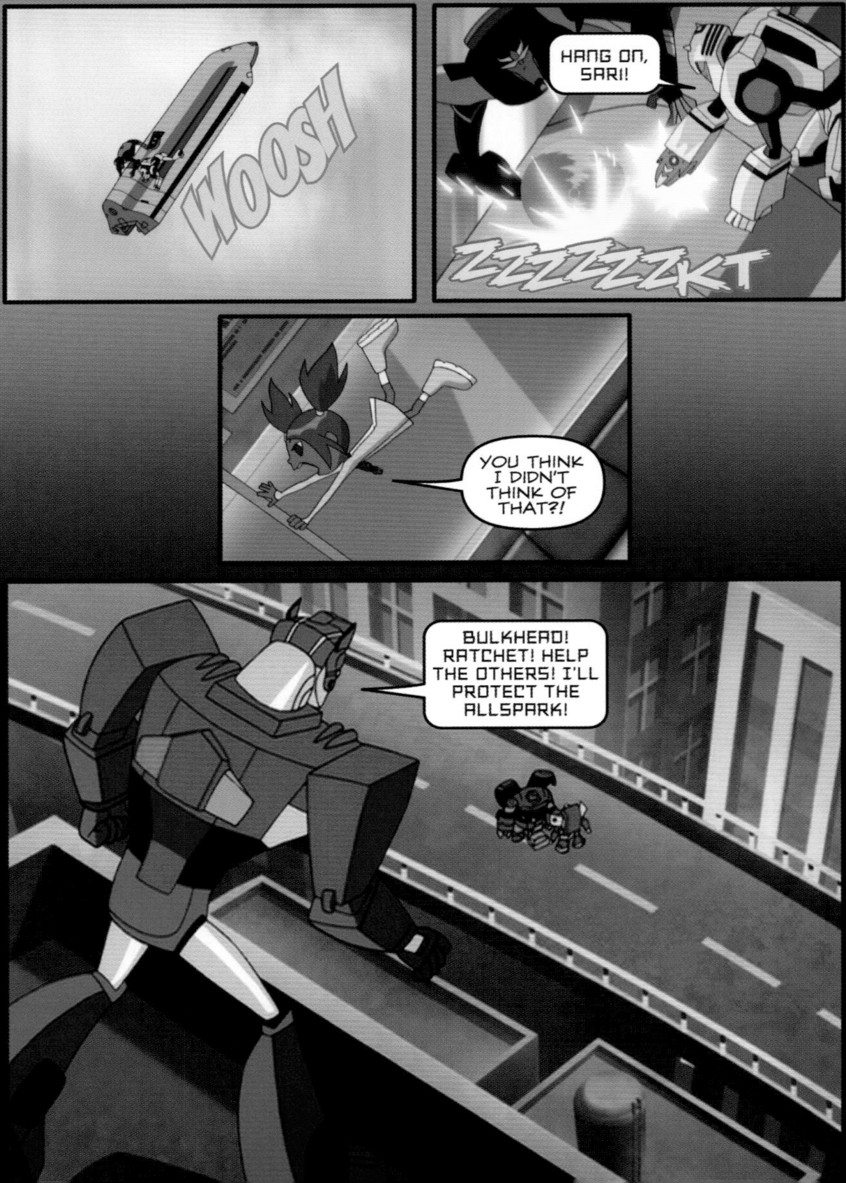
WOOSH
HANG ON, SARI!
ZZZZZZZKT
YOU THINK I DIDN'T THINK OF THAT?!
BULKHEAD! RATCHET! HELP THE OTHERS! I'LL PROTECT THE ALLSPARK!

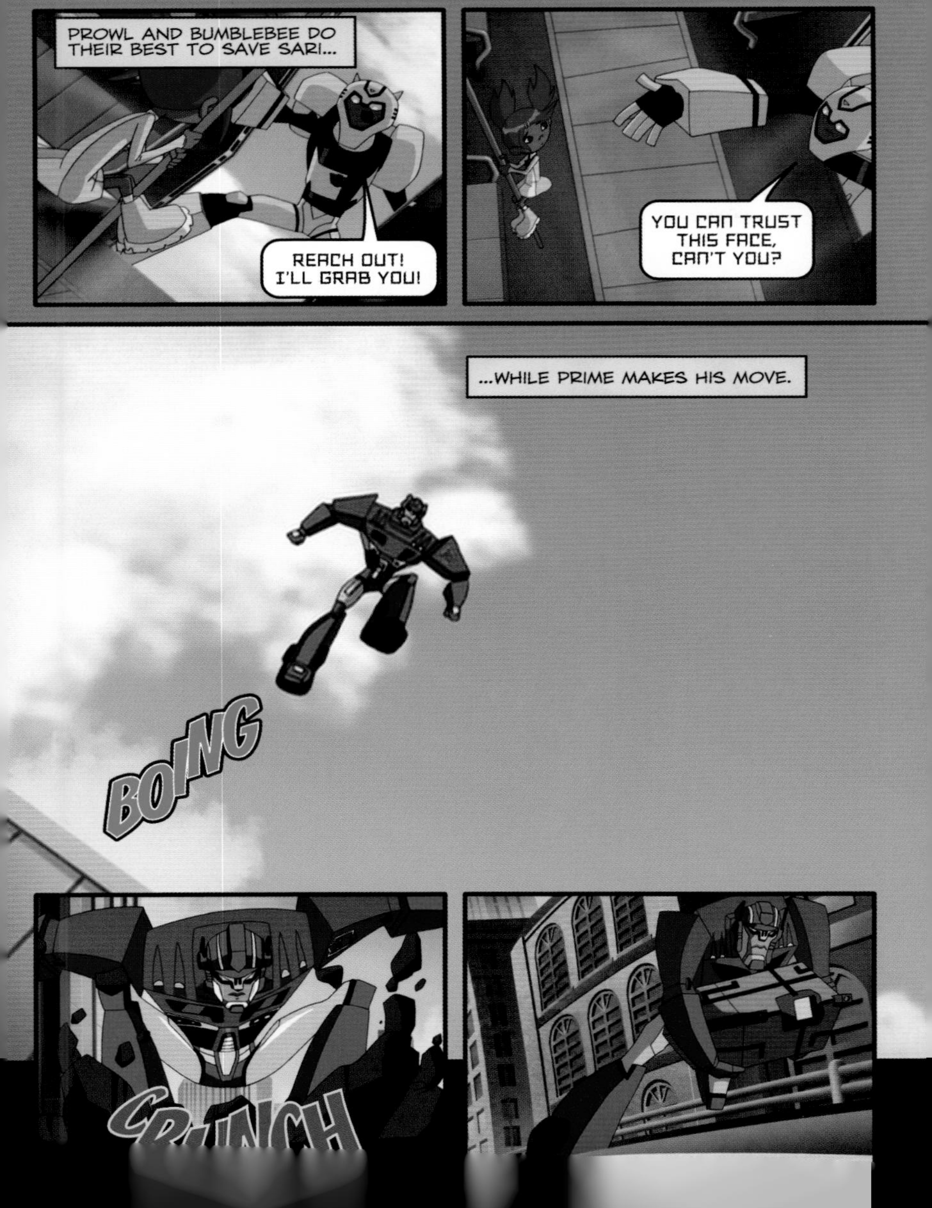
PROWL AND BUMBLEBEE DO THEIR BEST TO SAVE SARI...
REACH OUT! I'LL GRAB YOU!
YOU CAN TRUST THIS FACE, CAN'T YOU?
...WHILE PRIME MAKES HIS MOVE.
BOING
CRUNCH

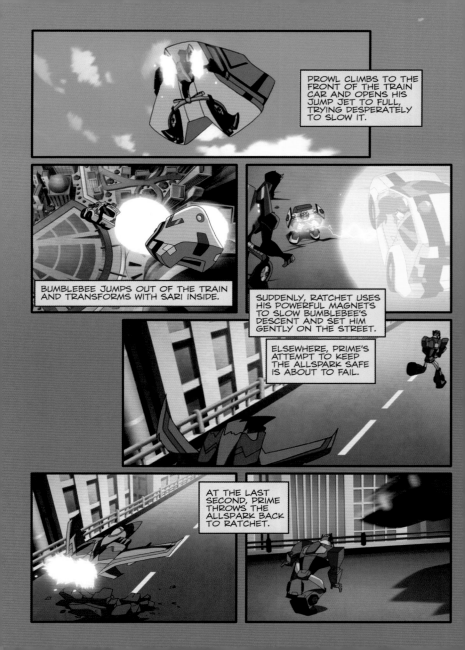

PROWL CLIMBS TO THE FRONT OF THE TRAIN CAR AND OPENS HIS JUMP JET TO FULL, TRYING DESPERATELY TO SLOW IT.

BUMBLEBEE JUMPS OUT OF THE TRAIN AND TRANSFORMS WITH SARI INSIDE.

SUDDENLY, RATCHET USES HIS POWERFUL MAGNETS TO SLOW BUMBLEBEE'S DESCENT AND SET HIM GENTLY ON THE STREET.

ELSEWHERE, PRIME'S ATTEMPT TO KEEP THE ALLSPARK SAFE IS ABOUT TO FAIL.

AT THE LAST SECOND, PRIME THROWS THE ALLSPARK BACK TO RATCHET.

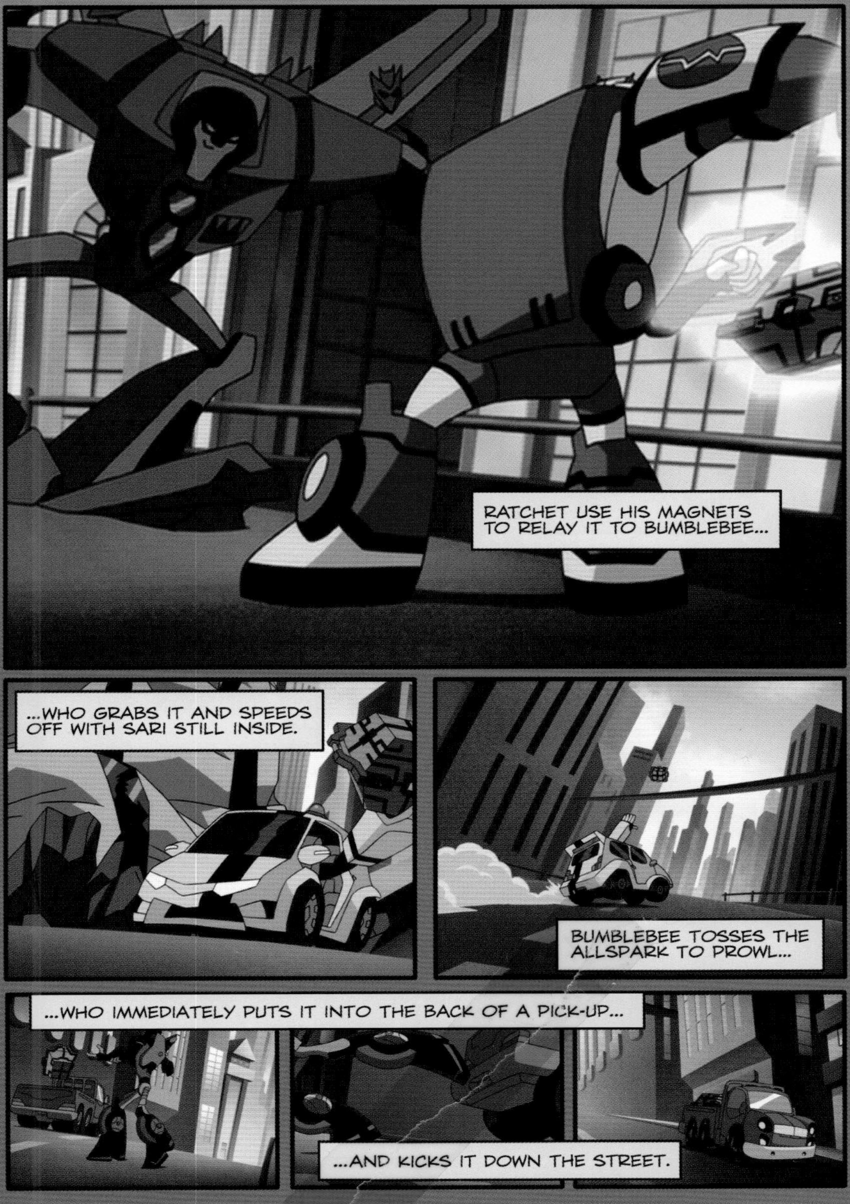
RATCHET USE HIS MAGNETS TO RELAY IT TO BUMBLEBEE...
...WHO GRABS IT AND SPEEDS OFF WITH SARI STILL INSIDE.
BUMBLEBEE TOSSES THE ALLSPARK TO PROWL...
...WHO IMMEDIATELY PUTS IT INTO THE BACK OF A PICK-UP...
...AND KICKS IT DOWN THE STREET.

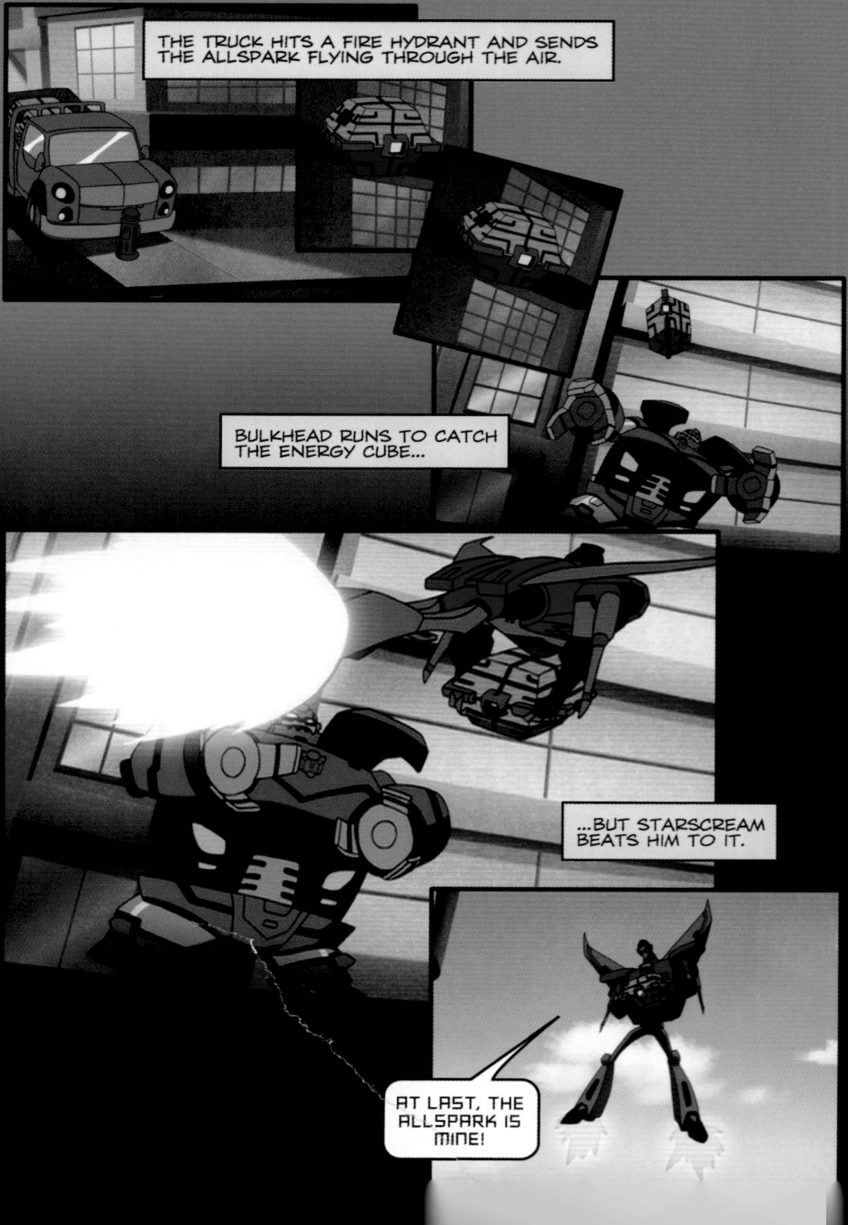
THE TRUCK HITS A FIRE HYDRANT AND SENDS THE ALLSPARK FLYING THROUGH THE AIR.
BULKHEAD RUNS TO CATCH THE ENERGY CUBE...
...BUT STARSCREAM BEATS HIM TO IT.
AT LAST, THE ALLSPARK IS MINE!

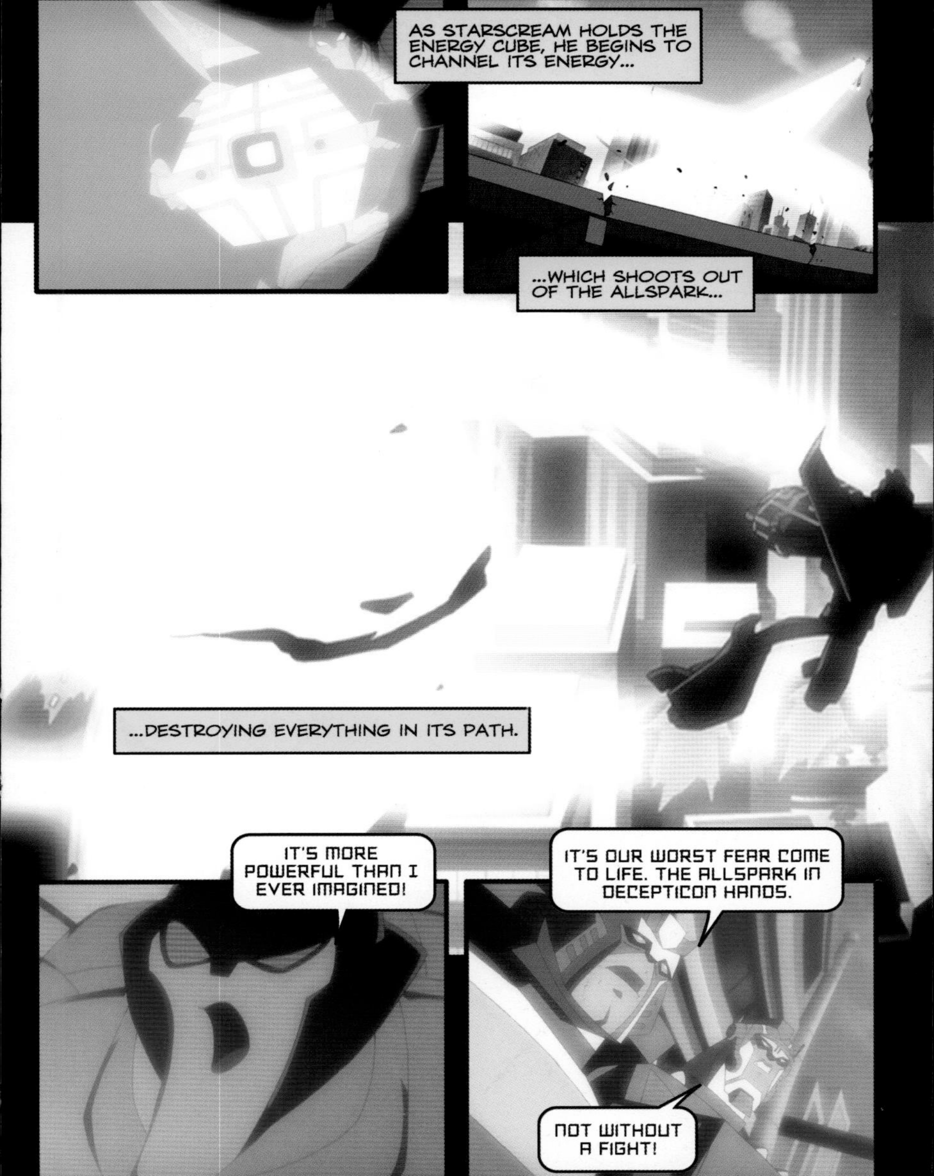
AS STARSCREAM HOLDS THE ENERGY CUBE, HE BEGINS TO CHANNEL ITS ENERGY...
...WHICH SHOOTS OUT OF THE ALLSPARK...
...DESTROYING EVERYTHING IN ITS PATH.
IT'S MORE POWERFUL THAN I EVER IMAGINED!
IT'S OUR WORST FEAR COME TO LIFE. THE ALLSPARK IN DECEPTICON HANDS.
NOT WITHOUT A FIGHT!

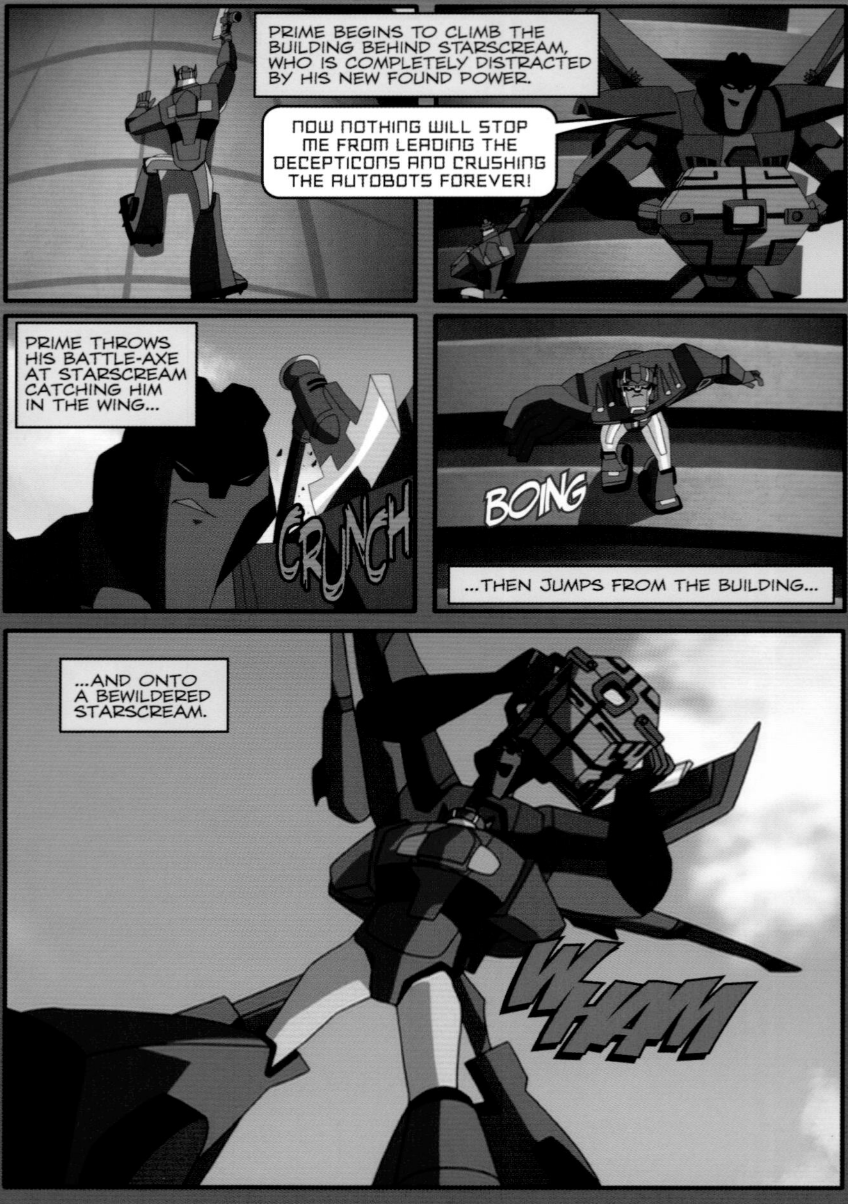
PRIME BEGINS TO CLIMB THE BUILDING BEHIND STARSCREAM, WHO IS COMPLETELY DISTRACTED BY HIS NEW FOUND POWER.
NOW NOTHING WILL STOP ME FROM LEADING THE DECEPTICONS AND CRUSHING THE AUTOBOTS FOREVER!
PRIME THROWS HIS BATTLE-AXE AT STARSCREAM CATCHING HIM IN THE WING...
CRUNCH
BOING
...THEN JUMPS FROM THE BUILDING...
...AND ONTO A BEWILDERED STARSCREAM.
WHAM

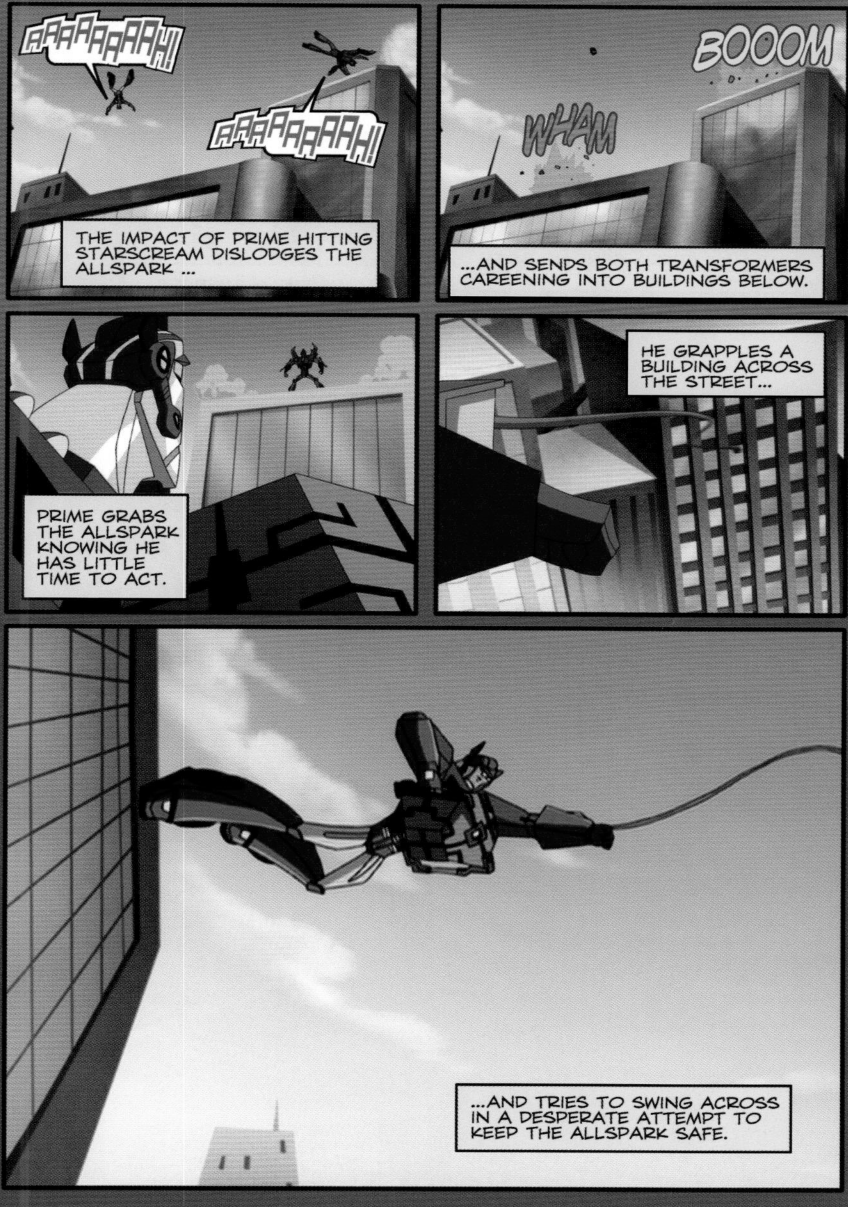
AAAAAAAAAH!
AAAAAAAAAH!
THE IMPACT OF PRIME HITTING STARSCREAM DISLODGES THE ALLSPARK ...
BOOOM
WHAM
...AND SENDS BOTH TRANSFORMERS CAREENING INTO BUILDINGS BELOW.
PRIME GRABS THE ALLSPARK KNOWING HE HAS LITTLE TIME TO ACT.
HE GRAPPLES A BUILDING ACROSS THE STREET...
...AND TRIES TO SWING ACROSS IN A DESPERATE ATTEMPT TO KEEP THE ALLSPARK SAFE.

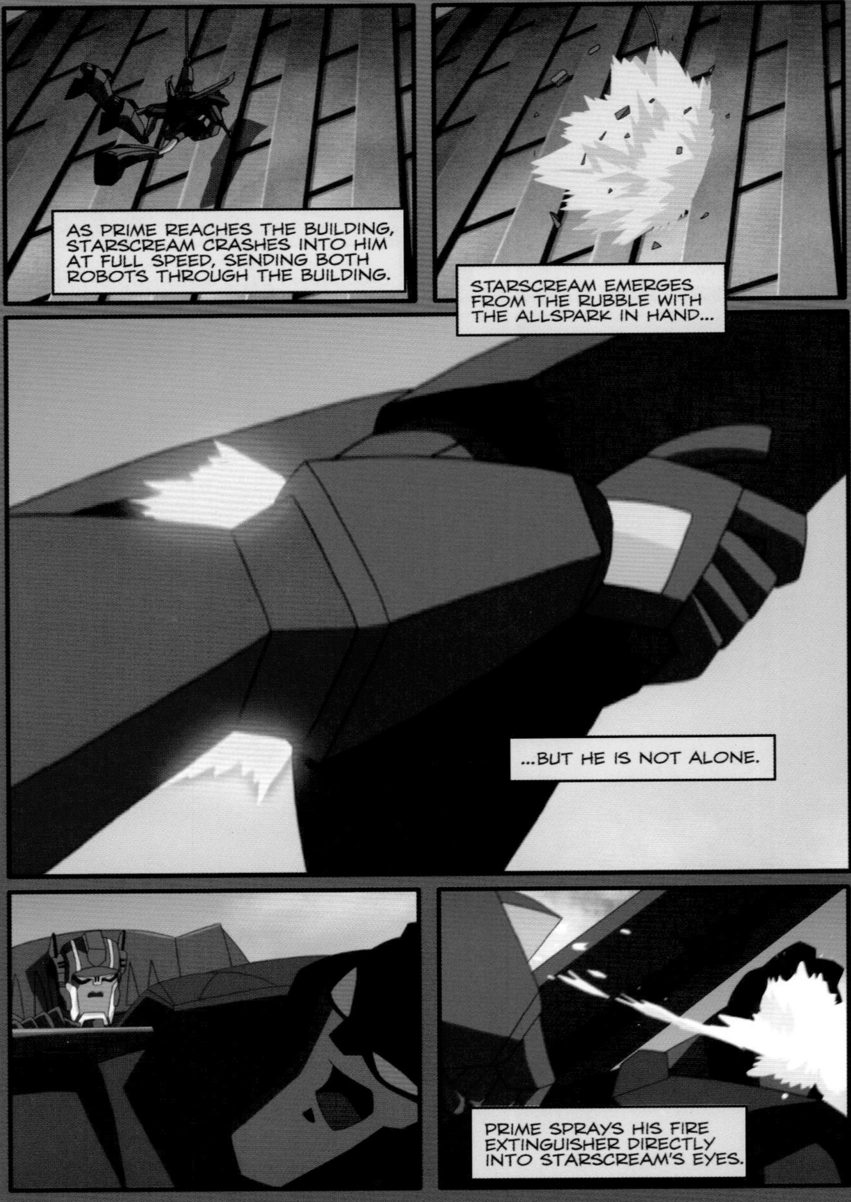
AS PRIME REACHES THE BUILDING, STARSCREAM CRASHES INTO HIM AT FULL SPEED, SENDING BOTH ROBOTS THROUGH THE BUILDING.
STARSCREAM EMERGES FROM THE RUBBLE WITH THE ALLSPARK IN HAND...
...BUT HE IS NOT ALONE.
PRIME SPRAYS HIS FIRE EXTINGUISHER DIRECTLY INTO STARSCREAM'S EYES.

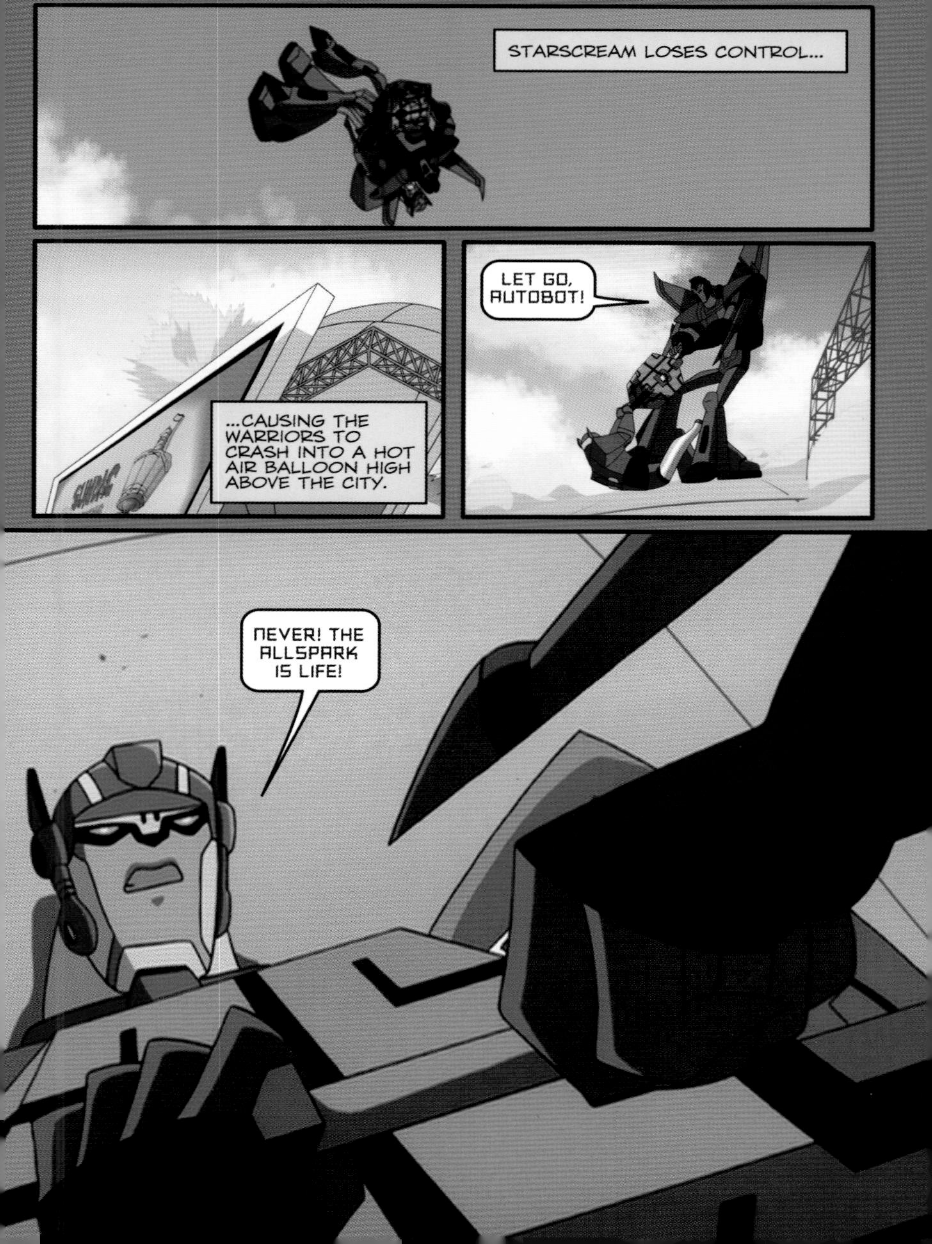
STARSCREAM LOSES CONTROL...
...CAUSING THE WARRIORS TO CRASH INTO A HOT AIR BALLOON HIGH ABOVE THE CITY.
LET GO, AUTOBOT!
NEVER! THE ALLSPARK IS LIFE!

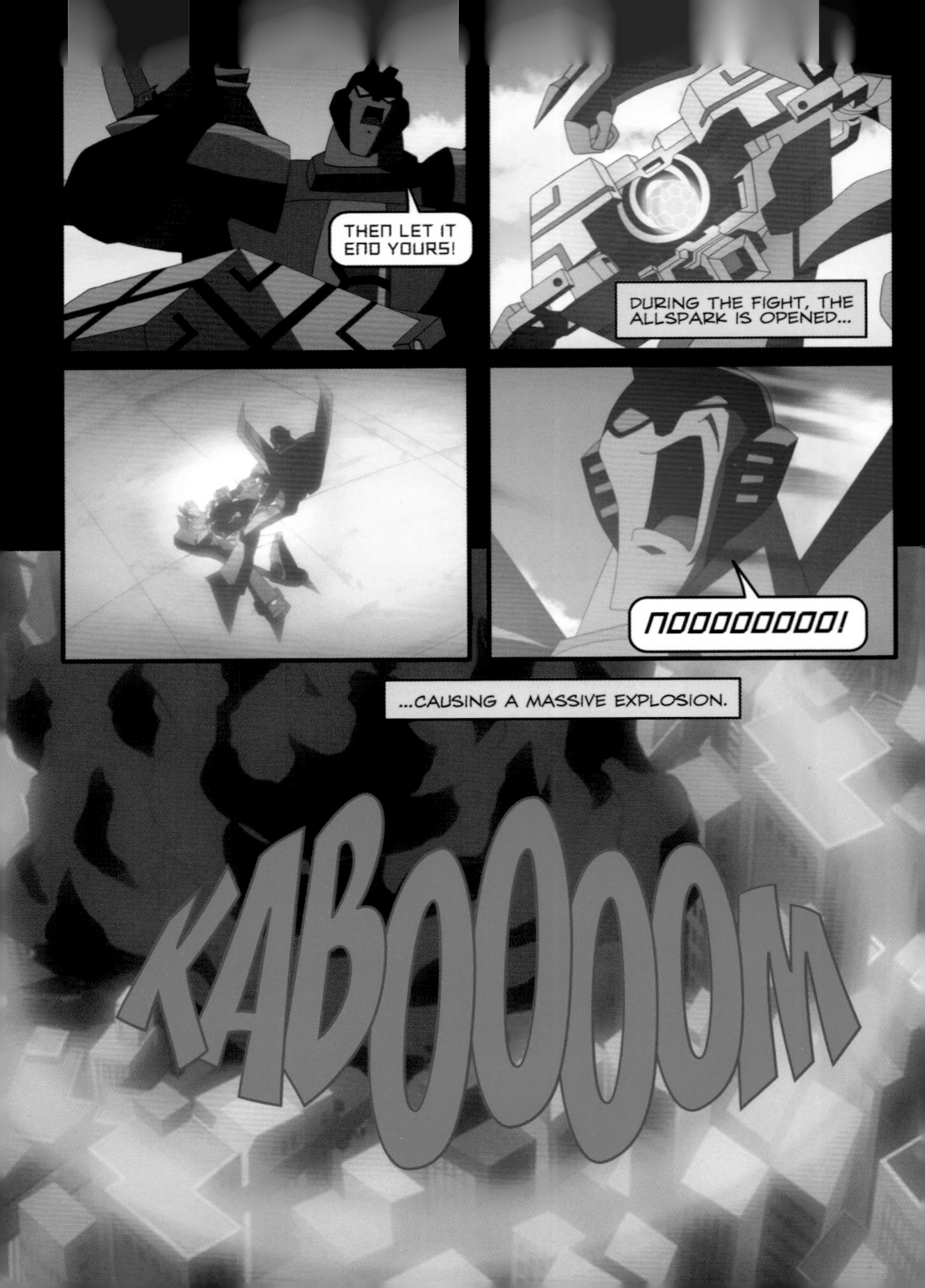
THEN LET IT END YOURS!
DURING THE FIGHT, THE ALLSPARK IS OPENED...
NOOOOOOOO!
...CAUSING A MASSIVE EXPLOSION.
KABOOOOM

WHEN THE SMOKE CLEARS, ALL THAT IS LEFT IS OPTIMUS PRIME HOLDING ONTO THE SIDE OF THE BILLBOARD ATTACHED TO THE HOT AIR BALLOON.

EXHAUSTED AND BATTLE WORN, PRIME LOSES HIS GRIP AND FALLS.

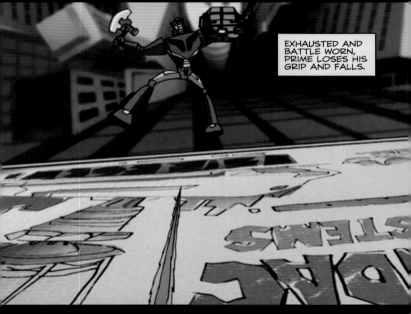

PRIME CRASHES TO THE STREET BELOW...

...AND DOES NOT MOVE.

CRASH

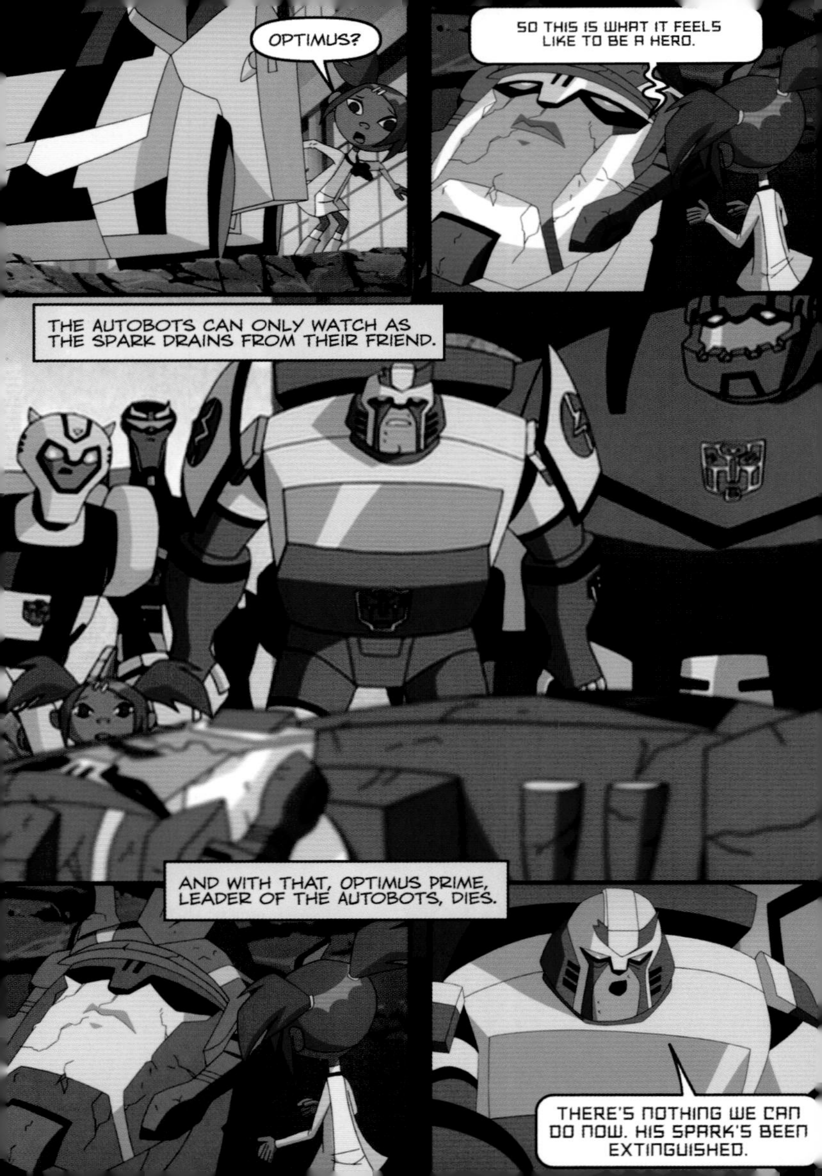
OPTIMUS?
SO THIS IS WHAT IT FEELS LIKE TO BE A HERO.
THE AUTOBOTS CAN ONLY WATCH AS THE SPARK DRAINS FROM THEIR FRIEND.
AND WITH THAT, OPTIMUS PRIME, LEADER OF THE AUTOBOTS, DIES.
THERE'S NOTHING WE CAN DO NOW. HIS SPARK'S BEEN EXTINGUISHED.

HE WENT OUT SAVING THE ALLSPARK. THAT'S WHAT MATTERS.

NO! HE CAN'T BE GONE. HE CAN'T!

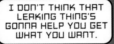

I DON'T THINK THAT LEAKING THING'S GONNA HELP YOU GET WHAT YOU WANT.

BUT I KNOW SOMETHING THAT CAN!

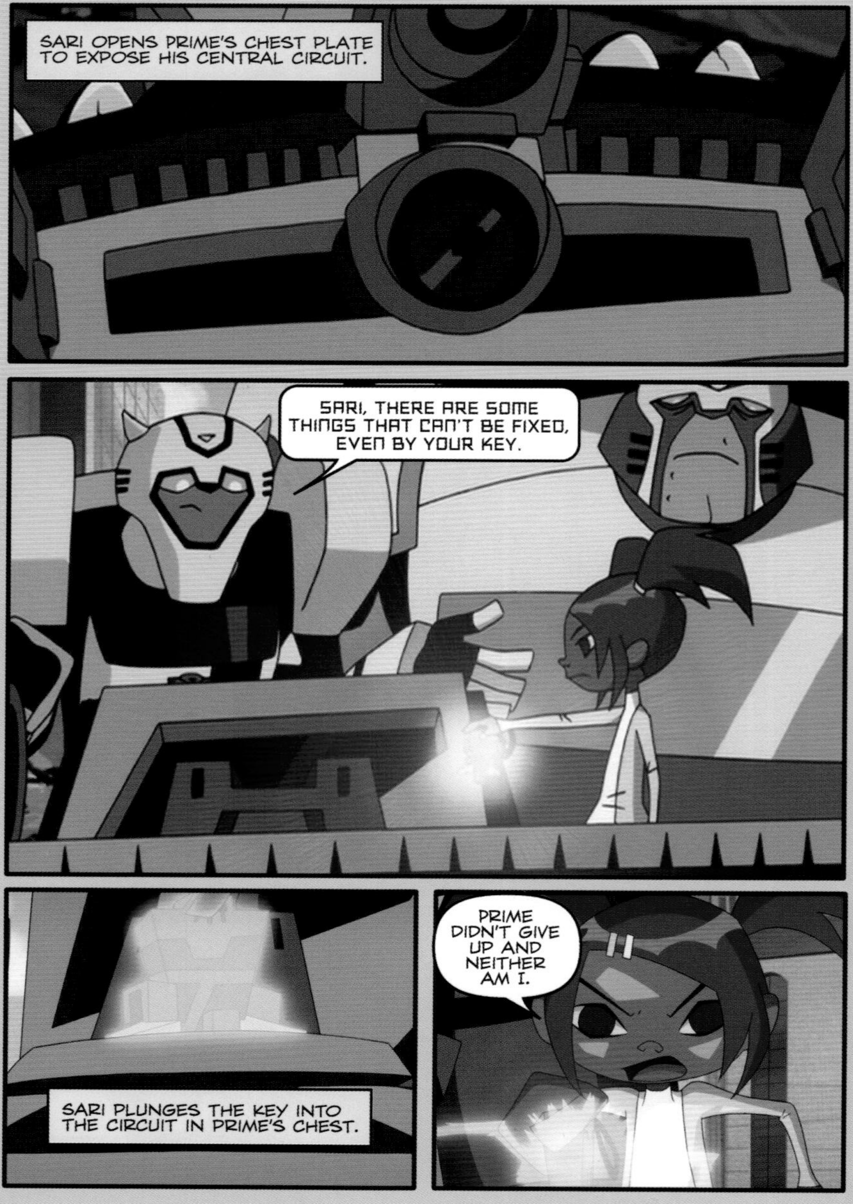
SARI OPENS PRIME'S CHEST PLATE TO EXPOSE HIS CENTRAL CIRCUIT.
SARI, THERE ARE SOME THINGS THAT CAN'T BE FIXED, EVEN BY YOUR KEY.
SARI PLUNGES THE KEY INTO THE CIRCUIT IN PRIME'S CHEST.
PRIME DIDN'T GIVE UP AND NEITHER AM I.

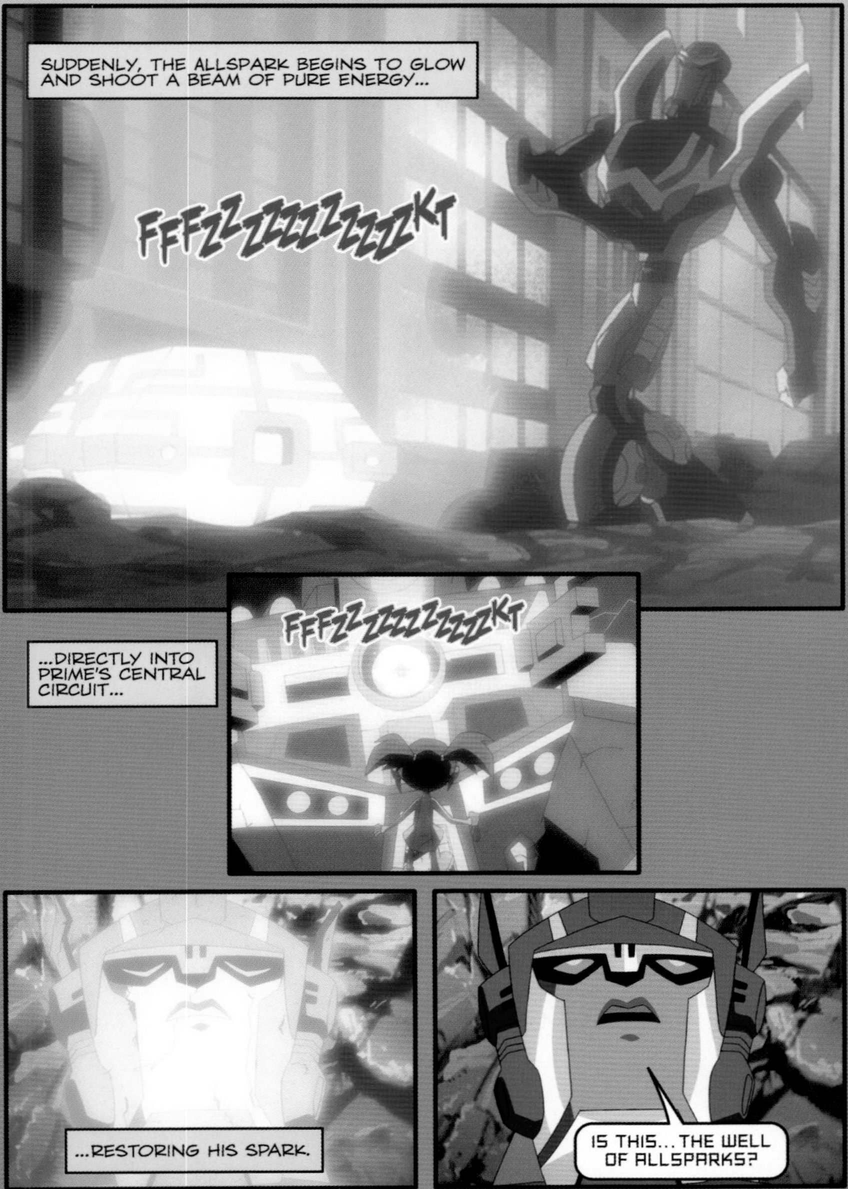

SUDDENLY, THE ALLSPARK BEGINS TO GLOW AND SHOOT A BEAM OF PURE ENERGY...
FFFZZZZZZZZZZZZKT
...DIRECTLY INTO PRIME'S CENTRAL CIRCUIT...
FFFZZZZZZZZZZZZKT
...RESTORING HIS SPARK.
IS THIS... THE WELL OF ALLSPARKS?

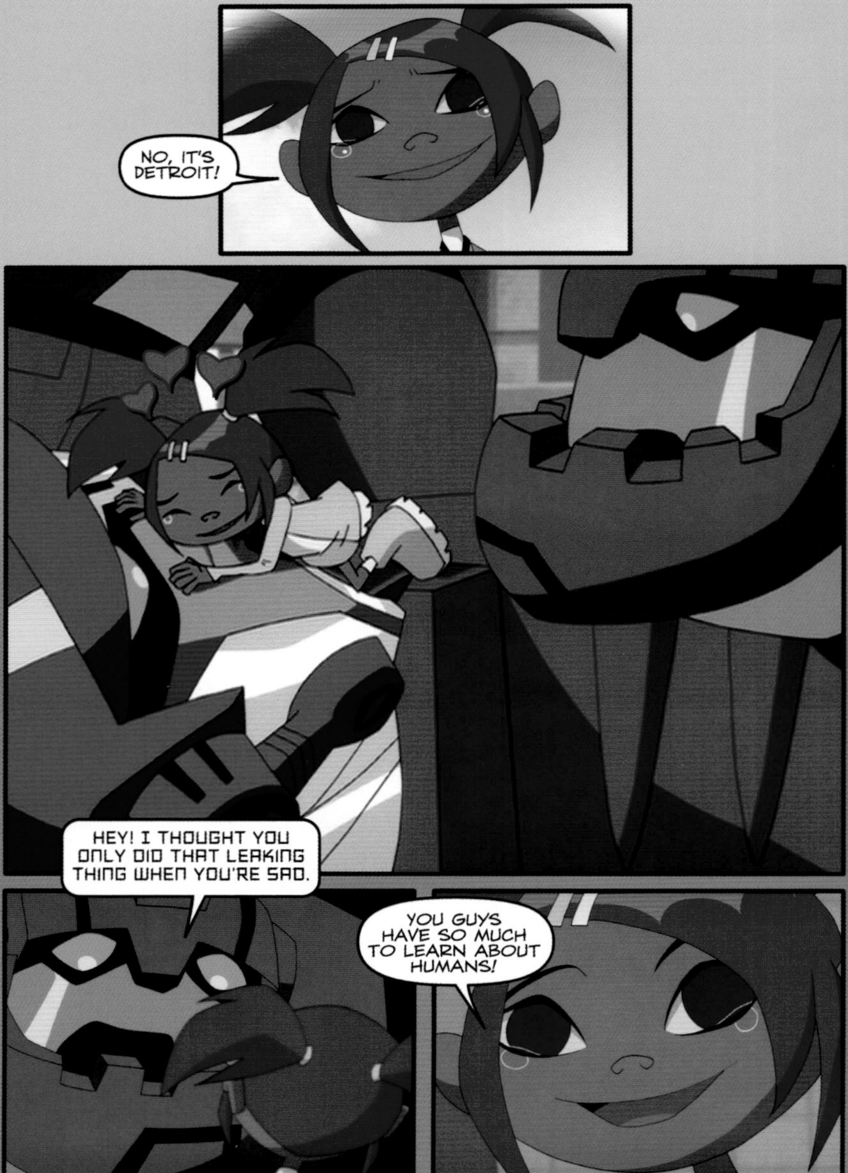
NO, IT'S DETROIT!
HEY! I THOUGHT YOU ONLY DID THAT LEAKING THING WHEN YOU'RE SAD.
YOU GUYS HAVE SO MUCH TO LEARN ABOUT HUMANS!

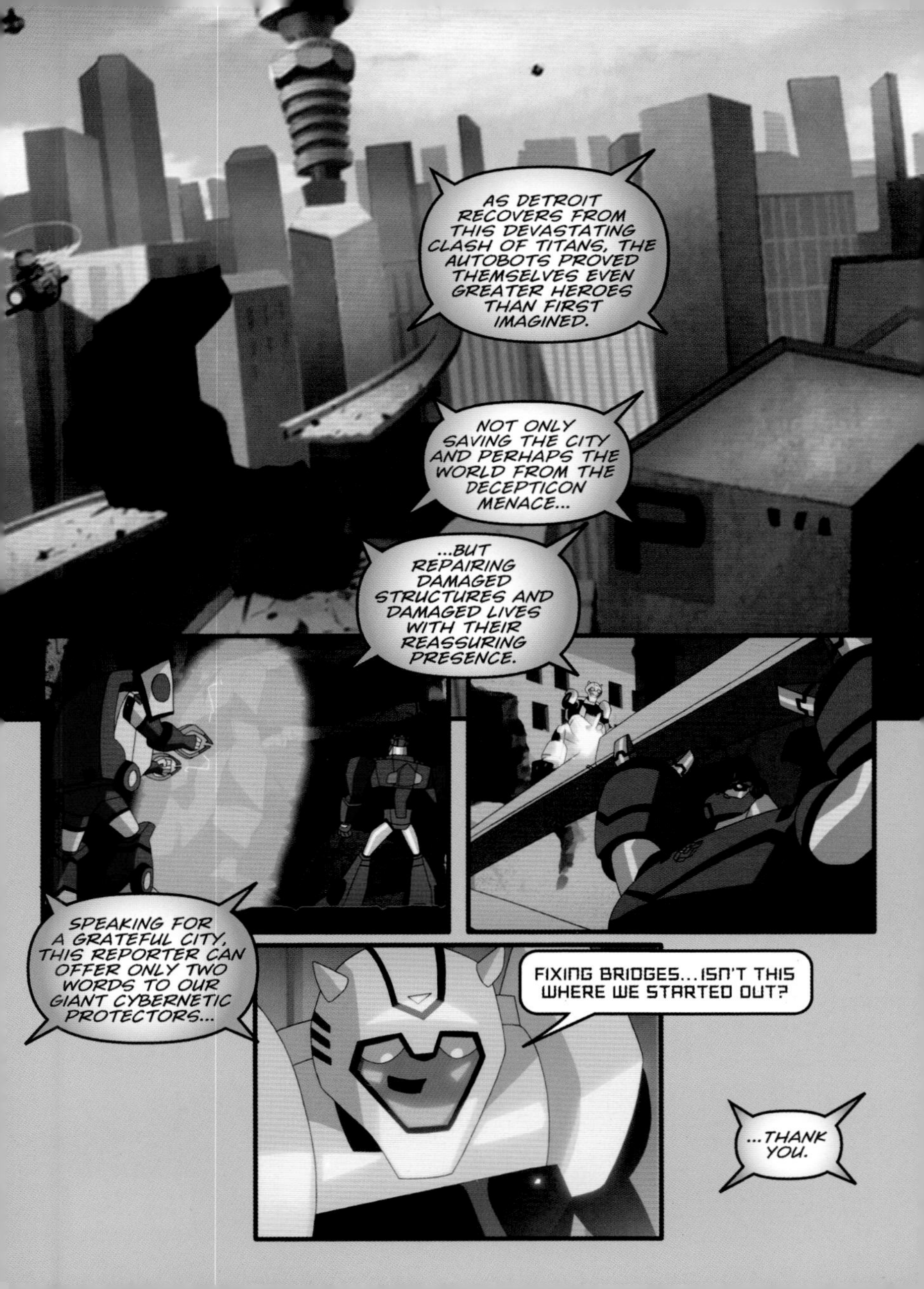
AS DETROIT RECOVERS FROM THIS DEVASTATING CLASH OF TITANS, THE AUTOBOTS PROVED THEMSELVES EVEN GREATER HEROES THAN FIRST IMAGINED.
NOT ONLY SAVING THE CITY AND PERHAPS THE WORLD FROM THE DECEPTICON MENACE...
...BUT REPAIRING DAMAGED STRUCTURES AND DAMAGED LIVES WITH THEIR REASSURING PRESENCE.
SPEAKING FOR A GRATEFUL CITY, THIS REPORTER CAN OFFER ONLY TWO WORDS TO OUR GIANT CYBERNETIC PROTECTORS...
FIXING BRIDGES...ISN'T THIS WHERE WE STARTED OUT?
...THANK YOU.

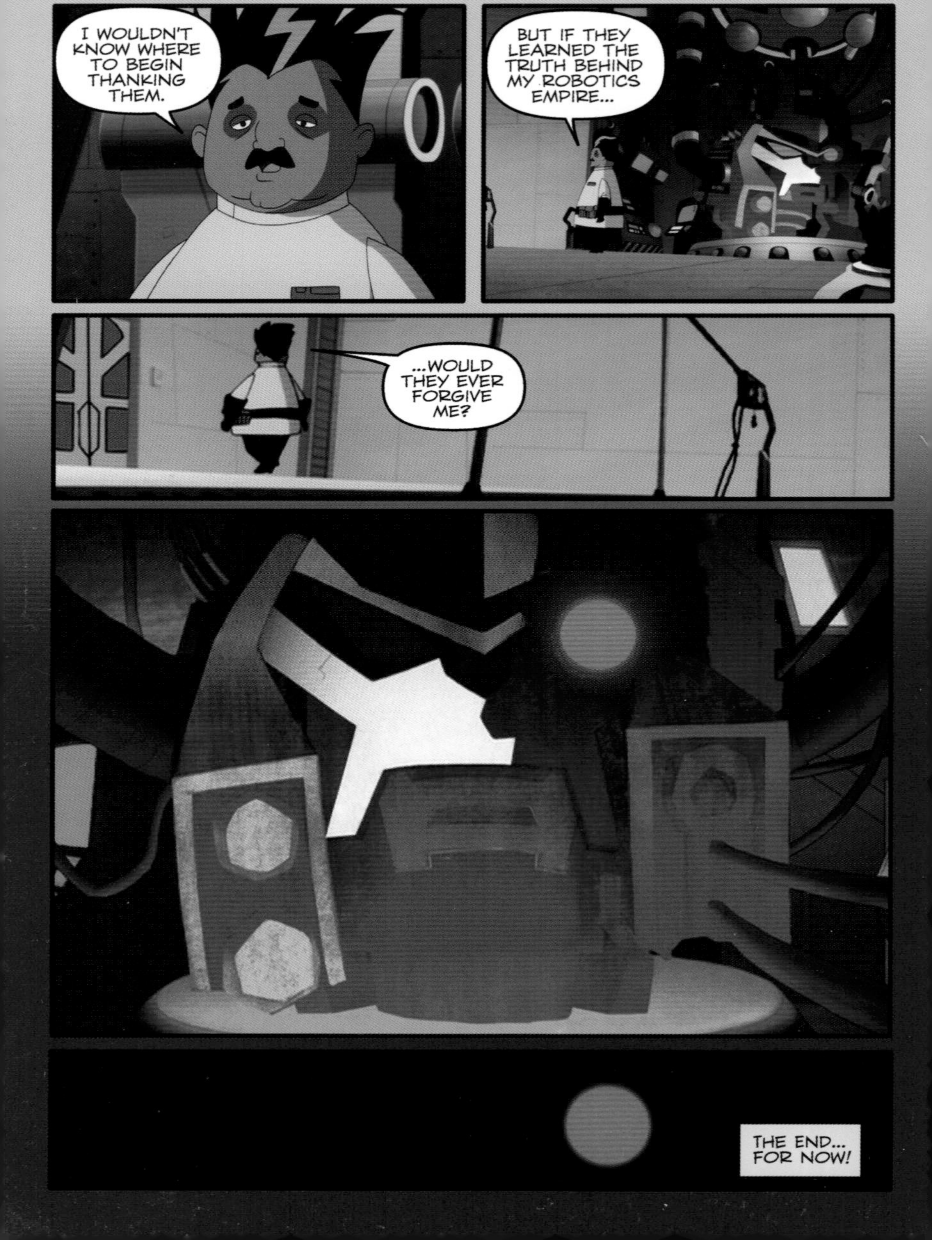

I WOULDN'T KNOW WHERE TO BEGIN THANKING THEM.
BUT IF THEY LEARNED THE TRUTH BEHIND MY ROBOTICS EMPIRE...
...WOULD THEY EVER FORGIVE ME?
THE END... FOR NOW!